Leaving Her Tears Behind

Madeline Dando

ISBN 9781910693797

Printed by Print2Demand, Hastings, East Sussex

Foreward

I would not have been able to write this story without the help, encouragement and inspiration that I received from my dear wife Brenda, my daughter, Caroline Wills, my sister, Helen Christian and my friends, Eroica Kelly, Valerie Hinkin, Jayne Frost and Ann Neville.

My childhood was spent in the East End of London and for the last twenty four years I have lived in Norfolk. I wanted to bring my memories, my dreams and my love of North Norfolk together into a powerful rollercoaster of a story.

It has taken me a long time to get to publication. I hope you enjoy reading this story as much as I did writing it.

Chapter One

11th January 1941

Sarah was having tea with her school friend, Jean, in Sally's Café near St Pauls. They sat behind dusty windows and mud-brown curtains as gentle rain caressed the dimly lit street outside.

'The fire brigade and hospitals are stretched to the limit. I can't imagine how they'll cope for much longer,' said Sarah.

'I know, London's been under attack for over four months. Every night the bombers come; it's been relentless.'

'The raids are getting worse, Jean. A whole street was demolished in Edmonton last night, goodness knows how many casualties there were.'

The girls met in the café every week, but today was different. Jean recently joined the Auxiliary Territorial Service as a cook and was waiting for her posting.

'Why did you volunteer?' asked Sarah.

'Because I thought it'd be more exciting than making parachutes,' Jean replied, draining the last drops from her teacup.

'I'm frightened, Jean,' Sarah admitted, as she counted out coins onto the table. 'I don't think I can carry on without you.'

Sarah hugged her tightly when they left the café, and heavy tears mixed with rain fell down her cheeks. There was an empty and forlorn look on her face, as if she never expected to see her friend again.

Jean looked away, trying to hide her emotions – she was stronger than Sarah and was not prone to crying easily.

'What happened to your idea about getting away from London and living in the country?' Jean asked.

'It's just a dream; things like that don't happen to people like us and anyway who knows what we'll do if England is invaded!' Sarah replied.

The girls parted with hugs and kisses and Sarah solemnly made her way towards Bank tube station. It was a cold night, the winter weather sapping at Londoners' spirits. The rain strengthened and teamed through the smog-filled air.

Sarah smelt burnt-out buildings still smouldering from the previous day's air attacks. She covered her mouth and nose with a woollen scarf. A passer-by coughed violently. He was choking on the smoke, which penetrated his lungs with his every breath.

An air-raid siren wailed as Sarah entered the station, amongst a large impatient crowd. Her slim five foot frame was crushed in the mayhem and she was lifted off her feet. Clinging to a woman's arm, she was carried past the ticket barrier.

'Don't worry lady, just breathe in,' said a man in a bowler hat.

Sarah landed by the escalator and rode down the long, moving staircase with people packed in twos and threes on every step. It was heaving with passengers below, but, using her elbows, she squeezed past people to get to the end of the platform. A train rattled into the station and Sarah looked at her watch. It was 7.59pm.

A bomb smashed into the ground above, causing an almighty bang and the earth shook violently as if it experienced a massive earthquake. Sarah immediately bowed her head and covered her ears as debris showered down from the ceiling. There were despairing screams and howls of pain, as a noise like rumbling thunder roamed the depths of the building in the bomb's aftermath.

In an instant, the lights went out. Sarah was terrified and thought she was going to die. Fortunately, because of the nightly blackouts, almost everyone carried a torch. Sarah's battery was low, but in a few moments an increasing trickle of light brightened the area.

Sarah looked along the platform and a sense of disbelief and bewilderment took hold. The top of the tunnel had collapsed by the entrance and a railway carriage was on fire. Wild flames camouflaged its crumpled roof as people lay motionless. Some were without arms and legs and there was blood seeping silently onto the platform from the dead and injured.

A thick, choking dust made Sarah cough, as the smell of burning, like piping hot creosote, smarted her nose. She was petrified, standing still and clutching her shopping bag tightly. It was her only comfort.

Some passengers knew there was an escape route via the Northern Line and a lift to ground level. It was a short distance from where Sarah was standing.

'This way!' a man in a shiny raincoat shouted out. He was holding an umbrella aloft.

People hastily followed, as pitiful screams continued to ring out along the platform. A clean-shaven man with short, reddish curly hair was pushed towards Sarah. He was tall and towered over her. She was trembling, and from the ghostly expression on her face, he realised she needed help.

'Are you all right?' he asked loudly, trying to make himself heard above the din.

'I'm afraid!' Sarah mumbled. She sobbed with her head bowed.

Sarah was shy and timid, but she let him put his arms around her. Her heart was beating rapidly, and her fingers were pressing into his back. She never thought she would be in the arms of a stranger.

'My name's Jimmy, I'll help you,' he said.

Sarah raised her head. Her long dark-brown hair was speckled with flaking paint and old brick dust. She was still shaking, but she smiled as Jimmy took hold of her arm.

He escorted her along the platform, crammed full of people, including passengers who dis-embarked from the train. Jimmy protected Sarah as best he could with the weight of his body. He guided her around the debris and injured passengers lying on the ground, while keeping sight of the 'umbrella man' in front of him.

'I hope the lift's still working,' he said.

'It is, I can hear a whirling sound; it's coming down the shaft,' Sarah replied.

An orange bulb was flashing above the entrance and people pushed and shoved even harder to get to the front of the queue.

The metal concertina doors opened with a cranking sound. They were pulled apart by an attendant from the inside. He was an elderly man dressed in a black railway suit. Passengers rushed forward, and Sarah was pushed into the lift.

Jimmy wrestled his way into the chamber and joined her. It was as full as it could be. The attendant closed the doors. He was hurried by a panic-stricken and intolerant crowd, until a man with a satchel shouted out.

'Stop! Someone's being trampled on.'

His deep, loud voice commanded attention. The doors were opened again, and two passengers stepped outside to make way. A woman was carried into the lift by a soldier, who struggled with her lifeless form. Sarah could see that she needed immediate help, before it was too late.

The doors were slammed closed again and a sudden jerk unnerved the passengers as the lift ascended. The weight inside was enormous, far exceeding its maximum capacity. An eerie whining sound exposed the pressure on the cables above, and after a loud clonk, it stopped.

'We'll never get out of here; we're all going to die!' a woman called out.

Some people screamed and others cried. Sarah clasped Jimmy's arm.

'Don't be scared, I said I'd look after you.' His smile was broad and comforting.

The attendant repeatedly pressed the operating button until there was another jerk and the lift dropped an inch or two. There were more cries and gasps of breath. Sarah's stomach churned before the lift ascended once more. The passengers were still and silent, frightened any movement might stall its operation again.

In a few seconds, the lift reached its summit. It was to be its last journey and the attendant pulled the doors open. The injured woman was carried out onto the street, cradled in the soldier's arms, and then laid on a stretcher.

'I think she's done for,' said Jimmy.

'It's not looking good, but I saw her fingers move. She clenched them slowly, so there's some movement,' Sarah whispered.

The station was on fire and the emergency services were on the scene. Medical staff were dealing with many people as best they could, in the acrid smoke billowing out of the flames. Sarah coughed and both her eyes and nose smarted. It took time for her senses to adjust to the pungent atmosphere.

'How many casualties are there?' she asked a passing policeman.

'The bomb hit the surface above the booking hall. There're many dead and injured,' he replied.

The ground shuddered again, as a bomb exploded in the next street and then another towards Tower Bridge. The atmosphere was violent and terrifying.

'Oh my God, London must be engulfed in flames!' said Sarah.

'It is most nights, but not usually in this part of the city,' said Jimmy.

As they walked away from the station, the drones of the planes lessened.

'I think the planes have gone,' she said, sounding relieved.

'Yes, it looks like the raiders are making their path down the Thames Corridor towards the docks, they're after the merchant ships.'

In the distance, searchlights combed the skies and Sarah heard the continuous thud of anti-aircraft gun shells. With so many enemy planes, she knew countless bombs would inevitably reach their targets.

Sarah sobbed again, and tears ran down her face. The wetness gathered in little pockets of grit and grime on her cheeks. She noticed Jimmy walked with a slight limp, but arm in arm they managed to tread a safe path along the streets littered with glass, pot holes and shrapnel.

It was not long before the 'all clear' siren sounded, which prompted the couple to hug again like old pals.

'Let me look at you,' said Jimmy.

He dried her face with a clean blue handkerchief he kept in his inside jacket pocket. He smiled at Sarah, but his comforting caused her to cry again.

Sarah and Jimmy sat down on a low-level wall in front of a burnt-out garage. It was still smouldering from a previous air raid and trickles of smoke were rising from the ruins. Fire engines and ambulances rushed by and there were sounds of bells ringing from emergency vehicles all around them.

In a quieter moment, Sarah heard someone crying.

'Can you hear that, Jimmy?'

'Yes, it's over there I think.'

They walked across the road through the gloom. There was a repugnant smell from water seeping out of an old pipe, and a door, from a half-demolished house, was still standing and banging in its frame. Sitting in the rubble were two children – a small boy in short trousers, aged eight or nine, and a younger girl with yellow ribbons in her hair, hugging a brown woollen teddy.

'Where're your parents?' asked Sarah.

There was no response. The children did not seem aware of the adults, as their little minds were traumatised. They appeared to be oblivious of what was going on around them. Sarah put her arm around the girl's shoulder and tears filled her eyes. The girl shivered as she snuggled into Sarah's body.

'It's all right missy, everything will be all right,' said Sarah softly.

An air-raid warden came by. She was keen to get the children off the street.

'What are these kids doing here?' she asked.

'We've only just found them,' Sarah replied.

The warden was rather abrupt and a little impatient.

'Well they can't stay on the street!' she said loudly.

Lacking any compassion, she took hold of a child in each hand, pulled hard on their arms and hurried them away.

'Do you think the parents are dead?' asked Sarah.

'I don't know, but I'm very worried.'

'I wonder why the children haven't been evacuated?'

'It's puzzling, but it's the parents who are missing,' said Jimmy.

Despite living with the war for a long time and used to hearing terrible news, the sight of these children distressed Sarah greatly.

'Oh my God, will it ever stop, Jimmy?'

Sarah sobbed again, and he placed his arm around her shoulder.

'It will be over one day, we have to believe that.'

The evening was horrific, but with the bombers gone, the tension in Sarah's body eased.

'What's your name?' asked Jimmy.

'Sarah Mays.'

'Where do you live, Sarah?'

'In Paxton Road, Tottenham, with my parents and my younger sister, Doris. I need to get a train home from Liverpool Street.'

'Do you work in London?'

'No, in a factory in Enfield. I'm a trained machinist but I was called up to make military equipment.'

'Do you enjoy it?'

'No!' Sarah laughed. 'I hate it. Every day I'm reminded how dangerous it is to bring matches, coins, rings or anything metallic into the factory for fear of an explosion.'

'It sounds very scary.'

'It is, occasionally something goes off. A woman lost the sight in her left eye a couple of weeks ago because of a hair pin.'

'That's terrible,' said Jimmy.

'It serves her right, she might have blown up the whole building. My uncle died in a major accident in a bomb factory fire in the East End in 1917 so I understand the risks. I keep telling the girls, we rely on each other.'

'Blimey! You women are really playing your part.'

'Do you think we all sit at home with our feet up, Jimmy?'

'Sorry, come on, I'll walk you to the station.'

On their way, people were assessing the air-raid damage. It was largely a business area, but there were many flats above offices and the pavements were covered with all kinds of debris.

In the distance, down Old Broad Street, flames were raging through buildings.

'Where are the fire engines?' asked Sarah.

'They must be occupied elsewhere, there've been lots of bombs this evening.'

Part of the front wall of a public house fell into the road and crumbled into a pile of bricks. Piercing cries rang out, as a man with his clothes in flames, jumped to his death from an adjacent upstairs window.

Sarah let out a scream, her body shaking once more. This was the worst night of her life.

'It's the Black Lion. I used to drink there, Sarah.'

Jimmy held her tightly with his arm around her waist, trying to calm her feelings and anxieties. They walked on and attempted to further explore one another's lives. Small talk, however, was impossible, as their minds were absorbed by the evening's events.

On reaching Liverpool Street station, the emergency services were dealing with the effects of another bomb. A small row of shops had taken a direct hit, and in the road a burnt-out bus lay on its side.

Sarah was relieved the railway was not affected, but the concourse was heaving with people. They were all trying to get home. Sarah's train was due to depart from platform four in seven minutes. The carriages were already in the station and Jimmy escorted her to where she usually boarded.

'I don't suppose you'd let me buy you a drink sometime?' Jimmy asked.

Sarah was startled. She was a little nervous of men and had not been on a date before.

'Why would you want to do that?'

'We've been through so much this evening. I'd like to know more about you,' said Jimmy.

Sarah's shyness prevented an instant reply. It took her a moment to make up her mind, in which time she thought, 'He's not particularly attractive, but he's been very kind to me.'

'I'll meet you at the Bricklayers Arms in Tottenham next Saturday at six o'clock,' she said, with a new-found confidence. 'It's on the high road near the football ground.'

Jimmy's face beamed. Hugging Sarah again, he put both of his arms around her and planted a kiss on her cheek. Sarah blushed and her lips broke into a tiny smile, but she was already wondering if she had made the right decision.

Sarah entered the carriage. It was occupied by eleven people and as the window was slightly open, the passengers had listened to their conversation. They were grinning, and Sarah was embarrassed, as she sat down between a woman wearing a thick brown overcoat and a man in a dark blue jacket.

'Will you be okay, Sarah?' Jimmy called out.

He noticed she was still shaking and wanted to be sure she would get home safely. Sarah replied with a slightly wider smile and the nod of her head as the train carriages jolted into motion.

Jimmy was out of sight in seconds and Sarah felt unsure. He was a stranger, but in the tube station carnage and on the war-torn streets, he had kept her safe. She would have been lost without him.

Sarah felt tired, her eyes shut intermittently as the train rattled along the track. The din was enhanced by steam whistles and oncoming trains, but when she reached her destination, she was asleep.

Fortunately, Sarah was awoken by a passenger, with an empty bird cage on his lap, wanting to make his exit. He brushed past her legs, before stretching his arm out of the window to open the door from the outside handle. She was shocked to see the name White Hart Lane on the station wall and hastily followed him out of the carriage.

Sarah searched in her bag for her purse, as it contained her ticket. It was missing. She thought, 'It must have been taken while I was crammed in the lift.' It only contained a shilling, but, being a kind soul, she hoped who ever stole it needed the money.

On reaching the exit barrier, the inspector was nowhere to be seen and she walked out on to the street. It was only a short distance to her home.

Sarah made this journey many times, but tonight was different. She was still reeling from the bombing and there was an uneasy atmosphere all around her. Sarah sensed from the forlorn look on people's faces, that their self-belief about good prevailing over evil was being severely tested.

Sarah burst into tears again as she thought about the hours before. She had witnessed people being killed and heard the most terrible screams and pleas for help. She had been powerless to assist them, but the sights and sounds were captured in her mind.

On arriving home, Sarah's parents were relieved. They heard about the bombing on the wireless and knew the Bank tube station was on their daughter's way home. As soon as she stepped inside the door, tears rolled down her mother's cheeks.

'Thank God you're safe, Sarah, so many people have died in London this evening.'

Sarah shook as she retold the evening's events to her parents. When she mentioned Jimmy, they wanted to know more about him.

'He was there at the right time and helped me,' she said.

'Where does he work?' asked her dad.

'I don't know.'

'Where does he live?' her mum enquired.

'I don't know, but I'm seeing him next Saturday.' Sarah giggled.

'Well, we'd like to thank him, it seems we owe Jimmy a debt for taking care of our daughter, he may have saved your life,' said her dad.

'I'm meeting him at the Bricklayers, but only for a drink,' she replied.

Chapter Two

As each day passed, Sarah worried more about her date. She had agreed to meet Jimmy on the spur of the moment, even though she hardly knew him.

On the day of the meeting, having put on her blue pinafore dress and combed her hair, Sarah sat down on her bed.

'I'm not sure I can go through with it, Doris.'

'You have to Sis, I know you said he isn't dishy, but he might be coming from miles away. You can't let the poor bloke down.'

Doris was much taller than Sarah. She had a round baby face and was always smiling. Doris idolised her sister and would do anything for her. As they sat chatting she was polishing Sarah's closed black shoes, ready for her date.

'I suppose so, but I'm dreading it,' said Sarah. Her face, a light complexion with chubby cheeks and beautiful lips, was beginning to redden with the effort of containing her woes.

It was pitch black outside when Sarah left home shortly before six o'clock and she approached the pub from the other side of the road. Jimmy was waiting for her by the entrance, leaning against a closed door with his arms folded. 'He's so confident,' she thought, whilst butterflies fluttered furiously in her stomach.

Jimmy smiled and kissed her cheek. Taking hold of her arm, he escorted her inside the pub.

'What would you like to drink?' he asked.

Her heart was still racing, and she was embarrassed. Sarah was not familiar with alcohol and did not know what to choose.

'You suggest something for me, Jimmy.'

He tempted her to a gin and orange and he bought a glass of brown ale for himself.

After a few sips, Sarah was a little light-headed, but it helped her relax; her nervousness faded away.

'It's a bit cloudy this evening. Maybe we won't get an air raid,' she said.

'I can't stop thinking about the bomb in the tube station, Sarah.'

'Yes,' she sighed slowly, 'it was really awful. In the newspaper it said one hundred and eleven people died.'

'I know, we were lucky to survive, but at least I met you Sarah. It's strange how things turn out sometimes.' He paused and looked at her directly with his dark brown eyes. 'Will you tell me all about yourself?'

'There's not much for you to know really. I'm twenty-one and I live in a small two-bedroomed basement flat. It's around the corner from the high road and is very noisy with traffic passing close by. My parents don't have much money, but they love me and my sister Doris and make sure we have what we need.'

'I can tell they mean the world to you,' said Jimmy.

'They'd do anything for me and Doris. My dad works for a rag-and-bone man. Five days a week he's out with a horse and cart on the streets, buying stuff for a pittance. I suppose we're poor, but my mum and dad are honest and hardworking; they always think of others.'

'If you could wish for one thing in the world, Sarah, what would it be?'

She hesitated, and shyly said, 'There is something, but it's silly.'

'Come on, tell me, I'd like to know.'

'No, I told you, it's daft.'

'You sound so sincere and have such a cheeky smile, Sarah. If I tell you mine, will you tell me yours?'

'Okay, you go first, Jimmy.'

He entwined his fingers and raised them to his chin.

'If I ever have children I want them to be proud of me,' he said.

Jimmy sounded sad, almost upset and Sarah thought, 'It's a strange thing to wish for.'

'Your turn,' he said. 'Go on, you promised.'

'Alright, when I was a child, I dreamed of living in the country.'

Jimmy laughed.

'That's why I didn't want to tell you. I knew you'd make fun of me.'

In an instant Sarah's smile disappeared. A tear or two dropped from her eyes and Jimmy reached out to hold her hands.

'Jimmy, I want children too, but I don't want them to struggle like my family. As much as I love my mum and dad, there must be something better than barely surviving and living in a poky flat. I want to move far away from here.'

Sarah was now more comfortable in Jimmy's company. The small amount of alcohol she consumed was causing her to both relax and giggle.

'Enough about me, tell me about you, Jimmy. I want to know everything.'

Before he answered, she enquired very abruptly, 'What's wrong with your leg?'

'It's an inch shorter than the other.'

Then he laughed and added, 'And vice versa.'

'Doesn't it worry you, Jimmy?'

'I only have four toes on this one,' he said, pointing to the shorter leg.

Sarah's smile disappeared.

'I'm so sorry,' she replied.

'There's nothing for you to be sorry about. I can get about okay, but balance is a problem if I lift anything.'

'Is that why you're not away fighting?'

Jimmy raised his eyebrows as if she was intruding into his life too much. They were enjoying their evening together, but this question troubled him.

'The War Recruiting Office won't let me. I'm apparently not fit for purpose, but many people think I'm a coward.'

'That's terrible, where do you work?'

'I used to be a postman in Norfolk, but I moved away from home. It was three years ago when I was seventeen. I'm now a warehouseman in a paper mill in Stratford.'

'Why did you leave home?'

'I didn't get on with my dad. He's tall and strong and doesn't have any patience. He often used to give me a good hiding for the slightest thing. I'd get smacked around the ears for arriving home five minutes late after playing out, or forgetting an item of shopping. I remember being hit hard for not shutting the garden gate.'

'Oh, Jimmy, I can't really believe it!'

'My dad also hurt my mum, Gladys. There were times when I lay awake in bed listening to my parents' raised voices. It frightened me as when they argued, my dad's temper got the better of him. My mum's hair was pulled, or her wrists were grabbed tightly. I've seen her pushed across a table and onto the floor. Sometimes I was terrified she might get seriously hurt.'

Sarah was shocked, coming from a loving home she found Jimmy's upbringing hard to comprehend.

'That's really awful, Jimmy. My parents have never given me or Doris more than a small slap on our arms or legs.'

'I'll never forget what my dad did to me and my mum. I'll never forgive him.'

'What's his name Jimmy?'

'Eddie,' he replied.

'Why didn't your mum leave him?' asked Sarah.

'She loved him and never complained. He always gave her money to buy pretty clothes and put food on the table. She thought her life was good and tolerated his anger. I told her to go a thousand times, but she said there was nowhere else to live and she'd never leave me anyway.'

Sarah was saddened further when Jimmy said his mum died in 1938.

'She contracted tuberculosis and I watched her breathing deteriorate. As the days went by she became more tired and her neck swelled. Then she got a nasty cough that got worse and worse until one day the strain on her lungs killed her.'

'Oh Jimmy, that's very sad, I'm so sorry.'

'It was the worst moment in my life, but after the funeral I decided to leave Norfolk. When I told my dad he said, "You're making a big mistake, my boy", and I knew what he was referring to.'

'What was that?'

'He was only forty-nine but very wealthy. After he retired in 1935 we moved to Cleybourne in Norfolk from Hackney. Dad told me he left school at the age of thirteen and trained as a carpenter. He used to go on about sweeping floors, cleaning tools and making tea for his superiors. I don't know how he did it, but he owned a thriving business by the time he was thirty-seven.'

'What did he do, Jimmy?'

'He imported veneer wood from Ghana and employed people to make cabinets, chests of drawers and the like. He said "the rich" bought them.'

'So, your dad thought you wanted his money?'

'Yes, he laughed at me when I told him I was leaving. I remember him saying, "Where will you go? You'd better think again my boy." I hate him. He never showed me any affection despite having time on his hands. Not once did he take any interest in my school work or play with me like other fathers do with their children. He barely spoke to me, unless he was in a temper and then I received the full force of his anger.'

'Do you have any regrets, Jimmy?'

'None at all. I left home the following morning. "It's you're bed, you'd better go and lie on it", were the last words he said to me as I walked out the door.'

'Yes, but leaving home is such a big thing. I don't think I'd be able to do it.'

'I don't mind telling you, it was a momentous decision, especially as I was going to move to the East End of London. It was a scary time with Germany on the march in Europe and there was talk of a war coming. My dad's friend, Jack, owns a property on Park Road in Leyton. I always got on with him and secretly he agreed to rent me a second-storey flat. He also helped me get my job in Stratford.'

After chatting a while, they realised it was getting late, and Sarah was keen to get home in case the bombs came. Jimmy offered to walk with her, but she decided to go alone. They parted, with Jimmy planting another kiss on her cheek, and agreed to see each other the following Saturday.

*

Sarah liked Jimmy and met him often in the weeks that followed. They went to pubs, dance halls and the cinema. When the planes came, and people were asked to evacuate, they stayed inside. Having survived the Bank tube station bomb, they felt destined to stay alive.

Sarah's parents were both fifty-one years old. They liked Jimmy and believed she was safe in his company. When calling for Sarah, he sometimes bought Mrs Mays flowers and cigarettes for her father.

One afternoon, however, Mr and Mrs Mays were shocked by Jimmy's aggressive behaviour. They were all walking home after seeing *How Green Was My Valley* at the Regal cinema, about two miles from Sarah's home.

A man in a cloth cap came up to Jimmy and whispered something in his ear. It seemed a harmless approach, but Jimmy was incensed and grabbed the man's coat collar and punched his face repeatedly. Then he knocked him to the ground and kicked him in the stomach.

'Please stop!' pleaded Sarah.

'There's more of that to come if he doesn't leave me alone!' said Jimmy.

The man was left lying on the pavement with blood on his face.

'That was rather heavy handed,' said Mr Mays.

'I'm sorry, but he called me a limping cheat for not going to war. I'm branded a coward because I'm not in the services. I want to fight for my country, but I'm told I don't meet their physical requirements. I can't help my disability, but I suffer the same intimidation every day. Why can't people mind their own bloody business?'

'I thought you were going to kill him, Jimmy. I don't care what he said, you must control your temper,' said Mr Mays.

Sarah was shocked by the violent outrage, but wouldn't have a word uttered against Jimmy. She understood the torment that sometimes raged inside him.

*

Mr and Mrs Mays knew Sarah was very happy. Since Jimmy came onto the scene she was noticeably cheerier. Whenever his name was mentioned, her eyes lit up and she talked about him constantly.

The relationship blossomed further, and Sarah and Jimmy enjoyed each other's company almost every day, despite the air raids that continued to destroy people's lives and property.

One evening while they were eating a fish and chip supper in their favourite café, Jimmy got to his feet. Putting his hands on the edge of the table, he pushed his chair back. Sarah noticed he was sweating.

'What are you doing Jimmy?'

He smiled, as he nervously put his hand in his inside jacket pocket and produced a small red square box. Sarah loved Jimmy and often thought about being his wife, but imagined any proposal would come after the war.

Jimmy sunk to his knees on the stone floor, to the cheers of onlookers. Sarah choked on a large piece of cod and was coughing when he opened the tiny casket. Her eyes widened at a diamond ring. It sparkled under the florescent light and she thought it was beautiful.

'I love you Sarah Mays, will you marry me?'

There were more cheers and Sarah was embarrassed, but her face beamed.

'Yes, I will, Jimmy Jackson!' She replied at the top of her voice and when he stood up, Sarah threw her arms around his neck.

The proprietor had not witnessed a proposal in his café before. 'Tea for everyone!' he shouted out spontaneously and people clapped.

While walking Sarah home, her usual smile disappeared, and she became very serious.

'What's the matter? You haven't changed your mind, have you?' asked Jimmy.

'No, but it's occurred to me, you'll need to talk to my dad and see if he wants you for a son-in-law.'

'Do I have to? You've already said you'll marry me.'

'I think you should. He likes George Stewart who lives across the road. We used to go to school together and had a kind of crush on one another.'

'George Stewart! This is the first time you've mentioned him. Why didn't you tell me before Sarah?'

'I didn't want to worry you. He's been away in Scotland for the last three years, where his father worked on an airbase. The family came home last week. My mum and dad get on very well with the Stewarts and they hoped one day me and George might be together.'

'Blimey! I didn't know there was a rival.'

'There isn't as far as I'm concerned,' said Sarah.

When they reached her flat, Jimmy was edgy. He was usually chatty and normally greeted Mrs Mays with a kiss, but his face was drawn and his hands were shaking.

'Hello Jimmy, are you all right?'

Jimmy ignored her question.

'Can I see Mr Mays please?' he asked, mumbling his words.

Sarah followed him into her home and planted a kiss on her mother's cheek. Her face lit up instantly. She understood why he was there and ushered him into the kitchen.

Sarah was close behind and Mrs Mays tried to hold her back.

'I think you should let Dad speak to Jimmy alone.'

'Not likely Mum! I wouldn't miss this conversation for the world.'

Mr Mays was seated at the table eating his dinner. Jimmy was often in this room and conversed freely with Sarah's parents. However, this was different and he trembled as Mr Mays put down his knife and fork. When spoken to, Mr Mays was in the habit of grinding his teeth.

Sarah could see how frightened Jimmy was. Asking Mr Mays for her hand was daunting enough, but he needed to prove he was a better prospect than the boy across the road.

Jimmy's face was ashen and he was pinching his right ear lobe. It did not take long for Mr Mays to realise why he was there.

'Is there something in particular you want to talk about?'

Jimmy was petrified seeing Sarah's father staring up at him and Mr Mays decided to put him out of his misery.

'For goodness sake, sit down boy; we can hardly discuss our daughter's engagement if you're in this state. Oh, and before you do, there're two bottles of brown ale in the cupboard over there – you might as well get them out.'

'What about George Stewart, Mr Mays?'

'George Stewart, who's he?'

Sarah fell about laughing and Jimmy was furious.

'You really are a naughty girl.'

Sarah laughed again.

Jimmy tried to be stern, but his face broke into a smile and they kissed passionately.

'Come and sit down you two lovebirds,' said Mr Mays, but then the joy on his face disappeared.

'Jimmy, I want your assurance you can control your temper. It's been bothering me ever since I saw you beat up that bloke in the high road. Your anger also worried Mrs Mays. I have to make sure our girl is safe.'

'I understand, Mr Mays. All I can say is, people won't leave me and my deformed leg alone. I've only lashed out on two occasions and both related to incidents during which I was accused of cowardice. I'd never lay a finger on your daughter.'

Mr Mays was still troubled, but he liked Jimmy and after calling his wife into the kitchen, he invited him into the family.

Sarah did not sleep a wink that night; she thought she was marrying the most wonderful man in the world.

*

A quiet engagement party, for family and friends followed a few weeks later, but Jimmy's father was not invited.

'I would like to meet Eddie,' confided Mr Mays to his daughter.

'So would I, Dad. I've been asking to go to Cleybourne for some time, but Jimmy always refuses. As far as I'm aware, he hasn't even told his dad I exist. He really detests him, and hasn't been back to Norfolk since before we got together. I don't think he'll want him invited to the wedding either.'

'Eddie has to come. If he doesn't, Jimmy will regret it for the rest of his life.'

'I know, Dad. I'll try and make it happen, I promise.'

Getting married during a war was not easy, and Sarah was particularly stressed about getting a dress. She did not have enough money, even for the material to make it herself.

One evening when she arrived home from work, there was a surprise waiting for her. On entering the bedroom which Sarah shared with her sister, she was amazed to see a beautiful white gown laid out on her bed. She ran her hands over the soft fabric. It was mainly of silk, but its puffed shoulders and sleeves were made out of lace.

There was a long veil lying beside it and on the floor a pair of white sandals with large side bows. Sarah had not seen the dress before. She guessed it was her mum's and rushed downstairs into the kitchen to thank her.

'Oh Mum, I love you so much!'

'I wasn't sure you'd want my old rags, Sarah.'

'I adore them, Mum.'

'You'd better go and see if it fits you then. I think it will. We're about the same size and height, but if it doesn't, I'm sure you can alter it. And we're both a size four shoe.'

Sarah tried on the dress in front of the bedroom mirror. She was overjoyed and returned to the kitchen.

'Mum, look! It's perfect.' Her face shone like a bright candle.

'Yes, it is, Sarah.'

Mrs Mays adjusted the sleeves with the tips of her fingers. Sarah hugged her mum again and would not let her go. While in the embrace, she tried to imagine she was walking down the aisle. It made her nervous thinking of all the people who would be watching. Then in her mind Jimmy was standing in front of the altar and she wished it was happening at this moment.

Sarah was as happy as a wasp in a jam pot and wanted to tell her sister. Doris was only fifteen, but she was her best friend and would be her only bridesmaid, as Jean was away with the Auxiliary Territorial Service.

*

June 1943

Guests were starting to receive their invitations to the wedding, taking place in September.

'I want us to invite your dad,' said Sarah as they sat in the café.

'No! We're not. I've told you all about my father. He's not a nice man and doesn't care about me. If he sees how we live down here, he'll say, "I told you it was a mistake". I wish it wasn't like this, but it is. He's not part of my life now.'

Sarah enjoyed a good relationship with her parents and loved them very much. She expected Jimmy's response, but was determined not to give up.

'I know you won't forgive him for the past, Jimmy, and I can't imagine how hard life was for you, but weddings are supposed to bring people together.'

Jimmy huffed and puffed. He was angry, his mouth sunken and his fingers clenched.

'I've nothing to say to him Sarah, he's not coming and that's final.'

Sarah rarely questioned anybody, but she was also getting annoyed.

'Regardless of what's happened, he's still your dad, Jimmy. You've lost your mum, do you really want to lose him as well?'

Jimmy was astounded. He stood up quickly, his arm swiping across the table, striking his tea cup to the floor with a loud clatter. His face was red with fury as he stormed out of the café.

Sarah was mortified and followed him.

'I'm sorry Jimmy, please come back,' she called out.

Jimmy ignored her plea and Sarah was left sobbing in the street.

Chapter Three

On Sunday, when Sarah was at home in her room, there was a knock on the front door.

'I wondered when you'd show your face, Jimmy,' said Mrs Mays.

'I'm sorry.'

Sarah was relieved to hear Jimmy's voice.

'We've not seen our daughter so upset before. I hope you'll make things right.'

Mrs Mays was blunt and her eyes were unforgiving.

Sarah came out of her room and ran into Jimmy's arms.

'I'm sorry, so very sorry!' she said, kissing him all over his face.

'No! I'm sorry. I overreacted; I shouldn't have walked out on you. I wasn't sure you'd want to see me again.' Jimmy's eyes were blood shot and he was nervy, but he creased a smile of relief.

'I won't ask about Eddie going to the wedding again, I promise,' said Sarah.

'No! You're right, we should invite him. He doesn't worry me anymore. I've moved on and I'm happy. I want you to see the ogre for yourself.'

'If you're sure, Jimmy.'

'He probably won't come, but if he does, all I ask is you don't expect me to socialise with him.'

A week later, much to Jimmy's surprise, the invitation was accepted and Eddie took it upon himself to invite a guest. Her name was Maggie and she was described as a friend.

'I think it's a bit of a cheek. It's so typical of my father, he always thinks he can do what he likes, Sarah.'

'It's understandable. If Maggie is his girlfriend, what's he supposed to do, leave her behind?'

'I should've been asked first, Sarah.'

'Yes, but this is the kind of behaviour you expect from your dad.'

*

The celebration took place in All Hallows' Church in Tottenham. It was a warm and sunny day with only a slight breeze.

Sarah panicked at home. All sorts of doubts ran through her mind and they made her nervous.

'I'm not sure about these puffed sleeves, Mum, and the dress feels a bit tight under the arms.'

'You haven't complained before, Sarah.'

'I can't help it. I'm not sure about my hair either. I wish it was straight now.'

Mrs Mays was not impressed. She had spent a long time pin curling and styling it into rolls and waves. Whatever she or Doris did or said it was criticised.

Sarah hardly slept the previous night. She was tired and irritable and even questioned her love for Jimmy. There was now less than an hour before the wedding service.

Her mum took a firm grip of Sarah's arms. 'Are you getting married or not?' she asked, fed up of listening to Sarah's moaning, and rapidly losing patience.

Sarah burst into tears. She ran out of the room into the arms of her dad.

'What's the matter Princess?' he asked.

'I don't want people staring at me.'

Her dad smiled and held her hands. 'Is this what all the fuss is about?'

Sarah nodded, and he stood back.

'Have I ever told my daughter how beautiful she is?'

Sarah shook her head as tears dripped onto her cheeks.

'It's quite normal for a bride to have a few nerves on her wedding day. I'm sure your mum had some. I know I did and Jimmy will too. Come outside, I've a surprise for you.'

With money tight in the Mays family, Sarah believed her father and her sister were to escort her the short distance to the church on foot. However, when she walked up the steps to the street from her parent's flat, Ginger, her dad's boss, was ready to chauffer her by horse and cart. He was wearing a black tunic with a black top hat.

The horse was dressed in a navy blue and white coat. The harness was shiny black, and the cart was freshly painted white. It was decorated with navy blue, crepe paper carnations.

Sarah thought it was perfect and all her apprehension disappeared.

'Oh, Dad, it's wonderful. Thank you so much!'

Sarah clutched his arm and kissed his cheek. She quickly got herself ready and after her mother left for the church, she spent a few minutes chatting to Doris. Her sister was quiet all morning and Sarah knew she was upset, even if she did not show it. They were always together at home, but from now on, Doris would be alone.

'I'll come back home often, I promise Doris. One day you'll find a nice man to spend your life with.'

Doris listened attentively with her tears in check.

'I don't think any boys will want me, Sis.'

Sarah had made her sister's dress out of some old curtain material. It was pink and flowery, and its delicate lace top and cuffs complimented Sarah's gown.

'Of course they will; you look stunning Doris, I wish I was as pretty as you.'

Sarah was ready for the biggest day in her life and neighbours gathered on the street to witness her departure.

'Old on a minute girl, I'll throw summit down to make it easier for yer to get up on the back,' said Ginger, in his broad Cockney accent.

He reached behind his seat and picked up an old wooden banana box. When he hurled it off the cart, people laughed, but Sarah's face was beaming, as her dad helped her up along with her sister.

The horse trotted down Tottenham High Road to clapping from well-wishers as she passed by. Sarah was embarrassed as young men whistled. She did not look at them, but Doris smiled and waved.

Mr Mays did not have much use for posh clothes and was dressed in an old brown two-piece suit. It only got outings for weddings and funerals, but the trousers were pressed and the jacket was brushed. It was acceptable for the occasion.

As they arrived at the church, Sarah looked at the magnificent building dating back to the twelfth century. The tall tower at the western end soared above her, the church an imposing landmark for the local community. Its eight bells were ringing out to mark her special occasion, and Sarah's nerves took hold. If her dad was not beside her she would probably have gone home.

'They're all waiting for us inside. I'm scared Dad.'

'They're your family and friends, my Princess.'

Sarah gulped. She was nearly sick, and her dad squeezed her arm.

'Remember what I said. Let's go in and show everybody how beautiful you are.'

Inside, Reverend Fred Wissington nodded to Mrs Smelling, a small-boned lady in a sparkling yellow dress. She played Mendelssohn's Wedding March and immediately Sarah was unsteady on her feet. The butterflies in her stomach were doing somersaults and she was light-headed. Her father, sensing her anxiety, gently squeezed her hand again and held onto her arm.

'We're doing this together, Princess. Imagine everyone is dressed as a clown.'

Sarah shrieked with laughter.

'What, even the vicar, Dad?'

This jovial moment was all Sarah needed, and at the far end of the aisle, as she had imagined, Jimmy was staring back at her. He was grinning; his eyes longing for her to take his hand.

The beautiful sound of the organ engulfed the building and Sarah took a deep breath. Slowly she walked next to her dad, with her sister two paces behind.

The Reverend welcomed the congregation into the church. People were focused more on him than the bride, because of his peculiar mannerisms. While talking, he entwined his fingers and moved both arms up and down in a chicken-like fashion. Sarah almost laughed when he pronounced them man and wife. With the Reverend's arms flapping she thought he was going to lay an egg.

After the ceremony and the signing of the registers, everybody gathered outside the church. Johnny Bins, a photographer and friend of the family, agreed to take Sarah and Jimmy's wedding photos. In return, Mr Mays was to repair his greenhouse. Sarah thought it a bit futile during the war, but Mr Bins was happy.

It was four o'clock in the afternoon and the sun's rays were hot for the time of year. Sarah was sweltering in her wedding attire, as the guests took it in turns to offer their congratulations.

Sarah's grandmother, Madeline, was ninety-two and walked slowly towards her. She usually used a stick, but was determined to do this unaided, having practiced for weeks in her flat. Madeline was wobbly on her feet and Mrs Mays was worried her mother might fall over.

She hurried towards her. 'Let me help you, Mum.'

'No! Don't fuss!' she shouted, gesturing her daughter to keep away.

Every step was a milestone for Madeline until Sarah was able to reach out and gently hug her. For a few seconds they stood clasped in one another's arms. Madeline then stepped back and smiled, as she unclipped a silver pearl and crystal brooch from her jacket. Sarah knew it once belonged to her great-grandmother. It was Madeline's prized possession and dated back to 1850.

'I didn't think I'd be around to give you this, Sarah,' she said.

'Thank you so much, it's beautiful, I'll always treasure it.'

While Sarah embraced her granny again, Mrs Mays noticed her mother was shuffling her feet.

'Granny's getting tired and needs to sit down before she falls down,' she said.

Mrs Mays tried to take her arm, but Madeline was stubborn and pulled it away.

'I'm not a child!' she shouted.

'You've broken an arm on four occasions. The trouble is you've no fear these days. The last time was when you fell off a chair while changing a light bulb.'

Madeline fumed at her daughter as the guests laughed, but with some gentle persuasion, Mrs Mays was able to escort her away.

At the end of the queue was a man in an expensive grey suit. He wore thick dark-framed glasses and his black shoes shone like polished silver.

'That's my father, Sarah,' Jimmy whispered as he got closer.

'Hello boy; I see you're still a bit tubby.'

It was not the comment of a man who missed his flesh and blood. Jimmy did not respond, but he shook his father's hand, held out in front of him.

'You must be Sarah,' said Eddie.

He kissed her cheek and she felt a slimy wetness from his lips on her skin.

'I've heard a lot about you, Eddie,' said Sarah.

'Not all bad, I hope. This is Maggie,' he said, placing an arm around her shoulder.

She was in her early twenties and gave a cheesy smile.

'It's very good to meet you,' said Jimmy.

'Thank you, it's a good day for a wedding,' Maggie replied.

'I hope it doesn't get any hotter,' said Sarah.

'I love your dress,' said Maggie, examining the material around the sleeves with her fingers.

'It's second hand, my mum's actually.'

'Yes, I can see that,' said Maggie. She inhaled slightly and grunted her disapproval.

Maggie was five feet two inches tall, with a pretty face and long golden hair. She wore a light blue swing tea dress, neatly decorated with polka dots, and royal blue sandals, which made her stand out in the crowd. She was very confident and spoke slowly and precisely.

Intentionally or not, Sarah was humiliated by Maggie. She thought, 'What a nasty woman. She's only my age but obviously thinks she's a cut above the rest. I wonder why she wants to be with a fifty-three-year-old man.'

As they chatted, Maggie's eyes were fixed on Jimmy.

'You must come and visit us, I'd make you very comfortable,' Maggie said smiling.

Sarah was annoyed. Her husband of less than an hour was being chatted up by his father's girlfriend!

'I can't place your accent,' Sarah said, interrupting the conversation.

'I'm from Stockport in Cheshire and moved down to Norfolk a while back.'

'Why did you do that?' Sarah asked.

The question annoyed Maggie. She glared at Sarah, as if it was an intrusion to ask.

'It's a long story. I met Eddie in Castle Acre and we're together now; that's all that matters.'

'Where's Castle Acre?' asked Sarah.

'It's a Norfolk village and she was the barmaid in the White Horse,' said Eddie bluntly.

'I was a waitress and a barmaid.'

'Oh yes, I forgot you served cheese rolls and the like,' said Eddie.

Maggie frowned at him. She did not want to talk about the past and changed the conversation.

'I don't suppose he's told you, Jimmy, but we're moving next week. Eddie has bought a property in the same village, but it's much closer to the sea. It's a beautiful Georgian house called Hemsley Grange. I fell in love with it instantly, didn't I, Eddie?'

'Yes, my love, you did.'

Eddie wished she'd stop talking, but she rambled on.

'There's an old windmill in the back garden and a cottage by the edge of the cliffs. We even own the village green. I told him he must buy it, didn't I, Eddie?'

Maggie was speaking in a raised voice.

Talking even louder so everyone heard, while locking arms with Eddie, she said boastfully, 'Tell Sarah and Jimmy how much land we've got, darling.'

'I think I own about ten acres, but it includes a large field that's rented out.'

'The property comes with a position in the community,' said Maggie.

'You mean you'll have a title?' Jimmy asked.

'Not quite, but we'll be very important people as most events and activities involve Hemsley Grange and its proprietors.'

As they all made their way to reception, Sarah thought, 'It would be easy to make up several titles for this boastful, gobby woman.'

The reception was in a pub called the Hotspur. Fortunately, Mr Mays knew the landlord. They both supported the local football team and were friends, so the refreshments were cheap and plentiful.

Simple gifts were given to Sarah and Jimmy. Mr and Mrs Mays had saved up to buy them a double bed, there was a selection of crockery, a large blanket, two cushions, a bread bin and Doris had made them a tea cosy.

Eddie gave them an envelope containing twenty pounds which Sarah thought was very kind, but Jimmy accepted it grudgingly.

'Thank you, Dad, it's very good of you,' he said, without any enthusiasm in his voice.

'There's always more if you need it; all you have to do is ask. I mean it boy, I've more money than I can use and I'd like to help.'

Jimmy's face remained glum. Sarah knew he was barely tolerating his father and realised the past would never be forgotten.

'You'll need all you've got to keep me happy, darling,' said Maggie taking hold of his arm with both hands.

'I think she'll take Eddie for every penny he's got,' said Sarah, as they walked away.

'She's a bit full of herself, maybe her nerves are making her talk too much.'

'I don't usually say horrible things, Jimmy, but I think she has a big mouth.'

Although a happy day for the couple, rationing limited the wedding breakfast even further than money. Nevertheless, friends managed to save some coupons and a tasty buffet was prepared.

A top table was set up in a private room for the bride and groom, the bride's parents, the bridesmaid, the bridegroom's father, his friend Maggie and the best man Tom. Other guests were seated on chairs and stools around small pub tables.

Maggie was placed next to Tom, and Sarah heard her ask him lots of questions about Jimmy. She listened to their conversation and was thankful Tom refused to discuss his friend with a stranger.

As soon as the buffet was over, the speeches followed and Mr Mays caused some embarrassment.

'I have to tell you Jimmy, my daughter snores like the sound of the Queen Mary.'

Mr Mays was slurring his words after consuming three bottles of brown ale.

'No I don't!' Sarah shouted out.

'Well, listening from the next room, I thought I was at sea last night.'

There were shrills of laughter and murmurs of despair.

Sarah covered her ears and wondered what her father might say next.

'Why don't you shut up and sit down before you fall down,' said Mrs Mays.

Tom lowered the tone further in his best man speech. He told a joke about a bride and bridegroom in a bath and then a story about Jimmy urinating on Tottenham station. The more lubricated guests laughed again, but his humour was not to everyone's taste. He quickly moved on to read the cards and telegrams from absentees.

One of the messages was from Sarah's friend Jean. It read:

I don't know where I'll be, it may be far away. I'll be thinking of you now on your special day.

Momentarily everyone was silent, as many of the guests, relatives and friends were away, serving in Her Majesty's Forces. There were tears, but these few words also provided comfort, turning the sadness in people's eyes to smiles of joy.

When the formal proceedings were over, Maggie and Eddie found a quiet corner to talk. Their relationship only spanned eighteen months, since their paths first crossed and Eddie had flirted with Maggie in the White Horse.

At the time, it had not taken Maggie long to find out Eddie lived comfortably in Cleybourne, and she wanted to know more about him. She took an interest in his conversation and on subsequent visits he bought her chocolates and flowers. Maggie overwhelmed Eddie with affection and their romance blossomed. Over the coming weeks she fulfilled his every desire and, before long, they were living together in Cleybourne.

Maggie realised Eddie wanted an easy life in retirement and a younger playmate to keep him company. Her aspirations were different. There was a reason for everything she did, as she pursued her own agenda. She thought, 'I'll make something of myself in Hemsley Grange with or without him.'

'It isn't a bad do is it?' said Eddie, looking around the wedding breakfast.

Maggie put her hands over her face and shook her head.

'You must be kidding. It's loud, boozy and the table manners of some of the guests are disgusting. Some people have been drinking tea from saucers and Madeline licked her plate.'

'You're priceless Maggie. This is North London for heaven's sake and I'm proud to say the guests are my kind of people. I'm glad we came, as I didn't realise how much I'd missed Jimmy. Sarah's a nice girl, but I think she's a bit timid. I hope she'll tend to his needs.'

'I doubt he'll get the same pleasures you do, Eddie.'

'You're so vain, woman. You always think you're better than others. I was embarrassed by your boasting.'

'I don't care, most of them are dreadful people. They'd live in a hole if they needed to. I wanted Jimmy to know we're moving up in society; he's your son after all.'

'It means so much to you does it Maggie? To rub peoples noses in the dirt? Even in the war, with their world collapsing around them?'

'It's not my war, Eddie.'

'What about back in Stockport? You never mention your family.'

'I've told you before, I don't have one.'

'What did you do when you left school?'

'Why all these questions? It doesn't make any difference.'

'I'd like to know, if I'm going to spend my life with you.'

'I worked on a horse stud. I used to clean out stables and exercise the animals. Is that enough for you?'

'Is that all?' asked Eddie.

'Alright! I worked in a smart restaurant some evenings.'

'Is that where you got your posh voice?'

'No, Mrs Gaynor, the owner of the horse stud taught me. She disliked my common tones, but I'm not common anymore.'

'You can't change your past, Maggie.'

'I'm not arguing anymore; Hemsley Grange will be the making of us. We'll be lord and lady of the manor.'

Eddie laughed.

'You can be Lady Muck if you like, I'm going to get another beer.'

Sarah did not notice her mum and sister leave the pub. A few minutes later they returned and the bride and groom were told to close their eyes while a cake stand and three boxes were brought in.

'Can we open them now, Mum?'

'In a minute, Sarah.'

The last of three tiers was carefully lifted into its place and the guests gasped at the sight in front of them.

'You can now,' said Mrs Mays.

A beautiful wedding cake decorated with swirls of blue icing was standing on a trestle table dressed with a blue table cloth and white crape paper carnations.

Sarah cried easily, but she was not alone. It was only a cake, but it was what it stood for. Sugar was a main ingredient and it was rationed, but with people's generosity the iced delight was made in secret at a neighbour's house. This was a tradition and nothing the war did was going to stop it.

Mr Mays sang 'God Save the King'. He did not know why, but it seemed the right thing to do. Everybody stood up and joined in and it was heard through the open windows and out onto the high road.

Sarah and Jimmy cut the cake. With their hands clasped together they made an incision into the bottom layer. Everybody clapped again and for Sarah it was an amazing day.

In the time leading up to the wedding, Sarah had thought about her childhood. She was a quiet, introverted girl who struggled at school. Her life expectations were low, but in less than three years she had been swept off her feet in the most unlikely circumstances.

Sarah shared a few moments in a quiet area with her mum, knowing her life would never be the same again.

'There've been so many surprises today,' she said.

Mrs Mays was calm and content. 'I've been waiting for this day all my life.'

Small tears of joy fell from the corners of her eyes. Sarah did not remember the last time her mum was so jolly. Her friend Winnie had lent her a pink and blue floral dress. It complimented her short black wavy hair.

'Sarah, I hope you'll be as happy as me and your father have been. We've nothing but our love for one another and our two wonderful children, but our lives have been truly blessed.'

'Oh Mum, I love you so much.'

'I love you too, Sarah.'

Mother and daughter held each other tightly. Singing and dancing followed, accompanied by Madeline's sister, Violet on the piano. She was ninety-three and wheelchair-bound, but her fingers were still nimble enough to play the favourite tunes.

It was early evening, and after changing out of their wedding clothes, Sarah and Jimmy were ready to leave the pub for their honeymoon. When saying goodbye, most of the attention was paid to Sarah, so Maggie grasped the opportunity.

Away from the crowd, she approached Jimmy. Without warning, she wrapped her arms around him and kissed his lips. There was no resistance and she realised he was powerless to stop her.

'Are you sure you wouldn't like to come to Norfolk, Jimmy?'

There was desire in her kingfisher blue eyes.

'The taxi's here!' someone shouted out.

Sarah looked for Jimmy and was surprised to see him chatting to Maggie. 'I wonder why he's talking to her,' she thought.

'Come on, we have to go,' she called out.

'You take good care of my Sarah,' said Mrs Mays.

'I will, I promise,' Jimmy replied.

The vehicle pulled away and, with a deep lump in her throat, Sarah watched her mum waving until she disappeared out of sight. She was upset she did not say goodbye to her dad but remembered with so much beer inside him, he was asleep on the floor behind the piano.

Chapter Four

The honeymoon was for one night in a hotel in Southend-on-Sea. With low clouds stretching across the south east of England, Sarah was hoping the bombers would stay away.

A thirty-minute journey took them to Stratford, where they were to board their train. The taxi driver was wearing a red-stained white shirt.

'What's that smell?' asked Sarah. She put a handkerchief over her nose.

'I had an accident with a tin of tomato soup this morning and haven't had a chance to clear it up,' he replied.

Sarah noticed the cab was filthy. The windows were thick with road grime, there was a liquid stain on the passenger seat and bits of food were lying on the floor.

While travelling, the taxi driver decided to tell a joke.

'Did you hear the one about a man sneaking a woman into a hotel room and a waitress hiding under the bed?'

'Will you stop him?' said Sarah.

She was feeling too apprehensive about the hours that lay ahead to listen to this horrible man. Jimmy closed the glass panel behind the driver's seat.

Sarah had not been separated from her parents before and leaving home was a much bigger wrench than she imagined. For the first time, it dawned on her she would not be going home to Tottenham. Her belongings were now in Jimmy's flat in Leyton.

On entry to the station, Sarah visited the toilet twice. When returning for the second time, she heard an engine approaching and hurried up the stairs.

'I didn't think you'd make it,' said Jimmy.

Sarah was out of breath and panting as the carriages came to a halt. There were few passengers on the platform and, with Jimmy carrying a dark brown suitcase, they boarded the train.

The compartment was empty and smelled musty. For some reason Jimmy patted the seats and dust, in tiny particles, rose from the green tartan fabric.

'What are you doing Jimmy?'

Sarah sneezed and coughed repeatedly.

Jimmy slapped her on the back and when she stopped they both burst into laughter.

'I hope you're not always going to slap me.'

'Only when you cough,' he replied.

Sarah giggled.

The dust settled again and they cuddled up on the least worn part of the seat. Sarah was worried about the wedding night. She kept crossing and uncrossing her legs and playing with the curls in her hair. She chatted throughout the journey to hide her anxiety.

The engine's speed varied greatly, it rattled along quickly for lengthy periods, but for some of the time it crawled and even stopped occasionally.

'It's so peaceful out here, Jimmy.'

'Yes, there aren't so many buildings to bomb. This is our day, let's be selfish and concentrate on us.'

Jimmy kissed her passionately and let his hands wander.

'Not on the train!' said Sarah.

She pushed him away after the slightest touch.

'No one can come in, and we're married, Sarah.'

Jimmy moved along the seat and sulked.

'I'm not comfortable with you doing it here, it's still a public place.'

Sarah quickly changed the subject back to Eddie and Maggie.

'I liked your dad, I know what you said about him, but he was nice to me.'

'He was trying to impress you. My dad is always charming when he wants to be. Please don't be fooled.'

'I know, but it's our wedding day and you wanted him to be kind to me. I thought Maggie was a strange lady though. Did you see them arguing?'

'Yes, she wasn't happy,' said Jimmy.

'After your dad stormed off I didn't see her talk to him or anyone else. Perhaps she was bored and thinks being in the back room of a pub is beneath her.'

'I don't know why, Sarah, she was a barmaid wasn't she?'

'Oh yes I forgot; she didn't like being reminded of it though. Maggie gave me the impression she liked you. Whenever we were close to her I noticed her eyes were focused in your direction.'

Jimmy laughed it off.

'I'm not surprised; I'm a big catch, you're a very lucky woman.'

'It's you who's the lucky one. What were you talking about outside the pub?'

'I was being sociable that's all.'

Sarah and Jimmy's train eventually rattled into Southend station. While they were walking along the platform, the engine let out a ferocious jet of steam. Sarah screamed and the driver laughed out loud from his cab.

'He did it on purpose,' said Sarah.

Jimmy glared at the man. His face was blackened with coal dust, but he laughed even more. Taking hold of her hand, Jimmy led her away from the train.

'Don't let that idiot upset you,' he said.

Without further confrontation, they exited the station building. It was only a ten-minute walk down the main road to the hotel, but Southend had not escaped the war. There was bomb destruction only a short distance away in front of them and their hearts sank.

'I hope our hotel isn't in ruins,' said Sarah.

'Try not to worry, it's probably okay, but what will be will be.'

Jimmy spoke to a policeman, as the immediate area was cordoned off and they did not know which way to go.

'Walk down there, mate, and turn right by Judy's Cleaners or what's left of it. Then go right again at the Pig and Whistle and you'll be back on Station Road.'

There was a chill in the evening air and Jimmy put his jacket over Sarah's shoulders. Walking down the darkened streets, they passed a large crater and mounds of rubble where properties once stood.

After the short detour, their hotel was in front of them. It was a two-storey property called the Victoria. It was just after ten o'clock when they entered the building through a heavy squeaky door. It was in semi-darkness, but a light from a white candle, almost burnt to its base, exposed a small reception area.

One room key was dangling from a piece of string on a hook behind the desk and there was a calendar hanging from a nail on the wall. Closer inspection revealed it had not been changed since 3 April. On the floor there was a waste bin over flowing with paper.

'What do we do now, Jimmy?'

There was not a service bell on the desk.

'I don't know, Sarah.'

She cast her eyes around the dingy surroundings. Pictures haphazardly decorated the walls. There was a washed-out blue rug on the floor inside the entrance and an armchair cluttered with newspapers. Most uninviting was the pungent smell of fish that filled their nostrils.

'Somebody's coming down the stairs,' whispered Sarah.

She heard shoes pounding the wooden treads and in seconds a man with broad shoulders and a thick neck arrived to greet them. He was holding a bucket and a long-handled brush.

'It's Mr and Mrs Jackson isn't it? Sorry to keep you, I'm Mr Coombs the owner. I heard the door go when you came in, but I was unblocking a toilet.'

He held out his hand to greet his guests, but his palm was still damp and his fingers were wet. Fortunately, Sarah was wearing gloves.

Mr Coombs did not stop talking. In a couple of minutes, he gave Sarah and Jimmy a potted history of his life. He told them he and his wife purchased the hotel in 1936 and described it as an elderly retreat, mainly for old biddies.

'The odd one drops off now and again, but the rooms are never empty for very long. Between you and me, I think its Mrs Mead who's stuffed up the bog. She spends hours in there and uses so much paper. She's been here since Christmas and this happens often. I think I'll charge her for two rooms in future.'

He was still talking as he handed Jimmy a form to fill in.

'I've put you in room twelve, which is next to Mrs Mead on the second floor. Is that okay for you?'

Jimmy did not have a chance to reply.

'I hope so, it's the only room I have, although I suppose you can share with Daphne Fielding. She's away with the fairies and wouldn't know if you both slept in her bed with her.'

Mr Coombs chuckled as if he did not care.

'Room twelve will do,' Jimmy replied.

Mr Coombs picked up their suitcase and led them upstairs. On entering the room, Sarah's spirits were deflated, as there was not a lock on the door. It had been removed leaving a large hole and there was not an inside bolt. The door wouldn't shut unless a small piece of wood lying on the floor was wedged under its bottom.

'I'm not sure I can stay here,' she said.

Mr Coombs laughed.

'Well, there's a war on you know,' he replied.

'Can't you see my wife's upset?' said Jimmy.

'It's up to you. Take it or leave it, but I'm not refunding your money. I didn't advertise a lock on the door.'

Mr Coombs was a horrible man, but Sarah and Jimmy did not have a choice. It was late in the evening and there was nowhere else to go.

When Mr Coombs left the room Sarah and Jimmy kissed. It was a sense of relief for both of them to be on their own. They purposely fell back onto the bed in each other's arms and the mattress creaked like an old wooden gate. Coming out of the embrace, they did not know whether to laugh or cry.

'I'm going to the bathroom Jimmy. When I get back would you mind freshening up while I get into bed?'

Toilet and bathroom facilities were situated down the corridor and shared with three other rooms on the same floor.

Someone was using the facilities and while standing outside the door, Sarah heard the continuous rustling of paper. It was like a fox in a dustbin, until the chain was pulled. Two minutes later it was tugged again, before a woman wreaking of body odour with long matted grey hair opened the door.

Sarah thought, 'It must be Mrs Mead,' and held her breath as she came out. Inside it was damp, the walls were decorated with fungus and there was an unpleasant smell coming from a puddle on the floor. She did what she needed to do as quickly as possible and returned to the room.

'You'd better hurry, Jimmy, in case Mrs Mead makes another appearance.'

While he was away, Sarah undressed. Fumbling with her shaking hands, she unfastened her bra and put on a pink lace nightie. She got into bed and lay on her back with the covers covering her shoulders.

On his return, Jimmy wedged the piece of wood hard under the door with the back of his heel. He hung his jacket on the handle to cover the hole left from the removal of the lock.

Sarah watched, as he took off his shirt and trousers and laid them on the floor. There was a tingling all over her body, as with his back to her he removed his pants. She was silently panting, her eyes wide and starry.

Jimmy tried to hide the surge of energy in his body. It was threatening to burst and he quickly turned out the light. The room fell into complete darkness, as the window was blacked out. Carefully he made his way along the side of the bed by feeling the covers, and Sarah moved to one side, so he was able to lie next to her.

As soon as he got in, the expected creaks gave way to a cracking sound like burning wood followed by a clonk.

'What was that, Jimmy?'

They both jumped up and rushed out of bed.

Jimmy put on the light and Sarah covered the top of her flimsy nightie with her arms. Jimmy put his hands over his favourite toy and they both laughed out loud.

'Look! A leg of the wooden bedstead has gone through a floorboard,' said Jimmy.

'Can we manage with three legs?'

'I don't know, Sarah, what did you think we would do with them?'

'The beds at an angle, Jimmy, you'll be sliding onto me.'

They laughed again and kissed passionately.

Sarah was now shivering in the cold of the night, as Jimmy examined the floor. He decided the bed would not move any further and she got back under the covers. He joined her and despite many more creaks the bed remained stable.

'I love you so much,' said Jimmy, moving his hands gently over Sarah's body.

She stayed silent and motionless out of both fear and anticipation. Reaching under her clothing with the tips of his fingers, Jimmy made his way up over her stomach. Sarah was finding it hard to both kiss him and prepare for the moments that lay ahead.

Sarah was breathing heavily, as Jimmy squeezed and stroked her so gently, she felt like she was floating on a cloud. He moved his hand down and gently inserted his fingers inside the top of her panties. She gasped as he reached a little lower. All thoughts of family, friends and the war were temporarily erased from Sarah's mind.

The air raid siren sounded. Unknown to them the weather conditions had improved enough for a bombing raid. Rising from their bed in haste again, they quickly dressed and made their way downstairs and out into the back garden. The hotel's shelter housed up to twenty-five people. There were benches to sit on, provisions to make tea and some basic supplies.

The elderly guests, many of whom found it difficult to walk, took a long time to get to the shelter. Some were still arriving when the 'all clear' was sounded. Fortunately, the bombs never came that night, although the drones of the planes were heard in the distance.

'I expect London and the docks are the targets again, Jimmy.'

'I suppose so, but at least the raids come less often now.'

Sarah and Jimmy returned to their room. Their honeymoon was a disaster. Everything was against them, so they decided to wait until they got home to consummate their marriage. They wanted to make love where they would be comfortable, in their own surroundings.

Somehow Sarah and Jimmy managed to get some sleep and in the morning they ate a hot breakfast. It was cooked by Mrs Coombs but did not look very appetising. Fried food was lying in fat on their plates, but they were hungry and forced it down.

'Mr Coombs, this is the worst place I've ever stayed in,' said Jimmy, when leaving.

Sarah stayed silent.

'You haven't stayed in many places then have you, Mr Jackson?'

This flippant reply incensed Jimmy.

'The food is disgusting as well.'

Mr Coombs laughed. 'Well, yes my wife can't cook. I never said she could.'

'Come on Jimmy, there's no point arguing.'

They made their way out onto the street and Mr Coombs called out, 'I assume you won't be returning then!'

On Sarah and Jimmy's journey back to Leyton, low clouds returned to dominate the sky. It was Sunday morning and when they reached the station it was heaving with people.

'Are the trains running?' said Jimmy to a guard on the platform.

'There was a fire by the track down the line, mate, but it's out now. You should get away in about half an hour.'

Ten minutes later, a shunting engine pushed eight empty carriages into the station and passengers opened the doors almost simultaneously. They quickly filled the seats and standing room in every compartment. The netted luggage racks above bulged with bags and cases.

Sarah sat with her arms tight against her body. She was squeezed between two large men in army uniform and was pleased to get to Stratford. The cocktail of cigarette smoke, coal dust and poor personal hygiene churned her stomach.

'Any longer on the train Jimmy, and I'd have been sick. My fried breakfast was whirling inside me.'

'Yes, it was oppressive, we'll feel better by the time we get home.'

They walked to Jimmy's flat in steady pouring rain. It was two miles and the broken streets reminded them they were in the grip of war. Bomb craters, demolished buildings and cracked roads were everywhere.

'I hate it, Jimmy, people dying all the time.'

Sarah was looking at a shelter blown to pieces, next to the remains of three terraced houses.

'It's hard, but we have to get on with our lives regardless. We owe it to the soldiers, sailors and airmen fighting for us,' said Jimmy.

Within days, Sarah was homesick. When she was alone, she missed her mother, although she only lived five miles from her home in Tottenham. Tears sometimes fell from her eyes, as she pondered over whether she was cut out to be a housewife.

Her life improved when she got a job in another munitions factory in Leytonstone. It was only one stop away from Leyton on the tube. Her employment hours enabled her to get home by four-thirty each afternoon.

Sarah was not impressed with Jimmy's living conditions. He was untidy and she constantly cleared up after him. When Sarah moved into his flat, there were remains of food on the floor, old dingy curtains hanging, a layer of grease on the inside of the oven and dust on every surface. There was also a washing-up bowl full to the brim with dirty crockery and clothes lay everywhere.

'Did you ever do any cleaning Jimmy?'

'I've always been on my own, so there's not been much point. That's why I wanted a wife. It's cheaper than a housekeeper and with benefits,' he said, jokingly.

'We'll have to see. I'll be tired out if I've to clear up after you every day, then I'll need a good night's sleep!'

Sarah was house-proud and did not understand how Jimmy lived in such a mess. It took her a few days of hard graft to clean the flat from top to bottom. Keeping it spotless was a challenge because of the road grime and the heavily polluted air.

As the weeks went by, Jimmy's temper troubled Sarah. Sometimes he was discontented with everything around him. He told her the barrage of abuse he suffered for not serving in the war was relentless and building. Initially, Sarah was very supportive and understanding, but Jimmy's behaviour got progressively worse and it worried her. He was now in the habit of drinking heavily in The Coach and Horses, every evening after work.

Chapter Five

'Why can't you come straight home, Jimmy?'

'Because I can't Sarah; you'll never understand how I feel.'

His steely eyes fixated on her as she dared to question him. Jimmy's friends in the pub understood the truth about his disability, but Sarah worried as his frame of mind was now unstable.

Every workday evening, Sarah thought about Jimmy walking home. She did not know what state he would be in and was concerned he might injure himself falling over debris on the pavement in the dark.

For these past few weeks, Sarah dreaded the moment his key turned in the lock, and on hearing his footsteps she drew breath. She cringed, listening to him struggling to walk up the narrow stairway.

Sarah and Jimmy's second-storey flat consisted of one bedroom and a lounge and kitchen combined. The toilet was in the back garden and shared with the occupants downstairs. There was not a bath.

Trying to act as normal as possible, Sarah planted a warm kiss on his cheek and removed the coat from his back. She noticed Jimmy's eyes were bloodshot and some vomit was on his tie and shoes.

Sarah, trying to disguise her concern, chatted about her day as she removed his dinner from the oven. Jimmy stayed silent as he watched her place it on the table in front of his favourite chair. It was next to the electric fire where his slippers were warming.

'Is it too much to ask you to eat with me? You're a bloody selfish cow!' he bellowed.

Sarah was startled as he raged at her. She had taken the brunt of his temper before, but this was the first time he had complained about eating alone. Jimmy was more inebriated than usual. He was swearing and shouting so much she was shaking.

'I'm sorry,' she said softly, trying to calm his anger.

Sarah was not able to prepare Jimmy's dinner for when he arrived home. It was dependant on his time in the pub, but at this moment she was not about to tell him. Jimmy had not abused Sarah physically before, but he reached out a hand and wrenched at her hair.

Sarah screamed. 'Stop it you're hurting me!'

Jimmy continued to pull her hair as Sarah yelped in pain. Letting go, he led her closer to the table with a firm grip of her arm.

'Look at it, it's been in the oven for hours, bloody hours, woman!'

His voice boomed around the flat as he shouted.

'I'm really sorry, Jimmy.'

Sarah struggled free and moved out of his reach, but Jimmy was not listening. He picked up his dinner and threw it like a back-handed tennis shot, catching her head with the side of the plate. The food splattered against the wall and the plate broke into pieces. Her head was stinging as she wondered what he might do next.

'Stop it, Jimmy, please stop it!' she pleaded.

The air raid siren sounded. For once Sarah was relieved to hear this dreadful noise, heralding yet more terror for the streets of London.

Sarah and Jimmy made their way downstairs out into the back garden where an old waterway tunnel served as a bomb shelter. Sarah carried blankets and pillows, as it was cold and damp inside. She also took containers for her and Jimmy's personal needs.

Sometimes, in this dingy makeshift shelter, four families huddled together for most of the night. Oil lamps lifted the darkness and when the light shone on Sarah's face, Jimmy saw there was a cut above her left eyebrow. He was now sober and mortified by what he had done.

A basic first aid kit was kept in the tunnel, in a black tin box by the entrance. Jimmy cleaned up Sarah's wound with TCP.

'How did you do that?' asked Dorothy Turner.

She was a nosy neighbour and an off-duty nurse. She noticed the nasty gash on Sarah's face.

'I caught it on a kitchen cupboard,' Sarah quickly replied.

'Oh, you poor thing, let me dress it for you.'

Living next door, she was used to Jimmy bellowing. Dorothy had listened to his angry tongue this evening and heard a crash; she did not believe the explanation.

'It's all right, I'll do it,' said Jimmy, continuing to dab Sarah's injury.

'I shouldn't have to lie for you,' she whispered.

'I'm sorry; I don't know what came over me. Please forgive me.'

Planes were soon heard in the sky. The frightening rumbling sound gathered in strength, but the aircraft did not come close. They released their horror far away and the 'all clear' siren indicated that the shelter occupants had survived another night unscathed.

Sarah was content to stay in the shelter. She may have been spared an onslaught from above, but she endured a frightening ordeal inside her home. Once back in the flat, Jimmy attempted to put his arms around her, but she rejected him.

'I don't want you near me.'

Sarah's woeful eyes expressed her disappointment. Jimmy's behaviour was now rational and remorseful.

'I want to comfort you, that's all.'

The size of their home meant they were always in close company, but they sat on opposite sides of the kitchen table.

'Please, Sarah, I love you.'

'Not tonight, Jimmy.'

Few words were spoken during the following days. They continued to sleep in the same bed, but every night Sarah turned her back on Jimmy. There were many women who wanted their men home from the war, but she wished Jimmy was away fighting.

For a while, he drank less and was more attentive, but Sarah was wary of him. Begrudgingly, she sometimes submitted to his sexual needs, but there was no passion in her lovemaking and Jimmy sensed her resistance. After several weeks, Sarah still did not warm to Jimmy. She wanted to forgive him, but her body would not let her.

*

August 1944

Jimmy was drinking heavily again. He was unpredictable and even frightening, with his shouting and acts of aggression. Sometimes he banged his hands on the table in anger for no reason and Sarah was petrified. Wanting to keep the peace, she tried to stay calm and tender to his every need.

One evening, after another drunken spree, Jimmy's intentions were clear as soon as he returned home. After entering the flat, he shut the door behind him with such force its surrounds shuddered, and a picture frame fell to the floor. Sarah prayed for an air raid, but it did not come.

Jimmy's large imposing frame dwarfed Sarah's as he limped and staggered towards her. She smelled beer on his breath and burnt tobacco on his cigarette-stained jacket.

'What are you doing, Jimmy? You're frightening me.'

The atmosphere was ugly and intense. Jimmy grinned and stayed silent while clenching his fingers. Sarah watched him open the bedroom door and she screamed as Jimmy reached out an arm. Sarah knew there was no escape.

'No, Jimmy! Please, no! This is wrong!' Sarah shouted.

He grasped her wrists tightly and she tried to pull away, but he was too strong and laughed at her. Having dragged her inside, he flung her across the bed on to the floor beyond.

'Don't do this!' she pleaded.

Sarah crouched with her elbows close to her chest and her hands on her face. She was horror-struck, watching his eyes bulging as he ground his teeth. Jimmy looked at her like a piece of meat.

He took off his jacket and tossed it over a chair. Sarah heard him breathing heavily, as he undid his belt and threw it behind him.

'No! I won't let you, Jimmy, it's the drink talking.'

Sarah cowered in the corner of the room. Unnerving her even more, he smiled as he unzipped his trousers. She took a gasp of air and let it out in a raging scream with all the vigour she was able to muster.

Jimmy didn't care. He stood over Sarah and lowered his trousers, revealing a bulge in his wet pants. He took them off slowly but deliberately and then, for the first time since arriving home, Jimmy spoke.

'You're not going to make a fool of me any longer!'

He was shouting and throwing his arms about.

'I'd never do that, Jimmy.'

Sarah watched his every movement with trepidation.

'Shut up, just shut up!'

Sarah wouldn't keep quiet. 'Please Jimmy, you don't have to do this.'

'I told you to shut up!'

Sarah begged him. 'Please don't hurt me, Jimmy.'

'I don't think you've ever wanted me, but you're going to have me now, whether you like it or not!'

Pulling Sarah back onto the bed by her right arm, he wrenched her shoulder and she yelled out in pain. Jimmy was oblivious to her suffering and incapable of stopping. He pinned her other arm down onto the bed covers, using his other hand.

There was nothing Sarah could do. Kneeling with his legs straddling hers, Jimmy grabbed hold of her blouse. Ripping it apart, the tiny buttons popped and scattered around the room. Tears were running down Sarah's face.

'Please don't, I love you, this isn't right!' she pleaded again.

Jimmy was unmoved and unrelenting.

'It's too late for all that lovey-dovey stuff, much too late.'

Clasping her bra in the centre, he pulled it upwards. She screamed out, as the straps cut into her shoulders and back until it snapped, relieving the pressure and exposing her breasts.

Jimmy was relentless and placed an arm over Sarah's chest. He used his other hand to remove her skirt. It was elasticated, and he pulled it down over her legs until it was freed.

Sarah was motionless. She was not going to provide any resistance. Whatever Jimmy was going to do, she wanted it over with quickly.

Releasing his grip on her upper body he used both hands to remove her knickers. Jimmy's body was awash with sweat and the odour from his armpits and lower body was overwhelming. Placing his lips on hers, as he lay on her body, she tasted his brown ale. She almost retched and found it hard to breathe.

Sarah clenched her fists, gritted her teeth and closed her eyes. She was shaking and it seemed like a lifetime with Jimmy's weight bearing down upon her.

After a few minutes, Jimmy rolled off Sarah, laid back on the bed and instantly fell asleep. Within seconds he was snoring and, for a moment, it was like any other night after he came home from the pub. Sarah sobbed uncontrollably.

With her body aching, she gingerly walked into the kitchen. She scrubbed herself until she bled and lay on the couch. Sarah shivered and comforted herself with a cushion and a thick woollen blanket. She did not sleep a wink and cried all night.

The following morning, Jimmy awoke as usual when the alarm clock went off at six-thirty. Walking out of the bedroom, he found Sarah sitting at the kitchen table drinking tea. He talked about the day ahead as if nothing had happened; using his drunken state to mask the wrongdoing he was guilty of.

'What are we having for tea tonight?' he asked.

Sarah's eyes were full of sadness and she did not look at him.

'I'll see what they've got in the butcher's. I've got rations for a couple of sausages.'

Despite her frightening ordeal, her anger gradually turned to guilt. 'If I'd been more of a wife it would never have happened,' she thought.

Sarah feared for the future, but she was not going to leave Jimmy. Times were hard and there was a war on. Also her parents wouldn't understand. They believed you marry for better or worse.

She picked herself up and got on with her daily routine, but at work she received the most terrible news. Her mother, father and sister had been killed in a bombing raid in Tottenham the previous evening. They were in their neighbour's shelter when it received a direct hit and the thirteen occupants died.

Sarah's mind was full of grief, she wanted to die there and then. She was allowed to go home and sobbed on the train. This was not an unusual sight during the war. There were many reasons for sadness, but people carried on with their lives.

'Can I help you, my dear?' asked an old lady with a walking stick.

She offered a comforting arm, but her kindness caused Sarah to cry even more. There was nothing that would console her. Sarah's world was torn apart. Regardless of what happened the previous evening, she needed Jimmy and wanted him home.

Jimmy did not to stop at the pub that evening and arrived early. Her usual dread of him opening the door turned to eagerness. As soon as he entered she cried and Jimmy hugged her tightly. He noticed her blouse was soaked with tears.

'What is it, Sarah?'

She was hardly able to speak, but taking her time, she managed to find the words.

'I can't believe I'll never see my family again.'

'Oh Sarah, it's the most awful news.'

'I can't go on without them, Jimmy.'

They sat down on the couch and she collapsed in his arms.

'I'll miss them too, Sarah. With my mum dead and my dad not around, they became my family. I'm so sorry, so very sorry. I know I did a dreadful thing last night. I can't really remember, but I know something bad happened, something really bad and now this. It's too much for you to bear.'

Sarah raised her head from Jimmy's chest and nodded.

'I do love you, Sarah, but my head gets full of such awful things and then the drink takes over. I know there's no excuse, but yesterday, when I got into work, there was a sheet of paper in my overalls. It listed the names of three people who previously worked in the factory and died fighting in the war. It was headed up:

To the Crippled Coward

Sarah was very forgiving and needed Jimmy. 'I know it's hard, but you have to stop drinking, whatever the provocation at work. Come home to me and if we comfort each other, we can get through this, we can get through anything together.'

'I promise.'

The next few days were even harder for Sarah. In her mind she tried to relive her years in Tottenham and her overriding memory was seeing how happy her mum was on her wedding day.

Sarah felt guilty because she was not with her parents when the bomb struck. She was frightened the future years would make her forget them and her sister.

Night after night, Sarah did not sleep. Jimmy made all the arrangements for the funerals and while she grieved, he ensured she was as comfortable as possible.

The funerals took place a few days later. People were used to death; it was the consequence of war. However, the loss of three family members captured the hearts of the community. As the mourners made their way to All Hallows' Church, the high Street was lined with people. Friends, neighbours and shopkeepers came together and this act of kindness warmed Sarah's heart.

A cold penetrating rain dampened the dismal proceedings, and by the time the coffins were lowered into the ground, the grass was sodden and caked with mud.

During the wake, the mourners reminisced about the past. Sarah was pleased to see her mum's sister Lily, who was unable to attend the wedding because of a broken ankle. Lily lived alone in Broxbourne and made the journey down to Tottenham by train. Her presence provided a tonic for Sarah. Regardless of any occasion, she always found something to be cheerful about.

She told Sarah many stories about her mum from their childhood.

'You may not believe it Sarah, but she ate spiders, stroked a lion's nose through a circus cage and she once put a bag of bad eggs under our mum's bed.'

'Did the lion mind being touched, Auntie Lily?'

'I think she must have been fed, otherwise she'd have bitten your mum's fingers off.'

'How about grandma, what did she say about the eggs?'

'She thought it was your Uncle Ted that did it. It's a shame, he died before you were born. He was so funny; you'd have loved him.'

'That's terrible. Didn't my mum own up, Auntie Lily?'

'She kept quiet and so did I. Ted was made to weed her garden for a whole summer; it was really funny.'

The more stories Lily told, the more Sarah laughed.

'It's difficult for you to imagine at the moment, but eventually all the wonderful memories you have of your mum, dad and sister will become a comfort to you.'

*

Two weeks later, Sarah felt nauseous and did not want her breakfast. When arriving at work, a severe tummy ache caused her to rush to the toilet. She tried to reach a cubicle, but her stomach was churning, and as she opened the door she was sick over the floor. This was now her daily routine and continued until she admitted to herself she might be pregnant.

A visit to her doctor and the result of a test confirmed her worst thoughts. Sarah was distraught, and her condition would become obvious sooner rather than later.

When Jimmy came home he was asked to sit down.

'What is it? You look petrified.'

Sarah was on edge, she fidgeted and her voice stuttered.

'I have some news, I've been to the doctor today and he's confirmed I'm pregnant.'

She was glum, but Jimmy was delighted.

'That's wonderful,' he replied.

Jimmy's face was beaming, but then he noticed her solemn face. It only took a moment for him to guess when the baby was conceived, and he tempered his enthusiasm.

'God bless you, Sarah,' he said.

Jimmy held her hands and planted a kiss on her cheek, but she did not warm to him. She walked over to the window and burst into tears. He followed her and placed his hands on her shoulders.

'It'll be okay, Sarah, I promise you it will.'

Sarah, however, continued to sob and thought to herself, 'I don't want a child born out of rape.'

Chapter Six

During the next few months, the news coming from the British Armed Forces in most parts of the world was positive. The end of the conflict seemed to be in sight. Sarah was relieved. The bombing raids were now infrequent, which meant less time spent in cold and cramped shelters.

One day, when she was at home alone, a letter addressed to Jimmy dropped onto the door mat. She felt something enclosed other than paper and as the envelope came unstuck in her hand she opened it.

Sarah was shocked to find a photo of Maggie, in a loose low-cut dress. Printed at the bottom in bold capitals was the name Miss Maggie MacArdle. From the letter, it was obvious Eddie was not aware of Maggie's correspondence. There was only a passing reference to him, but there were many compliments paid to Jimmy. Sarah read:

Come and live with us in Hemsley Grange. My home has plenty of room and we would really get to know each other.

Sarah did not care for Maggie's intrusion into Jimmy's life and questioned her motive. 'I wonder why she wants him to live in Hemsley Grange? Is the invitation for me too?' she thought.

After placing the letter and photo back in the envelope, Sarah sealed it and left it on the kitchen table. When Jimmy got home from work, he was surprised by the correspondence. He read it privately in the outside toilet.

'Who's the letter from, Jimmy?'

'It's only an old work colleague.'

'Why has he written to you?'

'To tell me his wife died of pneumonia. She used to cook me a meal sometimes.'

'Oh, I'm sorry. Has he asked you to go to the funeral?'

'It happened last week,' Jimmy replied.

Sarah hated being lied too. It made her worry that Jimmy harboured feelings for Maggie.

*

While she was pregnant, Sarah did not feel maternal. However, her expanding body mass increased her weight and restricted her movements. The resulting tiredness made her irritable.

Having given up work, Sarah rested more and with time on her hands she re-affirmed her belief she would not be a good mother to her baby.

Unknown to Jimmy, Sarah decided to enquire about adoption and went to the local library. She found the address of a charity which specialised in helping couples who desperately want children.

The office was situated in Edmonton in a tall double-fronted building, blighted with grime. Paint was peeling from every brick and plywood covered two blown-out windows.

'Surely this can't be the right address?' thought Sarah, but the black front door was open, and she walked into a long dimly lit hallway. Her heels gently tapped the stone floor with every step.

'Yes, can I help you?' A voice called out from a side room.

The office manager, Miss Watson, invited her in. She was about sixty years old, with large hips and thick eyelashes.

Sarah mumbled her words as she explained her situation. Miss Watson, now seated, was very dismissive. When Sarah tried to explain her circumstances in detail, she would not listen.

'You reap what you sow,' she said, with her arms folded. Miss Watson spoke with a raised voice and was aggressive and unsympathetic. Standing up behind her desk, she asked Sarah to leave. 'I've work to do, please see yourself out.'

Sarah was not going anywhere. She thought about the baby every day since her pregnancy was confirmed. She reasoned it would never be loved and would be better off with parents who wanted it.

Although intimidated by this woman, and with her hands shaking, she was undeterred. She planted them on the officer's desk and spread her fingers.

'This isn't easy for me you know. Do you think I've come to this decision lightly? This baby is part of me; every day I feel it inside my body.'

Sarah noticed the officer was addressed as Miss.

'You've not known this feeling, have you? Thinking about giving up your own flesh and blood. This notion has been going round and round in my head. It'll probably be the hardest thing I ever have to do in my life.'

Miss Watson was rarely on the wrong side of an argument, but Sarah moved her and she was invited to sit down. The words were not easy, but when she told Miss Watson she was raped and about the tragedy in her family, her attitude changed. She was an upholder of woman's rights and a strong believer in equality. Miss Watson became caring and supportive.

'Oh my dear, that's awful. I can't imagine how you've been coping with this burden.'

'I can't forgive Jimmy, but he's been very supportive.'

'So he should be, after what he did. What does he think about the adoption?'

Sarah had not discussed it with him and reluctantly lied, 'He knows it's the right thing to do,' she said.

Miss Watson sensed some hesitation in her voice and realised she did not want Jimmy involved at this time. This was highly irregular, but she trusted Sarah to gain his agreement if needs be, knowing they would both have to sign papers for the adoption to go ahead.

'This is a very unusual case Mrs Jackson. I can't promise anything, but I'll make some enquiries.'

A week later, Sarah was invited to a meeting with both Miss Watson and a welfare officer from the council. A laborious process followed, involving a series of discussions to establish, beyond doubt that Sarah was emotionally prepared to give up her baby.

Sarah was not sure how she kept her secret and anxiety from Jimmy, but finally she received the news she was waiting for.

In a further meeting, Miss Watson said, 'I'm pleased to confirm the adoption can go ahead.'

Sarah was relieved. The procedure was not designed for people like her. She thought, 'In different circumstances I'd give my baby all the love it needed,' and her heart skipped a beat.

'Thank you so much, Miss Watson,' she said.

'Normally our 'mothers to be' go into one of our homes prior to birth and even though you're married, Sarah, I still think it's a good idea. I've allocated you a place in Cotland in

Stamford Hill. You'll be transported from there to the Hackney Mothers' Hospital for the delivery.'

'I'd sooner stay at home, Miss Watson.'

'I know, but I think it's for the best. Afterwards you'll return to Cotland until adoption parents are found.'

'Why do I have to stay in Cotland?'

Miss Watson did not like being questioned and as in their first meeting she became agitated and raised her voice.

'Sarah, I must remind you we normally only cater for unmarried mothers. I've made an exception, but you must abide by my rules. Jimmy can come and see you, but it's not a good idea for you to bond with your baby at home.'

Sarah knew she was not going to change Miss Watson's mind and, in truth, a great weight was lifted from her shoulders. Now she needed to tell her husband but kept putting off this unenviable task. There were now only three weeks to the birth and Sarah decided she must talk to Jimmy.

Next morning, they were lying in bed when there was a noise coming from outside their window.

Jimmy got up and pulled back the curtains.

'Sarah! There're masses of people in the street. They're banging dustbin lids together, they're dancing and jumping around. Can you hear them singing?'

Sarah was hardly awake.

'Come back to bed, it's still dark,' she replied.

Jimmy opened the window.

'Listen, it's going mad out there. The war's over, it's bloody over, I know it is!'

He dived on the bed, cuddled Sarah and rolled her over the top of him.

'Careful, mind the baby!' said Sarah.

*

8th May 1945

It was VE Day and people were already partying early in the morning. Sarah and Jimmy made their way to central London by tube to join in the celebrations. Huge crowds gathered in Trafalgar Square and outside Buckingham Palace.

Sarah and Jimmy stood close to the statue of Queen Victoria and like so many others they let the stress of war release from their bodies. They embraced strangers, laughed, danced, swayed and sung.

Some people climbed trees, statues, railings or lamp posts; anything they were able to get a foot on. The party atmosphere was unrelenting, but at dusk Sarah and Jimmy decided to make their way home.

They had only walked a few yards when Sarah experienced some abdominal pain. At first it was an uncomfortable ache, but then she winced and doubled over.

'This shouldn't be happening, the baby isn't due yet, Jimmy.'

'Perhaps it's something you've eaten, Sarah.'

'It's more than that; I've never known such agony. I think it's coming out. I'm scared, Jimmy.'

Sarah grabbed his arm for support, while looking at swarms of people all around her and listening to the continuous din. The noise of exuberance, previously exciting, now frightened her as further pain raged in her body.

Not wishing to take any chances, they decided to go to the Mothers' Hospital. This was where Sarah's expected birth was registered.

'We'll not get a bus around here,' said Jimmy.

Sarah was in considerable distress, but somehow she managed to push through the crowd surging in the opposite direction. Holding onto Jimmy tightly, she squeezed past people who were still arriving to join in the celebrations. Eventually, they were away from all the euphoria and were waiting at a bus stop.

'How long will it be Jimmy? I think I need to get to the hospital soon.'

Sarah was crying, but Jimmy was powerless to help her. To their relief, in seconds a bus approached. It was packed with jovial passengers and as Sarah and Jimmy boarded, they were greeted with a rendition of 'Rule Britannia'. It was being sung with such passion, the conductor was not able to be heard. He had stopped selling tickets an hour before.

Sarah was getting contractions.

'I'm frightened, Jimmy.'

She felt uncomfortable and did not know whether to stand up or sit down. The singing lessoned downstairs, as some of the passengers shared her anxiety.

'You'd be better off lying down, dearie. I've got eleven children and always preferred to be on my back,' said an old lady.

She was sitting behind the driver, had bloated cheeks and thin bony legs.

'You've obviously been on your back a lot, if you've got eleven kids!' shouted a passenger at the back.

Some of the passengers laughed and at that moment Sarah cried out.

'Open your legs, girl, and give it a good push,' said a drunken man from three rows behind.

He was slouched in a seat, with the zip on his trousers half way down and his shirt tail hanging out.

'Why don't you shut up?' said Jimmy.

He comforted Sarah with his arm around her shoulder. She held on to him firmly, thinking she might not make it to the hospital.

The conductor told the bus driver what was happening and he sped along the road. People's stomachs churned as the wheels went over potholes and debris. This made the journey even more uncomfortable for Sarah, but within minutes the bus arrived at the hospital.

Sarah was relieved, but then thought, 'Oh no, Jimmy still doesn't know about the adoption!' Her mind was spinning with worry and as she entered the hospital her waters broke. Sarah sobbed.

'It's okay, sweetheart, we'll look after you,' said Prudence, a blonde nurse with hazel eyes, who rushed Sarah into the maternity area in a wheelchair. Her contractions were more frequent as the minutes passed by.

'I want my Jimmy!' she shouted as he pounded the corridors outside.

Sarah was tired after the exhausting day on the streets of London and needed to summon up all her remaining energy to give birth. She screamed intermittently as the pressure on her body increased.

'Not much longer, I can see the baby's head.'

'Are women really supposed to suffer like this, Prudence?'

'I think we are. It's the men who have all the fun. Come on, you can do it, one last push.'

Inside an hour, Sarah gave birth and Jimmy was invited in to see her with a beautiful tiny girl snuggled in her arms.

Sarah felt sad inside. She was going to give up her baby but was prepared for this moment. She was not going to change her mind and after some rest, she built up the courage to tell Jimmy about her plan.

Tears ran down her face. Mother, father and daughter were as close as they would ever be. Sitting on the edge of the bed, Jimmy put an arm around Sarah, as they both looked down at their beautiful baby. She was dreading this conversation and feared Jimmy would explode in anger.

'Jimmy, there's something I need to tell you; I should've told you a long time ago.'

'It's all right,' he said.

Sarah was not listening.

'I can't keep her; please don't make me.'

She was almost trembling as the words came out and hid her shaky hands under a blanket. Jimmy smiled and ran his hand gently down the side of her face.

'It's okay, Sarah. I know about the adoption.'

'What! How do you know?'

Sarah anxiously waited for an answer. She had not confided in anyone and her mind was all over the place wondering how he found out.

'I was searching for a knife I'd accidentally dropped into the rubbish bin. It pierced a letter you received from Miss Watson and I took it out.'

'Oh Jimmy, I wanted to tell you.'

'I was shocked, but I have no right to interfere. I understand why you want the baby adopted.'

Sarah was now very weary. At that moment a nurse came into the room. She was a small lady with black hair and a stern expression.

'Mrs Jackson needs some sleep and it's past visiting time.'

This was a statement, but it sounded like a command. She stood there with her hands on her hips. Her eyes were fixed on Jimmy and she did not move until he got up from the chair by the bed. After hastily saying goodbye to Sarah, he left the room.

The tiny bundle of joy was taken away by the night staff. She had dark brown curly hair, brown eyes and there was a large egg-like birthmark on her left arm. Sarah and Jimmy named her Mary.

The adoption process was put in motion at birth and, seven days later, Sarah left the Mothers' Hospital. She was taken in an ambulance to Cotland Home. Sarah used every ounce of willpower, but was unable to stop herself bonding with Mary. The baby was her life and she treasured every day knowing her child would soon be taken away.

'Mary's so beautiful, Jimmy. Look at her soft skin.'

Sarah got into the habit of running the back of her index finger over Mary's face.

'She's perfect, we'll always remember her like this,' said Jimmy.

Four weeks later, Sarah and Jimmy received the news they had been dreading. The baby was going to her new home the following morning and Sarah's face was awash with tears.

Sarah had been thinking about this moment ever since she gave birth and with her body shaking, she took hold of Jimmy's hands. 'I have to say goodbye to Mary alone,' she said. 'Please don't ask me why.'

Jimmy sobbed, as he looked into Sarah's woeful eyes. He held her tightly in his arms and reluctantly nodded his agreement.

The next day was one of the saddest in Sarah's life and now every second spent with Mary was as precious as the air she breathed. Despite the anxiety and heartache, she did not change her mind. Somehow, she stayed strong enough to give Mary up, but dressing her little girl for the last time was almost unbearable. Sarah knew that any minute her beautiful baby would be taken from her.

Sarah heard the sound of footsteps coming up the stairs and she cringed as she waited for the door to open. The handle grated as it turned and Sarah shivered. Miss Hudson, a lady aged about twenty-two with blond hair, came in.

Miss Hudson was kind and caring. She ran her hands down Sarah's arms.

'I'm so sorry, but it's time.'

'Please Miss Hudson, not yet.'

Sarah's blinking eyes were heavy with tears.

Miss Hudson remained calm and was now seated beside her. For a few seconds, Sarah wouldn't let Mary go and hugged her closely. Then, lifting her away from her body, she passed Mary to the nurse.

Having relinquished her child, she held onto her yellow blanket until the last fragments of knitted wool slipped through the tips of her fingers.

Miss Hudson stood there for a moment, so Sarah was able to kiss Mary once more. The baby briefly opened her eyes and Sarah managed to smile.

'Goodbye little one, I pray someday you'll know I did this for you.'

Miss Hudson took Mary away and strangely Sarah's tears dried up. She felt empty and worthless. She was full of guilt and then heard a noise outside. Through the window she watched, as a man with silver curly hair and woman in black boots got into a taxi.

'She's my little girl!' Sarah cried.

The muscles in her face were trembling.

Straining every emotion in her body, Sarah watched Miss Hudson hand Mary to the woman. She sobbed as the taxi was driven away and watched the vehicle until it was out of sight.

From that day on, she never forgot the smell of her baby and the warmth and softness of her skin. Most of all, it was Mary's eyes, wide open when she let her go, that were to haunt her memory.

Chapter Seven

While Sarah and Jimmy coped with their grief, Maggie and Eddie were enjoying a life of luxury in Norfolk. They had now lived in Hemsley Grange for two years. It was originally a very large estate, but now although smaller, it still retained its importance in the local community.

It provided employment for a servant, a cook and a garden/maintenance man. It boasted six bedrooms, a morning room, a sitting room, a sumptuous dining room with a mosaic ceiling, an enormous kitchen, a library, a sweeping spiral staircase and a magnificent entrance hall filled with valuable antiques.

As mistress of Hemsley Grange, Maggie was required to be at the forefront of most of the activities in Cleybourne, a role she assumed with ease. Her duties included chairing the monthly village hall committee meetings which were traditionally held in the Grange.

This was an onerous position initially, because of the negativity amongst the members. Maggie noticed from the minutes of previous meetings, that good ideas for the village were mostly rejected, due to the resistance of General Smythe and his wife.

The Smythes combined age was one hundred and seventy-two. They were both born in the village and perceived themselves to be upper class.

The General was well known for wearing double-breasted tweed jackets. He was a tall man with a few strands of silver hair and he constantly attended to his imperial moustache with a tiny black comb.

Mrs Smythe was only four feet seven inches tall and always clutched her husband's arm. Her head was a mass of unkempt grey hair. The other committee members appeared to be intimidated by both of them.

Any suggestions prompted whispers between the Smythes. Then Mrs Smythe would cough and the General would say, 'We don't do things like that around here.'

With stern faces, they would glare at the members around the table, and then rejection would be confirmed unanimously with a show of hands.

Maggie was shocked to find out that ideas dismissed recently were for a beetle drive and a raffle, to raise money for the Scouts. She also learned that the General's request for a donation for his bowls club was easily approved.

'Who do they think they are? They behave like Victorian school teachers, and in my house, but not for much longer,' thought Maggie.

Slowly, Maggie increased her influence on those around her. She invited the key players in the community to the Grange for drinks, to find out what their local concerns were. She listened, showed empathy and, growing in confidence, stood up to the Smythes.

At committee meetings, Maggie used her authority as lady of the Grange, to introduce change and after a while other members found their own voices. They voted freely for what they thought was right. At one meeting, the Smythes walked out, when despite their opposition, agreement was reached for the Scouts to use the village hall.

'It's disgraceful, an outrage, who does she think she is? I'll have words with Eddie,' the General muttered to his wife.

'I've never liked Maggie! Did you see those red shoes she's wearing? She's no taste,' remarked Mrs Smythe as they left the Grange.

Some of the community members did not believe what they had witnessed. Sophie, who usually doodled throughout meetings, was fraught with worry. She was a small, shy lady, aged sixty-five. Constantly sweeping her blue-rinsed hair away from her eyes, she spoke softly. Sophie was always concerned about other people.

'I don't know what's going to happen now,' she said, frantically scribbling on some paper.

'We're going to have Smythe-free meetings in future, that's what's going to happen,' said Maggie, rubbing her hands with glee.

Over time, local projects that had been rejected in the past were discussed again and where viable they were approved. Maggie's popularity was on the rise. She was talked about all over Cleybourne and many people, especially the ladies, now wanted to become acquainted with her.

At the Grange, demands on the staff increased with Maggie's insatiable appetite for work. She insisted being addressed as 'My Lady' and expected all of her demands to be fulfilled promptly.

'I think I preferred Lady Muck. You'll be thinking you've got royal blood next,' said Eddie.

'It's a matter of respect, that's all. They're servants, aren't they?'

'Servants you rely on,' he replied.

Maggie was relentless in her quest for change and wanted the local fox hunt banned from the estate.

'I hate the thought of any animal being torn apart for any reason and especially for fun.'

'I'm sorry Maggie, but it's going to happen, as it has done for the last sixty years.'

'You don't take an interest in much else around here. You don't ride and only want the hunt here because of your rich friends. Are you worried you'll lose face at the golf club?'

'It's a tradition Maggie, an old English pastime that must be protected.'

'Not everyone feels like that. Lots of people loathe the so-called sport and some farmers dislike horses trampling all over their property. They're frightened to say anything because of reprisals.'

'What reprisals, Maggie?'

'I'm not mentioning names, but you know that some farmers had livestock stolen last year.'

'If you don't like it, go out. I'm sure you can find a function to attend; it only happens once a year,' said Eddie.

Chapter Eight

The end of the war heralded the homecoming of the British Armed Forces. Sarah was unable to go back to the munitions factory, as she was surplus to requirements. All available work was taken up by returning servicemen. Fortunately, she was an experienced machinist and she got employment in a factory in Walthamstow.

Jimmy sulked; there was a sombre look on his face.

'It's only sewing on shirt buttons,' said Sarah.

'I should be able to provide for you. I wish you didn't have to work, that's all.'

'It's okay, Jimmy. I really don't mind. The factory's only a short bus ride away and you know the money will be useful.'

Jimmy was still employed at the paper mill. Somehow it survived the war unscathed, despite many fallen buildings close by. He told Sarah his colleagues were now supportive of his disability, and he was more relaxed and at ease at home.

Mary, however, was at the forefront of Sarah's mind. She often wondered if giving her up was the right thing to do and tried to imagine the kind of life her daughter was leading. Sometimes she sobbed alone, knowing she would take this burden to her grave.

As time went by, Sarah and Jimmy re-bonded. They went to the cinema, for walks in Epping Forest and spent time with friends. At night they enjoyed the closeness of each other's bodies and although passion still evaded Sarah, eventually they made love.

When Sarah found out she was pregnant again, she was eager to tell Jimmy. She waited outside their flat when he was expected home from work and was grinning when he arrived.

'I'm pregnant!' Sarah shouted out.

Onlookers cheered, but she did not care. Jimmy ran towards her, lifted her up and swung her around. The baby was not planned, but Sarah was ecstatic. She kissed him on his lips and his cheeks.

'You clever girl, how did you do that?'

'I think you helped in some way.'

This was a special moment, but back in their flat, Sarah considered what a new mouth to feed would mean. All her excitement melted away.

'We'll have to cut back, with me at home and only your wage coming in. It'll be hard, but we'll make every sacrifice necessary to care for our baby,' said Sarah.

'I'm sure we'll cope somehow,' Jimmy replied.

*

On 3rd February 1947, Robert was born in the Hackney Mothers' Hospital. In this familiar building, thoughts of Mary came flooding back to torment Sarah. All the hurt was still there, but somehow she managed to push these feelings away. At least this time she was taking her baby home.

'I'll make a crib, Sarah.'

'Really! Can you do that?'

'I'm not useless you know. My dad didn't do a lot for me, but I was taught some basic carpentry skills.'

Sarah's colleague from the sewing factory, Irene, gave her a pram, and neighbours and friends provided baby clothes. Sarah and Jimmy were now a loving family and within eleven months Robert was walking.

Sarah enjoyed watching him explore his surroundings. He loved touching bright coloured objects and giggled when he was told to stop. He also liked wiggling his ears which made Sarah laugh.

It was not long before Sarah was pregnant again and on 18th November 1948, Emily was born. Having lost both her mum and sister as well as parting from Mary, Sarah was pleased to have a female presence in her life.

With two children to feed, Sarah and Jimmy found money even tighter. Food was basic and with rationing continuing, even the essentials were not always available. Bread and potatoes were the mainstay of their diet. They also lived in cramped conditions, but were no worse off than many people in the East End of London

They continued to clothe their children with hand-me-downs from friends and purchases from the occasional visit to Walthamstow Market. Stalls stretched along the middle of the high street for almost a mile, selling a vast array of goods. They were sold cheaply, providing a lifeline to the local community.

On one trip, Sarah took Emily and her baby doll called Susie to a shop called the Dolls' Hospital, as its head was broken into three pieces and it had come out of its neck socket. Two days before, Susie had been left lying on the floor in the kitchen and Jimmy accidentally stepped on it.

Emily was three years old and Susie was her only doll. She took it to bed with her every night; it was her most treasured possession. Sarah and Jimmy did not have any extra money for such things, but they knew somehow the doll must be repaired.

When they entered the shop, a kind lady called Primrose wiped the little girl's tears, as she held the bits of Susie in her arms.

'What have we got here, lollypop?' she asked softly.

'It's Susie, she's not well.'

'Well, we must try and make her better.'

Sarah was asked to come back to the shop a little later. On entering for the second time, Susie was sitting in one piece on the counter. This time Emily cried tears of joy and hugged Primrose tightly.

'Susie was easily mended with some strong glue. It will smell a bit for a couple of hours, but there isn't any charge.'

'Thank you, Primrose, that's kind of you, I think Emily might sleep tonight for the first time in a while,' said Sarah.

*

1953

The nation was shocked when it was announced King George VI had died. Sarah cried in Jimmy's arms. He was much loved by the people, but this sad event gave rise to the Coronation of Queen Elizabeth II the following year in June 1953. The country was in need of a lift and this was a perfect tonic. It was like VE Day all over again.

Rows of people lined the streets of London for the Coronation procession, and in homes throughout the country the event was followed on the wireless. Televisions were a rare commodity, but Sarah's friend Carol was able to afford one of the very small screened sets.

Sarah watched the procession in a small untidy room packed with other local residents. Both the picture and sound were lost intermittently and Carol kept changing the aerial's position. She moved it in all directions trying to improve the reception.

'Why do you keep moving the aerial?' asked Sarah.

'That's a good question, all I can say is, it normally helps.'

Another neighbour, with a poodle in her arms, coughed and wheezed.

'It's probably her,' said her husband, lighting a half-smoked cigarette.

Sarah helped organise a party in the street. Parents were determined their children were going to enjoy a day they would never forget. Trestle tables stretched along the road and chairs were borrowed from people's homes.

Sarah helped lay out all the goodies people bought or made. The children sat down at two o'clock. They were amazed by the selection of food and their hands went everywhere, gathering the delights displayed in front of them.

Union Jack flags decorated windows, and bunting hung across streets and gardens in place of washing lines. Parents sang along to music from loud speakers, as the children filled their bellies.

Unfortunately, it rained for most of the time and small puddles formed on the tables. Some of the sandwiches were soggy, but nobody cared, nothing was going to spoil the celebrations. It was a wonderful day and the party atmosphere continued into the middle of the night.

The following morning, reality sank back in. People were still feeling the effects of the war both emotionally and financially. Sarah and Jimmy were finding it increasingly hard to cope.

'I've already tried to get some extra work, Sarah, but there isn't any.'

'We'll manage somehow, we always do Jimmy.'

They were discussing feeding their children, when a letter dropped through the letter box. From the printing on the outside, they knew it was from the council.

'You open it, Sarah, it can only be more bad news; I don't want to read it.'

Sarah peeled back the glued edge and took out a single sheet of paper. She studied it closely and read it over and over again.

Her smile got wider and wider.

'What does it say, Sarah?'

'We've reached the top of the council house waiting list!' she said joyfully, handing him the letter.

Jimmy dampened her enthusiasm.

'It's only a prefab, and the rent is more money a week than we're paying now.'

'We have to go and look at it, Jimmy. What harm can it do? We've been crammed in this flat for too long.'

'That's all very well, but we still can't afford it.'

Sarah was unperturbed.

'The letter says the prefab is in Lea Bridge Road on an estate called Porter's Field. The address is in Second Avenue. If I can get the kids babysat on Saturday, we can take the bus to Markhouse Road and walk the rest.'

Sarah was excited when she arrived at what could be her new home. She hurried into the kitchen and did not believe her eyes.

'Look Jimmy, the table pulls down from the wall,' she said, releasing the catch and lowering it on to its hinged leg.

She raced into the sunlit lounge and eyed the green fields in the distance through the large window. Then she rushed into the bedrooms.

'I never thought the kids would have their own space,' said Sarah.

When she stepped into the bathroom she cried. Not only was there a bath, but also a toilet, and she sat on the pink lid.

'What's the matter Sarah?'

'Is it really ours, Jimmy?'

'What the toilet?'

'The prefab silly, it's perfect.'

Jimmy realised there was no going back. He had not seen his wife so excited before and there was nothing he could say that would change her mind.

'You'd better go and tell the council we want it, on Monday, then we'll worry about how we're going to pay for it,' he said.

Walking outside, there was a garden all around the property, secured with wire fencing. Sarah calmed herself and took a deep breath.

'There are trees all around us and the air is fresher. The children will have a garden to play in.'

'There's also a vegetable plot at the back, Sarah, and look, a blackberry bush growing over the coal shed.'

A week later, they were ready to move and their possessions were transported from Stratford thanks to Jimmy's friend Pete who had a van.

Sarah's happiness was tinged with sadness when the postman delivered her last letter to their flat. She looked at it curiously, as she did not recognise the handwriting. Taking out a folded card, she read it was from the mother of her friend Jean. Their last meeting was in Sally's Café in 1941.

Sarah remembered it was the day she met Jimmy, and burst into tears.

'Whatever's the matter?' he enquired.

'It's Jean, she's dead. I only wrote to her last week, but she was killed a month ago. If I'd been told before, I'd have gone to the funeral.'

Sarah sobbed in Jimmy's arms.

'It's terrible, Jean went all over the world with the Auxiliary Territorial Service and the Royal Army Corps, but she was run over by a horse and cart in Tottenham while on leave. I can't believe it. Why is it when something good happens in my life, it's always compensated by something bad?' asked Sarah.

'I know you always think that, but I'm sure Jean wouldn't want you moping over her. It sounds harsh, but there's nothing you can do for her now.'

Although this was a terrible shock, the day marked a turning point in Sarah's life. Many challenges lay ahead. She and Jimmy were poor and their assets were few, but they were rich in love.

Chapter Nine

Sarah and Jimmy loved their new home, but the higher rent meant a reduction in the heating they could afford and less food on the table. Sometimes they went without meals so Robert and Emily were not hungry.

By chance, when Sarah's purse was empty, Harry Bond knocked on the door. His wife Sandra was a friend of Sarah and they often spent time together. Mr Bond was softly spoken and held his fingers and thumbs together when talking. He was the administration manager for Sewells Sewing Company Ltd. and was calling to take his wife home.

'I don't suppose you know anybody who wants some work, ladies? Two of our machinists are leaving on Friday and we need replacements urgently,' he said.

Sarah was desperate to get a job. She would do almost anything to earn some money.

'I'd love employment, but my two children make it impossible,' she said.

When Mr Bond found out Sarah was an experienced seamstress, he arranged for a machine to be delivered to Porter's Field so she could work from home.

The job was sewing the edges on bags for toiletries. It was very fiddly and did not pay well, but her earnings supplemented Jimmy's income. The machine also enabled Sarah to make some of her children's clothes. Then, as rationing ended, food choices improved and the Jackson family was at last able to eat a little better.

The prefab estate was on the edge of Leyton Marshes and one day Sarah took her children exploring. Rain falling during the previous week had made the ground boggy, so they ambled down the many paths that criss-crossed the marshland wearing wellington boots.

Robert and Emily loved the adventure and kept running out of sight along the twisted paths.

A silence would fall, then the children would jump out in front of her. Sarah pretended to be scared and Emily found it very funny.

'We frightened you, didn't we, Mummy?'

'You did, look, I'm shaking.'

Apart from the wetlands, there was the River Lea. Sarah pointed to a flat-bottomed boat moored on the other side. It was full of logs piled high and secured with thick ropes.

'Look, can you see the boat? It's called a barge. They help move food and wood from farms, forests and factories.'

'Where do the barges go?' asked Robert.

'All over the country, to wherever the goods are needed. However, it's Saturday today, so we won't see many barges, but there'll probably be rowers racing up and down the river instead. Look! There're two coming now.'

The boats approached at speed, with eight men in each vessel dressed in grey shirts.

'Are they racing, Mummy?' asked Emily.

'Yes, I think they are.'

'They're going very quick, Mum,' said Robert.

'Very quick and they're churning up the calm water into large ripples as they thrash their oars into the water. Come away children, you'll have it lapping over your feet.'

Robert noticed some perch and roach floating on the surface, and pointed.

'Unfortunately, the river's all dirty Robert. All the oil and waste from the factories goes into the river and it's killing the fish,' said Sarah.

Then Emily screamed.

'What is it?' asked Sarah.

Emily hid behind her mother as a rat, as big as a cat, scurried towards them. It was an ugly, pale grey creature with loose flabby skin which looked too large for its body.

'It's all right, it won't harm you Emily. It's searching for dead carcases in the mud.'

Sarah ushered her children away.

'It's horrible, I don't like it, Mummy!' said Emily.

'Don't worry, it won't come near us.'

Just then, Robert spotted a playground on the other side of a footbridge that spanned the river.

'Can we go to the park?' he asked.

'Oh yes, please can we go?' pleaded Emily.

It was getting late, but the children were persistent, and Sarah did not want to spoil a wonderful day. On reaching the far side of the waterway, there was a big slide. The children climbed it time and time again for the thrill of zooming to the bottom.

'Please be careful!' Sarah called out.

She was on edge watching them jostling to get to the top and closed her eyes when they attempted to slide down backwards on top of each other.

Robert and Emily also loved the swings and roundabouts, but the other main attraction was a massive grassed hill. They raced each other rolling down and when they reached the bottom, they were giddy for a few moments. When they tried to stand up, they fell over in fits of laughter.

The children wore themselves out and were ready to go home. Sarah gave Emily a piggy back, but Robert walked. He was jealous and whined constantly, as Emily purposely annoyed him further by singing nursery rhymes.

1957

The circus came to town. Much of the travelling show disembarked at Lea Bridge Road railway station, about a quarter of a mile away from Porter's Field. People lined the main road at the bottom of the estate and watched the procession on its way to an enormous tent, dressed in the colours of the rainbow.

Robert and Emily stood next to Sarah and enjoyed every moment. They did not believe they were so close to the animals. There were trucks going past that held lions, bears and tigers, and a parade of horses, zebras and elephants walked by.

Apart from the animals, there were clowns being funny, jugglers juggling, acrobats doing cartwheels and somersaults, ladies in pretty costumes and bands playing. People were laughing and clapping.

As soon as it was over, Sarah wanted to take her children home. Emily was holding her hand, but Robert was missing, and the immediate area was crowded with people. It was difficult for her to see further than a few feet away.

'Robert, where are you?' Sarah shouted loudly.

With so much noise around she was not able to make herself heard.

'Where is he, Emily?'

There was desperation in her voice.

'I don't know, but when you were talking to Mrs Laverty, he was chatting to a man over there by the lamp post.'

Emily pointed to the street light a few yards away.

Mrs Laverty was the mother of Robert's friend Kenneth. Sarah only spoke to her briefly.

'What man?' she asked.

Sarah's hands were shaking.

'I don't know, I haven't seen him before. He was wearing a black hat and sun glasses. I saw him looking at the animals with Robert and pointing at one of the cages.'

'Oh my God!' said Sarah.

'He's probably already gone home, Mum.'

They rushed back down Second Avenue, but Robert was nowhere to be seen. Sarah was distraught.

'Where an earth can he be, Emily?'

Sarah knocked on the doors of Robert's friends on the estate and the mother of another school pal added to her concern.

'The man was chatting to lots of children. I didn't see Robert, but he might have been one of them.'

Sarah was frantic. She needed Jimmy and sobbed in his arms when he arrived home from work.

'Robert's missing, we were watching the circus animals together, but when I looked he wasn't beside me!'

Jimmy took a firm grip of her arms as she was throwing them about and screaming. Her face was red and drawn.

'Stop it, Sarah. You don't have to do this on your own, I'm here now. We'll find Robert, okay?' he said.

Fortunately, the people in the prefab next door recently had a phone installed. Jimmy called the police.

While they waited, terrible notions passed through Sarah's mind. Robert, now ten years old, was a well-behaved boy, but he was very friendly and would talk to anyone. 'He must have been taken by somebody,' she thought.

Sarah was relieved when a police car came down the road. As soon as PC Judd opened his door she bombarded him with questions and demands.

'Most lost children are found, Mrs Jackson. Robert has only been missing for a short while and there's more than likely a good explanation for his absence,' he said, trying to calm her fragile nerves.

The policeman drove around the estate and made an announcement through a loudhailer. He asked all the residents of Porter's Field to inspect their homes and gardens. Within a few seconds people came out of their prefabs and after searching their properties, they formed small groups and combed a wider area including the railway line close by.

Sarah was scared, thinking her boy may be harmed. She was shaking with worry, sitting with her hands over her face.

'When you were watching the parade, Emily, was there anything Robert said that might help us find him?' asked Jimmy.

'No, I don't think so. He loved seeing the animals and kept laughing at the clowns.'

'Anything at all Emily? It might be important.'

'No, he loved it all. Oh! He did say he wished the tigers were walking along the road so he could see them properly, but he was joking.'

Sarah was up on her feet in a flash.

'Tell the policeman I'm going to the circus. Forgive me, Jimmy, but I'll get there quicker than you.'

She ran down Lea Bridge Road faster and faster with every stride. It was only half a mile away, but such was her desperation, it seemed like a lifetime before she reached the circus tent. It had been erected close to the River Lea the previous day.

After the procession, the entertainers went into their caravans which had arrived in the morning. The lorries with cages were placed in a secure pen, close to the back of the arena. The whole area was quiet, apart from the haunting and growling sounds of the animals.

The situation was getting critical because daylight was fading and the river was dangerous. There were painted signs on the bank warning of deep water. Sarah was breathless, but rushed around to the back of the tent and tried to enter the pen. It was locked and she pushed and pulled the entrance gate violently backwards and forwards until she was confronted by a circus steward.

'What do you think you're doing? You can't go in there.'

'It's my boy, I think he may be with a stranger near the tigers.'

The steward hastily opened the gate and they rushed towards the cages. Robert was with the man in the black hat.

'Robert, come here now!' Sarah commanded.

Immediately the man ran off. He exited the pen through a hole in the fence and made his way down the river embankment. PC Rudd arrived and gave chase, but lost sight of him on the marshes.

Robert walked towards his mother and was surprised when she hugged him tightly.

'Let's go home,' she said.

Sarah's heart was beating furiously as she thought what might have happened, but she did not scold him. He was safe and unharmed.

'Did you like seeing all the animals, Robert?'

'It's been the best day of my life, Mum. When I grow up I'd like to be a tiger tamer. The tigers are amazing,'

'That sounds very exciting, Robert.'

When they reached Porter's Field, Jimmy was waiting to greet him, but once inside, Sarah was not so forgiving. After more hugs she became annoyed and all her anxiety poured out. Robert was shocked to see his mother crying.

'Do you realise how worried we've been and how many people were trying to find you? You know you should never go off with a stranger,' she said.

'I'm sorry Mum, but the man said he was Dad's friend and it'd be all right if I went with him. He said he'd take me to see the tigers. He bought me an ice cream and was going to give me a ride in his car.'

Sarah cried again and held Robert firmly in her arms.

'Don't you ever go away with anybody again, unless you ask me or your dad first. Do you understand?' Sarah shook him gently.

Robert nodded.

'Promise me, Robert, promise you won't go away with anyone unless you ask first.'

'Your mum's right, it's very important, Robert,' said Jimmy.

'I promise,' he replied.

'I'll always stay with you and Daddy,' said Emily.

The panic was over and the family sat down for a late supper of sausage and mash.

Robert and Emily were captivated by all of the animals and the entertainers in the procession.

'Can we go to the circus please?' Robert asked.

'I want to see the lions,' said Emily.

'You've already seen them,' Sarah replied.

'I want to see the tigers do tricks,' said Robert.

Circus tickets were not expensive, but the family did not have money for such things.

'Not this time, maybe next year,' Sarah replied.

Emily cried. Her face was full of disappointment.

'All my friends will go Mummy, it's not fair!' she shouted and threw her woollen teddy across the floor.

'I'm sorry, but we can't afford it and you'll get a smack if you don't pick your teddy up.'

Jimmy hated seeing his children upset.

'I think we can find a way,' he said.

Sarah was flabbergasted, as Emily and Robert hugged him. When they were alone, Jimmy knew he would be rebuked.

'Well who's a popular man then? I have to tell the kids they can't have things time and time again, and then you say they can go to the circus. I thought we agreed a long time ago never to disagree in front of them.'

'I couldn't help myself, Sarah. I'm fed up having to say no. They're good kids, aren't they?'

'Yes, I know, Jimmy, but we still haven't got the money.'

Sarah and Jimmy tried to save up for the things they needed, but after paying the rent and having money for food, there was very little left. Somehow, they managed to find money for the insurance man every week. It was kept in a yellow teacup in the kitchen cupboard.

'I'll walk to work and back all next week and you can use my bus money to take them, Sarah. I'm sure there're some cheap seats high in the tent.'

'It's nearly three miles, Jimmy. You're on your feet all day and will be tired out, especially with your disability.'

'I'll manage, Sarah, we can't let them down can we?'

Sarah put her arms around Jimmy and kissed him.

'What was that for?'

'I don't need a reason, Jimmy, but you've given me one. You're a big softie and I love you for it.'

When Emily and Robert were taken to the circus they queued in a long line leading to the ticket booth. As they got nearer, a band played and the children were impatient to enter the tent. In a few minutes, they reached the entrance where a man with big pink plastic ears, wearing a yellow silky shirt was taking the money.

'Do you think he knows Noddy?' Robert asked Sarah.

'Shush!' She replied and they all giggled.

As they entered the arena, Emily and Robert cast their eyes everywhere. In the show ring there was an old red car with big headlights, some yellow buckets and two cannons. Sarah wished Jimmy was with her to see their excitement.

'Look, Mummy!'

Emily pointed every time something different happened. It did not matter if it was animals, jugglers or clowns. Emily and Robert loved everything.

There was a red kangaroo called Sydney that sat on its hind legs, with bright yellow gloves on its forelimbs. It punched volunteers from the audience. They were paid money if they lasted three minutes in a boxing ring without being floored. Clowns played recklessly with flour and water. There were bangs, screeches and siren sounds. Two people were even fired out of the cannons. Sarah's favourite was the trapeze artists who sailed through the air holding on to the flimsiest of swings.

The circus was exhilarating, but the event the audience remembered most was a tiger which sat on a stool inside a metal cage. The audience roared with laughter as it lifted up its right leg and peed all over a family in the front row! The water came out of the animal like a discharge from a fireman's hose and the smell was so pungent, people moved away.

This was the first live show Sarah took her children to see. On their way back to Porter's Field, Robert and Emily kept talking about the tiger. They believed what it did was part of the performance. They could not stop laughing about the family that got saturated.

*

Sarah was very imaginative in making meals for a pittance. By saving the odd penny here and there, she was able to take Robert and Emily to the beach for one day in the school holidays, when Jimmy was at work. They went by train to Chalkwell-On-Sea.

Sarah walked her children the mile and a half to Leyton station. It was a bright summer's day and along with other families, they waited patiently on the platform.

The signal went up and the station master, wearing a black uniform and a shiny peaked cap, came out of his office.

'Will all passengers please stand back!' he shouted.

He spoke through a loudhailer, but Robert and Emily did not need any encouragement. They had been scared before by the ugly sounds of a steam engine's pistons sliding up and down and its wheels clattering over the iron rails. Already standing behind their mother, they were holding their hands over their ears.

The train consisted of eight carriages, packed with excited passengers. Sarah ran along the platform with her children following behind. She managed to find a compartment with two empty seats and Emily sat on her lap. The station master blew hard on his whistle and the engine jerked. A ferocious jet of steam shot out of its funnel and into the air. There was a hissing sound as the wheels turned.

'We're moving!' said Robert excitedly.

Faster and faster the train sped on its way and the landscape soon changed from factories and houses to trees and fields.

Robert and Emily marvelled at the sight of sheep and cows in vast open spaces. When a train shot past in the opposite direction, the noise frightened them and their hearts fluttered, but they laughed out loud as if they were not afraid at all.

The time passed quickly with the family playing I Spy. When it was Emily's turn, she eyed a red slip under the skirt of a lady sitting by a window. She noticed Emily look at her and adjusted her clothing. Sarah and Robert took turns for ages trying to guess Emily's 'something beginning with the letter R'. When they ran out of guesses, Emily was asked to reveal the answer, but the slip was hidden from view.

'It's a red slip.'

'What are you talking about?' asked Sarah.

'I saw it,' Emily said and giggled.

'I think you're a silly girl.'

To the passengers' amazement, the lady by the window lifted up the bottom of her skirt.

'Is this what you're looking for?'

Sarah was embarrassed.

'You're such a naughty girl, say sorry to the lady.'

The smile on Emily's face disappeared. Saying sorry to a stranger was hard for a child, but at that moment the sea appeared in the distance. It came into view as the train made its way down the long embankment towards Chalkwell station.

Ignoring Sarah's request, Emily said, 'I saw the sea first.'

'No, you didn't, I did,' replied Robert.

The children argued.

'It doesn't matter, we're coming into the station,' said Sarah.

It was 10.25am and the sun's warmth was keenly felt out of the clear blue sky. With buckets and spades, the family walked over the rusty iron bridge and on to the promenade on the other side. With the sand in close proximity, the children ran towards the beach.

'Don't go near the sea!' Sarah shouted out.

Robert made sandcastles and dug such a big hole that he needed to be lifted out. Emily and Sarah built a witch's castle. They used straw lying on the beach to make a large cobweb and Emily placed seaweed in the middle. It looked like a scary spider.

Another treat for the children was a picnic, even though it was only jam sandwiches, homemade fairy cakes and warm orange cordial. Sand blowing in the breeze invaded their bread, but the children did not care. Nothing was going to spoil their day.

As soon as they finished eating and drinking, they were back on their feet, playing all sorts of games and running in and out of the sea. They tired themselves out and the rest of the day soon passed.

Robert and Emily did not want to go home. For them it was like being in a beautiful fairy tale they wished would never end.

'Come on kids, we have to leave now,' said Sarah.

It was 4.40pm and their train would soon be arriving in the station. They packed up their things and made their way off the beach.

Sarah stopped at a sweet stall and bought Emily and Robert pink sticks of rock, which they ate on the journey. They went home with memories of a wonderful day and slept well that night.

Chapter Ten

As time went by, Maggie's reputation became tarnished in Cleybourne. She flirted almost unashamedly with the local gentlemen because her relationship with Eddie was changing and she was lonely. Their tastes and aspirations in life were different and they shared few friends.

Maggie turned to alcohol. At first, she drank the odd gin and tonic, but after time, whisky was her temptation and her glass was rarely empty. Her only other comfort was Eddie's dog, Bailey, a chocolate Labrador that always stayed close to her chair when he was out.

For all Maggie's outward self-confidence, when on her own she worried about her life with Eddie. She thought, 'If he doesn't want me, I'll have to leave the Grange.' She did not wish to contemplate giving up the home of her dreams, where her position provided her with influence and importance in the community. She felt vulnerable and sulked in her own company.

On a rare occasion when Maggie and Eddie were in bed together, she lay awake considering the future. As usual, they faced away from each other and he was snoring after a heavy drinking session with the General. She thought to herself, 'I can't go on like this. I'm going to talk to him in the morning.'

Maggie was already waiting at the breakfast table when Eddie came down the stairs, doing up his shirt buttons.

'I need to speak to you!' she called out.

'It'll have to wait, I'm late for pheasant shooting.'

'You're always doing something Eddie, you've never got time for me.'

'I might say the same about you, you host more tea parties than the queen.'

Maggie came out of the room.

'Why can't you take me pheasant shooting?'

Eddie laughed out loud.

'You! Pheasant shooting! You'll be asking to kill the chickens next. Stick to your social duties. You're good at swanning around telling people what to do and pretending to be something you're not.'

Eddie opened the front door, but Maggie was behind him.

'I'm serious. I want to go shooting,' she repeated, taking a firm grip of his arm.

'Tell me Maggie, why on earth do you want to do this? You've not expressed an interest before.'

'Well I have now, God knows we should do something together.'

'Have you been drinking Maggie? Even for you it's a bit early, don't you think?'

'I mean it, I want to go shooting.'

Eddie smiled. There was a mischievous spark in his eyes.

'Okay Maggie, make sure you're ready early tomorrow morning.'

At seven thirty the following morning, they made their way out onto the estate with Bailey. It was misty and damp and Maggie was not prepared for the weather. It was late January and she was wearing a jumper over a tweed skirt, under a lightweight coat. She also wore casual suede shoes, when wellington boots would have been more appropriate.

Eddie laughed.

110

'You're not seriously going like that! We're walking, not going in the Range Rover.'

He was wearing a raincoat and thick waterproof trousers over some warm woollen clothes. He also wore a peak cap and walking boots. Maggie hated being berated and ignored him. Despite feeling cold and struggling not to slip over on the muddy ground, she was not going to back out now.

Maggie watched Eddie unlock a large metal shed attached to the back of the Grange. Inside was a cabinet, secured to the wall by four large bolts. Heavy duty keys were required to open its solid door.

Eddie took out one of three firearms.

'Take hold of that,' he said.

Eddie shoved it towards Maggie and she tried to take hold of it by the butt. It was much heavier than she expected and she dropped it. Eddie shook his head and picked it up.

'It's probably best if you hold the gun with both hands,' he said sarcastically, as he locked the shed.

Maggie frowned at him and she was uninterested when he tried to show her how to use it. Having already been humiliated for her dress sense she did not want to be told what to do. She kept huffing and puffing as he was talking.

'Maggie, if I don't show you how to shoot, you'll find it very difficult.'

Eddie attempted to wrench the shotgun from her.

'It can't be difficult if you can do it,' Maggie said, holding on to the gun tightly.

'Okay have it your way; let's find some birds.'

Maggie followed Eddie along a muddy path. It rained heavily the night before and large puddles obstructed their progress. Maggie watched Bailey walk slowly beside a hedgerow a few yards away. The dog continuously sniffed the dense undergrowth, searching for a scent and within a minute a pheasant shot out. It startled her as it flew into the sky.

Maggie screamed.

'Quick! Have a pop at that!' said Eddie.

She fumbled with the shotgun and tried to pull the trigger, but it was not loaded. It did not occur to her she would need to react so quickly, and Eddie laughed again.

'You didn't seriously think I'd let you loose with a live gun until I am sure you can use it properly, did you? You might have shot the dog, you silly woman.'

Maggie glared at him.

'You are such a bastard Eddie, I hate you.'

Maggie tried to slap him, but she lost her footing and fell to the ground, landing in the middle of a puddle in a tractor rut. When she got to her feet, much to his further amusement, her clothes and legs were covered in mud and she was soaked through.

'Now let me have the bloody gun and I'll show you what to do, Maggie.'

Standing very uncomfortably, with her legs apart, Maggie reluctantly handed it over. She was humiliated and angry, as Eddie went through the loading and handling processes, but this time she listened carefully.

Eddie could not resist one more comment about Maggie's dress attire.

'Are you going on anywhere straight after we've finished; perhaps a WI meeting?'

Maggie did not reply. She was furious and snatched the shotgun away from him. Once again, Bailey responded to her master's command and in a couple of minutes a pheasant flew out of a ditch.

'Quick! Do it now, woman!'

She lifted the shotgun, squeezed the trigger and a shot rang out. The pheasant was now far away, but standing at close range, Eddie took the full force of the four-pellet cartridge and fell backwards. He lay motionless on the ground with his legs open and his head to one side. Maggie knelt down and put a finger on his pulse. There was not a beat, as the ammunition had penetrated his heart. Eddie was dead.

Maggie ran her fingers along the barrel, while smelling the burned gunpowder like a Texas cowboy. Her lips broke into a broad smile, as the realisation sank in that she wouldn't see Eddie alive again. Maggie felt no more remorse than if she had killed a slug.

Bailey immediately lay beside Eddie with her head against his face. She stared at Maggie, with her woeful eyes and a tear or two dropped onto her nose. Taking hold of the dog's lead, Maggie wrestled her away and they walked slowly back to the house.

In these moments alone, Maggie considered what she would say happened.

'Giles! Giles!' she called out, while banging on the door.

He looked at her curiously, in her mud-stained clothes, as she pushed past him into the hall.

'Phone the police, Giles, there's been a terrible accident, Mr Jackson has been shot!'

Giles had only recently been employed at the Grange, as the house servant. He was a tall, thin man, aged sixty-two, with combed back grey hair. He always did his best, but he was nervous and forgetful. He hardly ever made conversation, but his sullen face and doleful eyes said a thousand words.

'Oh no! Do we need an ambulance, My Lady?'

'No, he's dead, do as you're told, man!'

Maggie sensed Giles was mortified. Unlike her, Eddie always treated him with respect and dignity. She joked to herself, 'It's a pity he didn't get shot, it would save me the trouble of sacking him.'

Detective Inspector James arrived within twenty minutes and Maggie asked Giles to invite the officer into the sitting room. She was shaking as he entered and took a moment to compose herself, by making a show of wiping away crocodile tears.

'This has been a terrible ordeal for you, Mrs Jackson, please accept my sympathy.'

The inspector assumed she and Eddie were married and Maggie didn't enlighten him.

'My foot slipped and the gun went off. It was only minutes before the accident my poor Eddie explained to me how to use it. I don't know what I'm going to do without him.'

After the body was inspected, it was taken away for a post-mortem. Meanwhile the detective inspector delved into Maggie's relationship with Eddie. He spoke to everybody she came into contact with and established she did not have many friends.

Maggie was worried about the investigation and spoke to Jess the cook.

'You didn't, by any chance, mention what I said the other day, did you?'

Jess noticed Maggie was agitated. She spoke quickly and defensively, but the usual aggression in her voice was missing.

'What was that, My Lady?'

Jess knew full well what she was referring to but wanted an answer. Somewhat reluctantly, Maggie was forced to remind her.

'I said I hated Eddie and wished he was dead.'

'Oh no, My Lady, I wouldn't say such a thing. It was only a joke, wasn't it?'

Maggie sensed some doubt in her stumbling reply, but she knew Jess would keep silent. Her job depended on it.

Police enquiries identified tensions between Maggie and Eddie, but they were not considered unlike those in many other domestic relationships. Accidental death was recorded on the death certificate.

Chapter Eleven

Maggie's attention turned to the future. Eddie was a wealthy man and, even before his funeral, she was impatient for the reading of his will. Eagerly she wrote to his son and explained what happened, hiding her excitement about seeing him again.

When Jimmy read the letter, he did not show any emotion and handed it to Sarah without a word.

'Such terrible news, I'm so sorry,' she said.

'I've told you many times, he doesn't mean anything to me. The old man will finally meet his maker. How I wish he'd died years ago, instead of my mother. We'll not be going to his funeral.'

Sarah was upset. She knew eventually Jimmy would receive some correspondence from Norfolk, but she didn't think it would come from Maggie about his father's death.

'Please don't turn on the tears, you only met him once.'

'I can't help it, Jimmy. Any chance of some reconciliation has now gone forever.'

'Oh, come on, Sarah, I know you love happy endings, but life isn't a fairy tale. It was never going to happen.'

Sarah believed blood was thicker than water and that over the years he and his dad should have been there for one another. How she wished her parents and sister were alive. She thought about them every day.

'Please, Jimmy, we have to go to the funeral. If we don't you'll never be at peace with yourself.'

Jimmy hesitated. Despite his negativity, the news disturbed him. Sitting quietly for a few seconds, he read the letter again, but to Sarah's dismay he did not change his mind.

'No, I won't do it. It would be hypocritical to mourn a man who, over the years, gave both my mother and me so much grief. It'll bring back too many bad memories. Even now I'm thinking about him hurting my mum for no reason, other than he'd been drinking.'

Sarah understood his torment. She would never forget how Jimmy had abused her, but she was not about to remind him.

'I know it will be hard, but regardless of what happened in the past, he's still your dad. We have to go.'

Sarah was so insistent that Jimmy begrudgingly agreed and somehow they managed to scrape together enough money for the train fare.

In Hemsley Grange, Maggie did her best to pretend she was missing Eddie. She instructed Giles to keep the curtains drawn and in the company of others, while always dressed in black she often burst into tears.

Giles witnessed Maggie's joviality when she was alone. She even sang in the bath, but he quietly got on with his work. The bereavement did not affect her appetite either, she appeared to be eating and drinking in celebration.

February 1963

On 6th February, Sarah and Jimmy left their children with their good friends, Debbie and John, who lived a short distance from the Porter's Field estate. Sarah had known Debbie since they were at school together in Tottenham.

It was the first time Sarah was separated from Emily and Robert and she hated leaving them. She knew they would be fine, as her friend's children were of similar ages and they were at school together, but it was a terrible wrench.

The journey to Norfolk was long and tiring. It involved three trains and they did not arrive in Cleybourne until late afternoon. Maggie had invited them to stay at Hemsley Grange and arranged for a taxi to pick them up at the station.

When Sarah got her first glimpse of the property, she was overwhelmed. As the vehicle approached the entrance, she eyed a stunning carpet of snowdrops each side of the long driveway.

'Blimey Jimmy, look! It's guarded by two large bronze eagle statues. Maggie boasted about this place, but I think she's undersold it.'

'We've never worried about material things, Sarah. They don't have any real value in life. It's who you are and not what you have that matters.'

'I know, Jimmy, but you can't help looking, can you?'

Sarah then marvelled at the splendour of the upstairs windows with their ornate balconies, as she got out of the taxi. Feeling nervous, Sarah gulped when the door opened.

'Hold on to me, Jimmy,' Sarah whispered, grasping his arm.

Maggie had instructed Giles to be on hand when the taxi arrived, and he had watched it approach through a downstairs window. The servant lived on the premises and occupied two rooms on the top floor. Sarah noticed he was shaking as he invited them inside.

As Sarah entered the hall, her eyes looked everywhere. She was overwhelmed by the decorated walls, paintings and antiques. There was a full set of armour standing outside the dining room and a tiger skin on the floor, but it was a beautiful walnut grandfather clock that mostly drew her attention. Its gold hands were enormous.

Maggie heard the Jacksons arriving. She was longing to see Jimmy and was determined to make an entrance. After purposely waiting a few seconds, she slowly strolled down the wide spiral staircase with her head held high, as if it was carrying a heavy book.

Sarah and Jimmy watched Maggie's every step. Her hair was loose and her long pearl necklace swayed until she reached the large hall in which they were standing.

'Giles, haven't you taken their coats, man? For goodness sake get a grip!' she shouted.

'Yes, My Lady.'

Giles assisted Sarah, then Jimmy handed him his jacket. They were both shocked and embarrassed.

Maggie instantly cried and bowed her head. Her face was solemn as she approached Sarah and Jimmy.

'I don't know what I'm going to do without my Eddie.'

'This is such an awful time for you,' said Sarah.

Maggie dabbed her face with a polka dot handkerchief and held it with an outstretched hand for Giles to take away.

Then, impulsively, Maggie leaned forward, wrapped her arms around Jimmy's neck and kissed his lips. Coming out of the embrace and out of Sarah's eye line, she stroked his back with the tips of her fingers. She heard him draw breath and knew she unnerved him as she had done at his wedding.

'This is a sad time for both of us, Jimmy, but I must make the most of you being here. I'm determined to make a fuss of you.'

Turning her attention to Sarah, she kissed her on both cheeks.

'It's so good of you to come all this way, you must let me know if there's anything you need.'

'I can't imagine I'll want for anything, not in a place like this,' said Sarah.

Privately she was disgusted by Maggie's behaviour, but very forgiving. Sarah thought, 'She must be grieving badly, her mind is all over the place.'

A thin smile crept out of Maggie's lips as she thought, 'I've got to put up with this meek excuse of a woman for three days.'

Sarah continued to look in wonder around the hall.

'Where are you, Giles?' Maggie called out, in her pretentious voice.

He rushed out of the kitchen, still holding a plate he was wiping dry.

'Ah, there you are, show Mrs Jackson around the house.'

'Yes, My Lady.'

Giles escorted Sarah into the Victorian sitting room.

'Don't get lost and try not to break anything!' Maggie shouted. 'The man's a nightmare. Yesterday he broke my favourite painted vase. Also, I'm fed up with telling him to do things twice.'

'Do you want him to do things twice, Maggie?' asked Jimmy with a smile.

She raised her eyebrows and inhaled. 'He gets everything wrong and for some reason, he seems to be frightened of me. Eddie liked him, but I don't understand why.'

Maggie moved closer to a door leading out of the hall.

'You come in here with me.'

She encouraged him to squeeze past her into the morning room. He felt her breath on his neck and could smell her Chanel.

'This is a lovely place to sit when the sun is rising over the green. You'll see it tomorrow, if it's a clear day, although the weather forecast isn't good.'

Jimmy sat down on a leather couch with rolled arms, a little distance away from Maggie.

'Come closer, Jimmy. I won't bite, not today anyway,' she said suggestively.

Maggie sensed Jimmy's nervousness. He stayed still, so she moved towards him. She smiled and ran her hands down his arms with their faces barely apart.

'If there's anything you would like while you're here, anything at all, Jimmy, you only have to ask.'

Maggie crossed her legs causing her skirt to rise above her knee. She sensed he was appalled by her behaviour, but he did not take his eyes off her. She thought, 'He's already falling under my spell.'

Jimmy wanted to leave the room and stood up.

'You must have lots of things to do, Maggie, I'll ask Giles to show me around the house,' he said.

'I should have hosted a village green committee luncheon today, but my heart wasn't in it. I postponed it until next week.'

'I'm sure they'd be able to manage somehow without you. Surely they must have assumed Eddie's death would devastate you?'

Maggie's ears pricked up. She interpreted his comments as a little flippant.

'Alright, I admit it, we didn't always get on; I'm sure you can relate to that. By the time he died, I didn't really know him. We rarely talked and got on with our own thing.'

'So, you're glad he's dead.'

'You can't miss what you don't have. I'm lonely and have been for a long time.'

'I'm sure you'll enjoy his money, Maggie. When's the will being read? Oh yes, the day after the funeral. I'm surprised you're waiting that long.'

Sarah and Jimmy were shown to their room on the second floor. It was as big as the perimeter of their prefab and its large window looked out over the drive and the village green. In the centre of the room was a large four-poster bed. When lying on the red eiderdown, their bodies sunk into the sumptuous mattress. Soft pink silk pillowcases matched the sheets. They had not laid on such extravagance.

'This bed must weigh a ton, Jimmy.'

'Yes, but I bet it hasn't been through the floorboards.'

'Oh yes, I remember. Can you believe it happened nearly twenty years ago?'

'Thank goodness we don't have to worry about Mrs Mead in the toilet!' said Jimmy, but his facial expression changed.

He was melancholy and sat up. 'We're all right, aren't we Sarah?'

'What do you mean, all right?'

'Twenty years is a long time. We've been through a lot together, but this place makes me realise we haven't come very far.'

Sarah smiled and took hold of Jimmy's hands.

'Have I ever asked you for anything?'

'No.'

'Why do you think that is?'

'I've always tried to provide for you, even though it has been hard sometimes.'

'Jimmy you've given me everything. We have our love and our two kids. That's all I've ever needed and what some people would die for.'

Tears fell from Sarah's eyes and she cried in his arms.

123

'What is it, love?'

Sarah was very hesitant. The words would not come out of her mouth. Since the day of the adoption, Mary was only spoken about a couple of times and not for years. Rightly or wrongly they both dealt with their grief separately, in their own way.

There were many occasions when people referred to their two children and it did not upset Sarah, but today for some reason it was different. Funerals do strange things to people. Sometimes they heal old wounds and bring people together. They can also rekindle bad memories and emotions, best left locked away.

Sarah had given birth to three children and every day she thought about the baby she gave away.

'It's Mary, isn't it?'

'I can't help it Jimmy, I can't bottle it up any longer. I wonder where she is and what she's doing. She'll be eighteen this year.'

'It was an awful time, my love, but we made a decision to let her go. There was a war on, we were poor and very young. All we can do is hope she's having a good life.'

While comforting each other, Sarah managed to compose herself. She dried her face with a small white handkerchief she kept in the sleeve of her jumper.

'I know, but I often feel so guilty. Sometimes I want God to punish me.'

The brass bell above the four-poster bed rang. The sound was like the noise heard on railway stations to warn of an approaching train. Maggie told them it signified dinner would be served shortly.

Quickly they opened their suitcase, took out some fresh clothes and made themselves presentable. There were two washbasins in an adjoining room.

Arm in arm, Sarah and Jimmy walked down the wide staircase, feeling like a king and queen. At the bottom, standing in the hall, Giles was holding a tray containing glasses of champagne. It was the first time they tasted the fizzy drink and Sarah did not like it.

'Is this the real stuff, Jimmy? If it is I don't want it. It's like sour lemonade.'

'It's real all right, quick there's no one here, give it to me.'

Sarah thought Jimmy was going to drink it, but to her surprise, he poured it into a large ornate porcelain vase by the staircase. It was very old and there was a small crack down one side. It was decorated with water lilies and contained a spider fern. The liquid soon disappeared into the soil under its foliage.

'I bet it's not the first alcoholic drink the plant has enjoyed over the years,' said Jimmy.

'That's probably why it's so healthy.'

Sarah was giggling and then froze when she noticed Maggie behind her. She did not know how long her hostess had been standing there and worried she may have seen the champagne being wasted.

Maggie was wearing a tight-fitting blue satin blouse over a short red skirt with a long slit at the front. Putting her hands on her hips, she smiled at Jimmy.

'I hope your room is comfortable. I slept on the bed many times when Eddie was alive. He was such a noisy snorer, I often left him alone.'

Maggie realised her close presence continued to make Jimmy feel uncomfortable. He could not stop looking at her.

'The room is beautiful,' said Sarah.

Maggie noticed she was holding an empty glass. 'Giles, where are you?'

'I won't be a moment, My Lady!' he called out.

He was making final preparations in the dining room for the evening meal and took a few seconds to arrive.

'Ah, there you are. I've told you before not to call out, just come when I command you. Haven't you noticed Mrs Jackson's glass is empty? She's a thirsty woman; top her up, man.'

Once again, Sarah was appalled by Maggie's behaviour. Giles opened another bottle of champagne and because he was so nervous, he was unintentionally shaking it. When removing the cork, the liquid shot out and, to Sarah's delight, in Maggie's direction.

Maggie roared!

'You stupid, stupid man!'

He stood there with his right hand over the top of the bottle. The champagne was still bubbling and seeping out from between his fingers and dripping onto the carpet. Maggie's face was wet and blood-red with anger. Somehow, Sarah managed to stop herself from laughing.

'Go and get me a towel, man. I don't want to look like a saturated cat all evening!' she bellowed.

Giles walked towards the downstairs bathroom.

'Quickly, will you?' Maggie loudly commanded again and he hastened his step.

'I don't know what it is with that man, I'll sack him after the funeral.'

Giles returned with a tea-cloth and attempted to wipe her chest where the wetness was most prevalent.

Maggie drew breath and angrily pushed him away. 'For goodness sake, man, what do you think you're doing?'

'I'm sorry, My Lady, is there anything else I can do for you?'

'You're a fool, Giles, leave the room now!' she yelled.

Sarah found the incident hilarious, but she was concerned for Giles. She found him to be helpful and charming, but he was unable to get anything right for the lady of the house.

Maggie was not as wet as she first thought and, after dabbing a few spots, she calmed down. It was time for supper and they made their way into the dining room.

Sarah's attention was immediately drawn to the ceiling, decorated with beautiful red and yellow floral tiles. She was also enchanted by three twenty-four piece chandeliers hanging above a sumptuous table.

On Maggie's instruction, Giles only set three places at the far end, but when full, the table accommodated twenty-eight people. In the centre there were three painted glass vases, full of spring flowers.

'I hope you don't mind, but I took the liberty of choosing the meal for this evening.'

'That's kind of you, Maggie,' Sarah replied.

'Jess is our cook. She's been here a number of years and when Eddie bought the property, he decided to keep her on. She lives in the village and works five hours a day, except weekends. Apart from the cooking, she helps Giles with the cleaning.'

While they were chatting, Jess entered the room; she was a well-rounded, middle-aged woman, with her hair pulled up into a bun. Jess was very messy and sometimes it was possible to tell what she was cooking from the stains on her apron.

'Excuse me, My Lady, are you ready to be served, please?'

Maggie raised a finger, indicating her approval, which prompted Giles to push a shiny brass-handled trolley into the dining room from the kitchen. It squeaked like a baby blackbird, causing Maggie to moan at him again.

'I told you to fix that noise, Giles. Don't you ever take any notice of what I say?'

'You only told me yesterday evening, My Lady. I've been getting ready for your guests today.'

Maggie hated being spoken back to, especially by a servant in front of company.

'That's it, he's definitely going next week,' she said.

Sarah thought Giles was badly treated, but at this moment she was only concerned about her evening meal. She was not used to fine dining and when she sat down, there was a selection of unfamiliar cutlery in front of her. It was lined up with precision to the edge of the table and shone as if it was polished every day.

Sarah did not know which utensils to use first. She was frightened to touch any of them, until her memory recalled a film called *The Toast of New Orleans*, in which Mario Lanza was shown what to do in preparation for a lavish party.

'Use the knives and forks from the outside, Jimmy,' whispered Sarah.

Maggie exhaled loudly in exasperation at the table setting.

'I don't know why we've got all this cutlery; you'd have thought it was the Lord Mayor's banquet. I've told Giles it doesn't matter now Eddie isn't here, but he won't listen.'

'Maybe Giles thinks things should stay the same until after the funeral.'

'He's not paid to think.'

Maggie was irritated, but Sarah did not care. She felt a little more relaxed and took a sip of the white wine that was poured in front of her.

Giles re-entered the room with his noisy trolley, containing three bowls of prawns with horseradish cream and lime. He had covered the wheel axles with butter to lessen the annoying sound.

'Wouldn't it be easier for Giles to deliver the dishes by hand?' asked Sarah.

'I prefer my food to be pushed to the table,' Maggie replied.

The delicious entrée was followed by a large thick gammon steak with new potatoes and green beans. Sarah and Jimmy were not able to afford to eat such tasty food at home. After two courses, Sarah was full, but somehow she managed to find room for a fresh fruit salad and cream dessert.

Sarah was feeling light-headed. She was not used to drinking and was flushed.

'Thank you so much for making us welcome and feeding us so well,' she said.

Her cheeks were red and she was slightly slurring her words.

'Don't thank me, it's Eddie's money, or at least it is at the moment.'

Maggie chuckled and Jimmy frowned at her. For the first time, Sarah sensed Maggie was not missing Eddie. She camouflaged the look of disgust on her face with her napkin, pretending to remove a smudge of food from her mouth.

They all retired to the Victorian sitting room, which amongst its contents contained blue upholstered chairs, a sideboard and a burr walnut boudoir grand piano. On the wall there was a beautiful cherub and heart wall tapestry.

'Do you play the piano?' Sarah asked.

'No, I don't, it hasn't been used in all the time I've been here; such a shame really.'

While they were relaxing, tea was served by Giles.

'Where's the Victorian china? I've told you before, it's always to be used when we're in this room.'

'I'm sorry, My Lady, do you want me to change it?'

'No, it's too late now. If we wait any longer I'll likely die along with Eddie. We'll have to manage, as I often do with you around.'

Once again, Sarah thought Maggie's conduct towards Giles was disgusting and understood why he was so nervous in her company.

After making further complaints about him and people in the local community, Maggie eventually got around to discussing the following day's funeral arrangements.

'The cars will be here at 10 o'clock in the morning. Eddie's paid for them and our flowers as well.'

Maggie smiled and laughed again, but Jimmy was outraged.

'If you don't mind, we'll pay for our own tribute. My dad and I may not have seen eye to eye, but he was never tight with his money. It's the least we can do and so should you.'

Maggie shrugged her shoulders.

'I've never known the deceased pay for their own flowers; it doesn't seem right somehow,' said Sarah.

In the bedroom, Jimmy was still seething at Maggie's behaviour.

'I'd no idea what she was like, Sarah.'

'Why would you, Jimmy, you're never in her company?'

'I know, but she showed her true colours today. My dad's death and tomorrow's funeral don't seem to be worrying her at all.'

'Perhaps she's putting on an act to hide her grief, Jimmy.'

'I don't think so, you never think badly of anyone. The more she speaks, the more I think she's an ungrateful selfish bitch.'

'That's a bit harsh.'

Jimmy laughed.

'What is so funny?'

'I just thought about the champagne incident. When Giles tried to dry Maggie's blouse with a tea-cloth, I nearly wet myself.'

'The poor chap didn't know what to do, I don't think he should've dabbed her chest though,' said Sarah.

'It was instinctive behaviour; he didn't mean any harm.'

'Maggie would probably like it if you did it, Jimmy.'

'Don't be silly. I certainly wouldn't want to.'

Over time, Sarah had lost some of her timidity. She was still reserved, but the adoption process, all those years before, taught her to stand up for herself. Maggie was a snob, a flirt and a bully and, unknown to Jimmy, prior to coming to Norfolk, Sarah decided to find out more about her past in Stockport. Her last name, MacArdle, was unusual and by using her neighbour's phone, Sarah easily located her family.

She spoke to Maggie's father and was extremely disturbed by her findings. They would shock Jimmy, so she decided to keep them secret. She reasoned, 'We'll be home in a couple of days, and not likely see Maggie again.'

Chapter Twelve

The day of the funeral was met with clusters of dark clouds and heavy precipitation. It had rained for most of the night and puddles had formed on the Grange forecourt. It was cold and gloomy for early February and a mist drifted in from the sea into the village.

Sarah and Jimmy dreaded meeting Eddie's friends and associates. They did not want any breakfast and a cup of tea was their only nourishment.

In contrast, Maggie was full of joy. She bounded down the staircase and skipped into the dining room. Her mannerisms shocked Sarah. She watched her tuck in to bacon, eggs and toast. For Maggie, the funeral was of little consequence, it was the reading of the will that occupied her mind.

'Thank you, Giles,' said Maggie, as he placed a pot of coffee on the table.

Today she was friendly and chatty. She appreciated he was doing his best to capture the sadness of the day, while carrying out his duties.

Giles was bewildered by her unusual kindness.

'Thank you, My Lady,' he replied, as he left the room.

As the minutes ticked by, Maggie's mood changed. Her hands shook and tears dripped down her cheeks.

She gave Sarah an unexpected hug and said, 'I hope we can be close friends in future.'

'We'll have to see; Norfolk is a long way from the East End of London,' she replied.

'That woman is unbelievable,' said Sarah, while alone with Jimmy.

'Has she upset Giles again?'

Sarah was getting ready for the funeral, after breakfast.

'Maggie's always upsetting Giles and now she wants me and her to be bosom buddies.'

'I think her mind's all over the place. She doesn't know what she's saying at the moment,' Jimmy replied.

The cars arrived at 9.50am. Carnations were draped over the hearse and decorated both sides, but their beauty was masked by the rain beating against the windows. The undertaker stepped out of the vehicle into a puddle. His shoes were sodden, but undeterred he took off his black top hat and bowed his head.

'Would you like to ride in the hearse, ma'am?' he asked.

'No, I'll go with Eddie's son and his wife in the Bentley.'

The two vehicles were driven slowly away from the Grange, out onto the main road and through the village to St. John's Church. This elegant building dated back to the fourteenth century. It boasted two large stained-glass windows behind the altar; they were over eight feet tall.

There were mixed feelings about Eddie. He had tended to socialise in high circles, where he was friends with the elite in the vicinity. He did not have any time for ordinary folk, or the day-to-day running of the estate.

Nevertheless, out of respect and despite the poor weather, many people came out of their houses and shops. They lined Cleybourne High Street for the funeral cortege and bowed their heads as the vehicles passed by.

The church was packed for the service. As Maggie, Sarah and Jimmy made their way down the aisle behind the coffin, the silence was only broken by people's whispers and the sound of coughing which echoed around the building.

The service was undertaken by Reverend Fiddy. He was a tall, slim man with short ginger hair and a jaundiced face. He expressed his sadness about Eddie's death and invited everyone to stand for the first hymn, 'The Lord Is My Shepherd'.

The organist was Mrs Fiddy. She first met the Reverend when he came to the village in 1943. They married two years later, when the war was over. She had long, brown hair and an unusual birthmark on the tip of her nose. Unfortunately, arthritis in her fingers affected their mobility and many wrong notes were played, but the gathering managed to navigate its way in song through the musical mire.

When everyone sat down, Reverend Fiddy talked about the deceased's life.

'Eddie rarely came to church, but I knew him from the bowls club. You might be surprised to hear he came from humble surroundings in East London.'

Maggie was shocked. Eddie never discussed his earlier years with her. She fidgeted with her clothing, fearing further embarrassing revelations.

Reverend Fiddy continued to provide details of Eddie's working life and people found it hard to believe he was once a carpenter's mate. It was no consolation to Maggie that he eventually became very wealthy. Whispers were heard growing in the pews, which were interrupted by the Reverend so he could continue with the service. The congregation prayed before standing again; this time for, 'Abide with Me', with the unwelcome help of Mrs Fiddy.

With umbrellas aloft, thirty-eight mourners made their way to Eddie's final resting place. The grave was at the far end of the cemetery and on a strengthening wind, the rain gathered momentum as they walked along a well-trodden stone path.

Maggie was last to arrive. It was a token gesture to a man she never loved. Nevertheless, he bought her a position in society and she was sorry they had drifted apart.

Once everybody gathered, the coffin was lowered into the ground. Gentlemen's hats were removed and the funeral party bowed their heads. The interment process was completed with words of comfort and prayers from Reverend Fiddy. Apart from Sarah, who sobbed in Jimmy's arms, there were no tears, just an acceptance by everyone they would not see Eddie again.

While walking away from the grave, Sarah noticed Jimmy's lips were twitching and he gripped her hand firmer than usual.

'I think deep down your dad's death has disturbed you,' said Sarah.

'I'd like to have said I was proud of him, but sadly my memories are of an angry, aggressive man who I want to forget.'

'I know Jimmy, but if it wasn't for him, I'd never have met you. That's something to be thankful for.'

The wake was held in the Grange, where Jess prepared a cold buffet. Some of the invited village folk chatted about the future of the Grange. Unknown to them, Sarah listened to their conversation from the morning room.

'Maggie does think a lot of herself. I'm sure she believes I'm beneath her,' said Miss Ward, who worked in the baker's shop.

'I get that feeling too, but Maggie's done a lot for us. She got rid of the Smythes,' remarked Miss Tidy.

'She's a bit flirty. My husband told her not to put her arm around him, for the third time, only last month,' said Mrs Johnson.

'Yes, but Maggie's harmless,' replied Miss Tidy.

'I don't know about that, now Eddie's dead she'll be after every man in the village,' said Mrs Johnson.

One by one the guests left the Grange and Maggie was delighted when the front door was finally closed.

'Thank God it's over; I swear over half of the people only came for a free lunch and to snoop about.'

'More inappropriate words at an inappropriate time,' thought Sarah.

Whilst Sarah and Jimmy went to freshen up, Maggie got in touch with the solicitor, John Barker, who was Eddie's friend and his executor. Work commitments prevented him from attending the funeral, but he was tasked with reading the will.

'Would you mind bringing our meeting forward to later today, as Eddie's son and daughter-in-law are keen to get back to East London?' she asked on the telephone.

Maggie was impatient and wanted Eddie's wishes revealed as soon as possible. Mr Barker had other meetings planned, but he, too, wanted the reading over with swiftly.

'It'll have to be five o'clock, that's the best I can do,' he replied.

When Sarah and Jimmy found out, they were flabbergasted.

'Surely my father should be allowed to rest for at least one day!' said Jimmy.

'I'm sorry, but I thought you'd both want to get everything over with as quickly as possible.'

'It does mean we can go home tomorrow, Jimmy. I'm missing the children.'

Sarah was uncomfortable in such luxurious surroundings. For her the fairy tale was over; she wanted to get away from Maggie and back to her prefab where she belonged.

'I suppose so. It's a bit sudden, that's all,' Jimmy replied.

Mr Barker arrived early. He was a very tall man, standing over seven feet, and towered above Giles when he opened the front door. The solicitor was shown into the sitting room where Maggie, Sarah and Jimmy were waiting.

Tea was served and this time Maggie did not moan at Giles, even though he forgot spoons for the sugar. She was exuberant and did not want to wait a moment longer than necessary. Her mind was fixed entirely on the will.

Mr Barker, however, was slow and deliberate in his actions. Unbuckling his briefcase he searched for the document.

'Sorry, it's been a long day; it's in here somewhere,' he said with a little chuckle.

Sarah noticed Maggie inhaling and exhaling. She did not appreciate Mr Barker's flippancy. Eventually he located the item contained in a long brown sealed envelope.

'Ah! Here it is.'

Mr Barker smiled with a curled lip, as he carefully put a fingernail under some Sellotape and pulled it off.

Maggie was fiddling with her pearl necklace and playing with her bracelet as he put his hand inside and removed the will. Her face was sweating and she was bursting with excitement.

Sarah was relaxed, but she thought the solicitor was taking pleasure from Maggie's anxiety, as he took time to peruse the document. He turned the pages over one by one.

'Read the will!' said Maggie, abruptly.

Mr Barker looked over his reading glasses and cast his eyes around the room.

'I'm required to read it to Maggie MacArdle, Jimmy Jackson and Sarah Jackson. Can I assume we're all here?'

'Yes, yes we are,' said Maggie.

'The value of Mr Jackson's estate is very substantial. Apart from property, the deceased made some very speculative share investments. Some people would say foolish at the time, but they've provided rich rewards.'

Maggie's face was glowing with expectancy.

'Yes Mr Barker, go on,' she pleaded.

'Before proceeding I wish to clarify something again. Please will you confirm you're Miss MacArdle. There're many people in Cleybourne who think you're married to the deceased and that your name is Jackson. I don't know why they should have this impression.'

'Yes, I'm Miss MacArdle,' she snapped back with eyes that could cut the solicitor in half.

'Thank you, it's for the record, you understand.'

Maggie breathed heavily again while rocking on her seat like a small child.

'Eddie updated his will last month. It's as well he did, as otherwise his final wishes wouldn't be aired today.'

Now sitting forward, Maggie's mind tormented her and she tempered her enthusiasm. For the first time, she doubted her inheritance.

For Sarah there were different emotions, as she considered the possibility that Jimmy might get a little nest egg.

'I'm now ready to read the will,' said Mr Barker.

'Eddie has dealt with smaller donations first. He leaves £500 to both Mrs Fiddy and Mrs Smythe.'

Maggie rubbed her face hard with the palm of her hand and interrupted the solicitor again. She was unable to contain her emotions.

'Why on earth did he want to leave money to Mrs Smythe? She's such a snotty woman. Eddie knew I loathed her; that's why he's done this.'

Sarah thought, 'If Maggie thinks Mrs Smythe, is snotty I wonder what she thinks she is?'

'Can I go on please, there's so much to get through?' said Mr Barker speaking with authority.

Maggie was now playing with a tassel that had come loose on a cushion, as Mr Barker consulted the will again.

'Let me see, where was I? Oh yes, £1,000 is left to each of Canine Park, The Cleybourne Bowls Club and St John Ambulance.'

Maggie now silent waited anxiously for the solicitor to come to the next provision.

'The main benefactor is Mr Jimmy Jackson.'

Mr Barker's words were delivered cheerfully. He bordered on being unprofessional as his lips widened into a broad smile. Maggie stood up and clenched her fists. She was so aggressive, the solicitor worried she might strike him.

'No! I won't stand for it. He can't do this to me.'

The smiles on Sarah and Jimmy's faces were enormous. They were astounded and waited to hear the details.

'Your provision comes next, Miss MacArdle; will you please sit down and let me continue.'

'Eddie wasn't thinking straight when he died; the will won't stand,' said Maggie.

'Oh, please believe me, it will. I persuaded Eddie to go to his doctor. It's on record he was of sound mind the day he changed his legacy.'

Maggie glared at Mr Barker.

'Mr Jackson, you're to receive nearly all of your father's property. In addition, you've been left a substantial amount of cash and many large investments. When your father and I discussed his estate, your inheritance was valued at £350,000.'

Sarah cried and Jimmy put his arm around her. Not once did it cross her mind this might happen, but it was going to change her life forever. It was easy to understand why Maggie was angry, but from her recent behaviour, Sarah realised why she was not the main beneficiary. She was an uncaring, selfish woman and Eddie had fallen out of love with her.

Maggie collapsed in a chair with her head in her hands. She was sobbing and Sarah tried to comfort her, but Maggie pushed her away.

'I don't want your sympathy.'

Casting her swollen blood shot eyes towards Mr Barker, she was at breaking point.

'Where am I supposed to live?' she shouted at him, while pulling her necklace so hard it snapped and the pearls scattered around the room.

'I was coming to that, Miss MacArdle, when you interrupted me yet again. Are you prepared to be quiet or shall we leave the rest of the will for another day?'

Maggie shrugged her shoulders.

'You've been left Mr Jackson's cottage, Miss MacArdle.'

Getting to her feet again, she cried out, 'I'm not going to live in that shack! The Grange is my home, my beautiful dream home. I persuaded Eddie to buy it.'

The cottage was situated next to the cliffs and used to have a long back garden, but coastal erosion had dramatically altered the landscape.

'It's an attractive property with an outstanding view of the sea. From the main bedroom you can also look down to the rocks and the sandy beach.'

Maggie wouldn't be charmed.

'You're an estate agent now are you, Mr Barker? I'm not swapping the Grange for a dingy cottage; I won't leave here.'

After watching her complaining for a few more seconds, Mr Barker decided to continue with the reading, speaking loudly to make himself heard.

'You're also to inherit Mr Jackson's cars. He owned two Rolls-Royces, a Bentley, a Lotus, a Mercedes and a Land Rover, which are all of substantial value. If you sell them and invest wisely the money will provide you with a large monthly income, but there's a condition.'

'What condition? Has Eddie not humiliated me enough?'

'You must vacate Hemsley Grange within two weeks, or these assets will also become the property of Mr Jackson.'

'So that's how much he thought of me. The bastard wants me to leave my home.'

Eddie only ever drove the Land Rover, but Maggie was aware of the other vehicles. They were kept in a large lock-up garage on the estate. She frowned at the solicitor; lifting her eyebrows and puckering up her lips.

'After all I did for that miserable man, I've been given scraps to live on.'

'They're hardly scraps, Miss MacArdle.'

Sarah and Jimmy did not stop smiling and caught Maggie's eye, who was now stalking the sitting room like a caged cheetah.

'Look at yourselves, sitting there as if butter wouldn't melt in your mouths. You're just a couple of East End paupers who can't even hold a fork properly. Did you think I didn't notice last evening?'

The solicitor's job was finished. He placed two copies of the will on a table before leaving. Maggie slammed the door behind him and then continued her assault on Sarah and Jimmy.

'You'll never be able to run Hemsley Grange. You need class and breeding.'

Sarah remembered being humiliated by Maggie at her wedding and now she was being chastised again. However, she was armed with information about Maggie's past that could destroy her and she was ready to seek revenge.

'Where did you get your breeding, Maggie? It certainly wasn't in Stockport.'

Maggie was shocked and speechless. Standing up to her was a daunting prospect for Sarah, but she summoned every ounce of her courage.

'What are you talking about?' asked Jimmy.

'I did some digging, like her father who's a gravedigger,' she replied.

Maggie was open-mouthed and silent.

'You might think we're nobodies, but we're decent honest people.'

'How did you find out?' asked Jimmy.

'The telephone is a wonderful invention and with her unusual name it was easy to track her down. Her father was mortified when I mentioned her name. He said she can rot like a rat in a trap.'

Maggie's eyes narrowed, as she fearfully waited for more home truths to be revealed.

'Her parents did everything possible for her, Jimmy, but nothing was ever good enough for you, was it Maggie?'

'Stop it, you know nothing about me.'

Sarah was unrelenting.

'You treated your family worse than chicken fodder. Your father told me you wished them dead.'

Maggie tried to slap Sarah, but Jimmy took hold of her arm. Maggie's face was morose; she was petrified and crying.

Sarah smirked. 'You like hurting people, don't you Maggie? Is that why you pushed your sister Marie down the stairs?'

Maggie laughed off the accusation, but her cheesy smile and her guilty eyes gave her away.

'I don't believe it,' said Jimmy.

'Oh yes, she did! She's a real box of surprises.'

'Shut up, it's all lies!' Maggie bellowed.

'Holler as much as you like; it won't stop me telling the truth. Marie will never walk again, Jimmy. She was paralysed from the waist down and Maggie was thrown out. Her parents disowned her and that's why she's in Norfolk.'

'I didn't push her. We argued and she fell. I left Stockport because I wanted too.'

'Make your own mind up, Jimmy. I wasn't going to tell you, but the circumstances have changed and she's made me so mad. I thought you should know what joy this woman has brought to the world.'

'Are you going to expose me?' asked Maggie.

She slumped back on her chair.

'What? Tell the villagers you're nothing more than a common barmaid? I think they deserve to know. Listening to some of them today, I know they think you're a tart anyway,' said Sarah.

'It's none of their bloody business!' snapped Maggie.

'You can stop worrying, we won't blacken your name, unless you give us cause to. From now on, however, you'll treat me, my family and the employees in this house with respect; is that understood?' said Sarah.

Maggie's facade was destroyed. Sarah had calmly dismantled her dubious reputation.

'Is that understood?' she said, repeating her command with vigour and authority.

'Yes, I will,' she replied softly.

'I didn't hear you, Maggie.'

'Yes!' she yelled.

Maggie was shattered. She realised the bricks she built in the community were tumbling down around her.

'I think Eddie gave you two weeks to get out of the Grange. As you brought the reading of the will forward to this afternoon, you have a fortnight from today. We'll leave in the morning and when we return with our children, we expect you to be gone. Meanwhile you'll not sack Giles or anyone else,' Sarah commanded.

Chapter Thirteen

Sarah's mind was overburdened with thoughts of the inheritance and sleep was hard to find. She tossed and turned and at 2.45am, sat up in bed.

'Are you awake, Jimmy?'

He was dozing and opened his eyes.

'There's so much to do. You've got to leave your job, we've to pack everything up and there's the neighbours and friends to say goodbye to. Do you think we should have a party? I don't want us to go over the top.'

Sarah was speaking quickly and Jimmy gently put his hand over her mouth. He kissed her on the cheek and smiled.

'Stop it, Sarah! These are good things, you don't have to worry. We'll deal with them all, one by one. They'll be nothing compared to our new responsibilities here.'

'Yes, I know Jimmy, I've been thinking about that. Have you looked through the diary? It's bursting with meetings arranged for the current year. Maggie's involved in almost everything that moves around here. I don't think I can be 'lady of the house'. I can't be posh. Do we have to move to Norfolk?'

'My lovely wife; you're kind, considerate and honest; the people of Cleybourne will adore you. If a barmaid can do it I'm sure you can with ease. You'll be like a summer's dawn compared to Maggie.'

'I'm not so sure, it's a massive job.'

'Well I suppose we could sell the Grange, but neither of us have family back home.'

'I'm not a born leader. The thought of chairing committee meetings doesn't appeal to me, Jimmy. I'm not strong enough.'

'Oh yes you are. Have you already forgotten how you demolished Maggie yesterday evening? I've not seen you like that before, but if you can stand up to her, the villagers will melt in your hands. Sarah, we have an opportunity to live a life away from the grime and the hustle and bustle of London. What about your dream to live in the country? You haven't mentioned it for years.'

'With so much going on in our lives and the constant struggle to bring up the children, I dismissed it a long time ago.'

'Well, now we've an opportunity to make it come true.'

Sarah put her arms around Jimmy. She never envisaged holding a position of influence in a community, but she knew he was right.

'I suppose it's a good place for our children to grow up, in clean unpolluted air by the sea.'

She smiled broadly and Jimmy was ecstatic. He rolled Sarah over and out of the bed onto the floor. They laughed out loud, as they lay side by side on the carpet.

'That's settled then, but you're right, running this place won't be easy. You'll need Maggie's help.'

Sarah's face was aghast.

'No! I don't want that scornful woman anywhere near us, Jimmy. I don't think she'll want to help anyway.'

'Maggie can provide the advice, information and introductions we need to run the estate. We'll have to keep an eye on her, but she'll do anything we ask to avoid people around here knowing where she came from.'

Sarah felt more relaxed and was ready to sleep, but then she thought about the children and sat up again.

'Oh my goodness, Robert is taking his GCEs in two months. We can't put him in a new school, not now, it'll be too disruptive.'

'Yes, my love, but we'll have to find one for Emily. Stop worrying, we'll sort it all out.'

'Perhaps Debbie and John will let Robert stay with them until he finishes his exams, Jimmy. I don't think they'll mind and we can pay them now without any problem.'

Sarah was shivering in the cold night air, so they snuggled up under the bed covers. Realising they were the main characters in a rags to riches story, they lay silently, wondering how it might end.

The next morning, Sarah enjoyed a large breakfast. Maggie was surprisingly friendly for a woman who expected so much and lost almost everything.

'This belonged to Eddie,' she said, handing Jimmy a brown leather wallet.

His name was embroidered on the front in large black letters.

On opening it, there was more money than he had ever seen before, other than in a post office.

'There must be £200 in here!' said Jimmy

He placed the wallet on the table in front of him and pushed it away.

'Its money, that's all. You'll get used to it and need lots of it to live here. Oh, I've ordered a taxi to take you home,' said Maggie.

'We have train tickets,' said Sarah.

'The owners of Hemsley Grange don't travel by train, unless they have to.'

While they were talking, Sarah asked Maggie if she would help her with the estate and as anticipated, she agreed. After the shocks and revelations of the previous day, Maggie picked herself up. She thought to herself, 'Assisting Sarah is an inconvenience, but at least I'll be back in the Grange and I'll see Jimmy. Despite everything, I know he's attracted to me.'

In return, Maggie was given a month to move into the cottage. Sarah and Jimmy were then able to take their time moving to Norfolk and Robert would be away from them for a shorter period.

Once Sarah and Jimmy were back home in the East End of London, news of the inheritance spread amongst their friends. They did not want to show off, but their new-found wealth was a source of local interest, leading to envy and jealously.

'You know nothing about running an estate, Sarah. How can you and Jimmy manage Hemsley Grange?' asked Debbie.

'I know it's mad, but we've some help and will manage somehow.'

'I've known you since we were kids, doesn't it frighten the life out of you?'

'Pretty much, but I've more confidence now, Debbie. You know I've always wanted to live outside London.'

While Sarah and Jimmy were away, Maggie told the villagers she had not been married to Eddie and that most of his estate was left to his son. People were amazed she was not bequeathed the Grange and found it hard to believe she was taking up residence in the cottage. They sensed from the tone of her voice she was angry.

'Well that's a shocker, Maggie,' said Mrs Fiddy.

'I have to get out of the property next month, but I've been left other assets. I don't mind telling you, Eddie has betrayed me, but I'm not destitute, not by a long way.'

Maggie decided it was about time she looked at her new home. While she was with Eddie, she did not visit it once. It was fully furnished and was previously let out in the summer months.

As she walked down the narrow path to the cottage, with Bailey by her side, she passed the disused windmill. The building was in a bad state of repair. Its sails had been removed long before Eddie owned the property and its wooden cap was all but destroyed.

Maggie reached the cottage by walking down a long uneven gravel path. It was guarded by a wooden arch partly covered by a sleeping rambling rose. The front door was painted bright red in contrast to the white window frames on each side. It was unlocked, but the door was stuck to its frame. It took all of Maggie's weight pushing against it to gain entry.

The musty smell of the empty, dingy dwelling filled her nostrils as she explored inside. She was saddened as she made her way up the stairs. Exposed treads creaked on every step as she thought about Hemsley Grange. Not even the stunning view from the main bedroom consoled her.

Casting her eyes to the right, in the distance there were the high cliffs near Sheringham. Down below there were rocks scattered on the beach and old crab and lobster pots lying in pools of water.

Maggie sat down on the bed. The mattress was soft and it sagged in the middle. She ran her fingers over the white sheets and pillowcases. They were made of cotton and were wearing thin. The luxury she enjoyed in the Grange was now a thing of the past. She cried and Bailey, sensing she was unhappy, came up close to her.

Maggie was overwhelmed by bitterness, revenge and desire. She thought to herself, 'I'm going to get my home back whatever it takes. I know Jimmy likes me; he can't keep his eyes off me. It's me he wants, not Sarah. We'll live in the Grange together.'

Chapter Fourteen

Time away from the Grange gave Sarah and Jimmy the opportunity to consider the future. They spent almost every spare moment talking about their new life in Norfolk and Sarah kept asking the same question.

'How are we going to cope, Jimmy? All those people in Cleybourne are relying on us. I'm frightened.'

'We've discussed this a thousand times, Sarah. We're no different from the previous incumbents. Eddie didn't have any pedigree and we know where Maggie came from.'

Sarah was not only troubled by her responsibilities at Hemsley Grange, she was also worried about leaving the East End of London. Life was hard, but she always coped. There was a sense of achievement in bringing up two children, sometimes against all odds.

'We've so many happy memories here, Jimmy. Even during the war years, the feeling of belonging and togetherness amongst friends and neighbours was cherished.'

'We'll create new memories and as you said, Norfolk is a great place for our children.'

When Robert and Emily were told they were moving home, their reactions were different.

'You can stay here Robert until your GCEs are completed. Debbie and John have agreed to look after you,' said Sarah.

Robert needed little persuasion. He was good at woodwork and metalwork and excited about working with his dad on the Hemsley Grange estate.

Emily, however, was very upset. Despite her humble life, she loved the prefab and was mortified at the thought of saying goodbye to her friends.

'I'll never see them again, Mum.'

She was very dramatic and waved her arms in the air as she sat at the kitchen table.

'You can invite them to come and stay in our new house in the school holidays.'

Emily wasn't listening.

'I don't know where Norfolk is. It might as well be in another world, I don't want to go!' she shouted.

Emily was fourteen. She was slim, with long wavy chestnut hair and beautiful almond-shaped eyes lined with dark lashes. She was highly intelligent and usually well behaved, but like most teenagers, she expressed an opinion on everything and challenged authority. She also possessed a fiery streak and was not afraid to show it.

Regardless of Emily's objections, the Jackson family was moving, but they wanted their daughter to be happy.

'Friends are important, Emily. I'm sure you'll make new ones,' said Sarah.

'I don't want new ones, Mum, I don't need them.'

Emily slumped on the table.

'In future you can have nice clothes, go out more and you'll have a bedroom all to yourself.'

Emily was not easily bought.

'Why can't we move to a bigger house around here? It's all right for Robert, but I'll have to go to a new school.'

Sarah was desperate to appease her daughter.

'If you were able to choose something to make you happy, what would it be, Emily?'

'Nothing will, I want to stay here.'

'There must be something you've always wanted. Name it and it's yours.'

Emily pondered over the question for a few seconds, then smiled.

'I'd like a horse, Mum. I've loved them ever since we went to the circus.'

Sarah was amazed.

'A horse, you really want a horse, Emily?'

'Yes, there's nothing else.'

For a long time, Emily had pestered her parents for a puppy. In recent months, she had cut out pictures of Scottie dogs from magazines and left them lying all over the house. She even sneaked them into her dad's lunchbox from time to time. Emily was always refused, because of the upkeep cost, but now money was no longer a barrier.

Sarah only took a moment to decide. 'There's plenty of space at the Grange,' she thought.

'I'll talk to your father. I promise you'll have your horse,' she replied.

Sarah and Jimmy wanted their daughter to be happy. The request was granted and her acceptance of moving was a huge relief to both of them.

Before departing for Norfolk, Sarah wanted to revisit some special places, so Jimmy booked a taxi to take them out. First, they went to All Hallows' Church in Tottenham where they were married and memories of a wonderful day came back to them.

In particular, Sarah recalled her grandmother walking unaided to give her a brooch and the beautiful wedding cake surprise. There was, however, another reason to visit All

Hallows' Church. Sarah wanted to pay her respects to her mum, dad and sister who were buried in the graveyard. She rarely went there, because of the bus or train fare, and she knew this visit would disturb her.

Except for the area where recent burials had taken place, it was untidy, strewn with fallen leaves and twigs. It upset her and she weeded the family graves using her fingers to pull out the unwelcome roots. There were two resting places; one for Sarah's parents and one for her sister. They were side by side.

Close by there was a water tap, and using an old cloth found lying over a fence post, Sarah cleaned the headstones. She stood back and looked at the inscriptions she chose. On her parents it said 'Forever in Our Hearts' and on her sisters' were the words 'My Best Friend Always and Forever'. Sarah was moved to tears, as she inserted spring flowers in matching porcelain vases.

'I've never said it, Jimmy, but I've needed them so much over the years.'

'I know, Sarah, it's been hard for you and it saddens me they didn't see their grandchildren.'

Jimmy put an arm around her shoulder and then kneeling down, Sarah said to her dad what she always did when her parents were alive, 'Look after Mum.'

Walking back to the taxi, Sarah did not know if she would ever return, but she felt a presence in the graveyard. She did not know if it came from God or her parents, but it gave her the strength to embrace her new life.

Sarah's next destination was Bank tube station. It was her first visit since the day she met Jimmy and she felt uneasy as she entered the booking hall. She remembered the explosion, the awful carnage and how lucky she was to survive. Standing on the Central Line platform she clasped hands with Jimmy, in the same place she did on that fateful day.

A train rumbled into the station and for a split second, Sarah held her breath. She was still haunted by screams and cries of desperation. Tiny tears wetted her cheeks and she hugged Jimmy, as people around them were going about their business.

'Mind out of the way!' said a man in a black trilby hat, who was impatiently trying to board the train.

Sarah was standing in front of the open doors, blocking the entrance, but she did not care. People fumed as they pushed past. They would have found it difficult to believe what happened all those years ago.

Next was Buckingham Palace and Sarah's thoughts about VE Day swamped her mind. She remembered the release of stress, recollections of lost loved ones and the celebrations that were everywhere to be seen.

Sarah was tearful again.

'What is it?' Jimmy asked.

'It doesn't matter.'

'Whatever it is, it's clearly upsetting you. What is it?'

'You know what happened that day, it wasn't just the end of the war, was it?'

Jimmy tried to console her, but she kept crying.

'I want to go to Cotland,' said Sarah.

'There's no point, why do you want to?'

'I know it sounds silly, but it was where I held Mary for the last time; we're moving far away, I have to go.'

Arriving at the maternity home, Sarah stepped out into the car park. She walked a few yards to where she remembered her little girl being handed to strangers. Sarah was silent, as she gazed up at the window she had looked down from. She stood there silently, hardly moving a muscle. Sarah was all cried out for Mary, but there was a feeling of emptiness inside that she had endured for eighteen years.

'We can go now,' said Sarah, after a brief interlude.

Hastily, Jimmy took hold of her hand and they walked back to the awaiting taxi. As it was driven away, Sarah did not look back. It was an absorbing and emotional day, but it provided Sarah with some closure. She was now able to draw a thin line under her life in the East End.

When the removal day arrived, it was dry, and a small red van, driven by Jimmy's friend David, pulled up outside their prefab. Hemsley Grange contained beautiful furnishings, but there were a small selection of family possessions and items of sentimental value they did not want to leave behind.

Whilst riding away in the taxi, Emily and Jimmy cried. Sarah somehow stayed strong and offered comfort and support.

'Come on you two, dry your eyes, we're going on a great adventure. Don't let the neighbours see we're having doubts.'

Emily and her dad did their best to compose themselves. They sat up straight and waved at the well-wishers.

At the time, milk was being delivered by a man in a white coat with his horse-drawn cart. The sound of both the removal van and the taxi spooked the animal. It lifted its hind legs in panic causing most of the bottles to fall off the wagon and land in the road. Broken glass and spilt milk lay everywhere.

'No good crying over spilt milk!' Sarah said, as she laughed, causing Jimmy and Emily to laugh too.

The incident lightened the mood and it was the family's last memory of Porter's Field.

Chapter Fifteen

Prior to the Jackson's arrival at Hemsley Grange, Maggie moved into her cottage. She tidied the garden and hung baskets of flowers each side of the front door. Inside there were new curtains everywhere and in the sitting room there was a thick piled brown rug on the varnished floor in front of the fireplace.

Maggie also purchased a new mattress, red silk sheets and white pillowcases for her bedroom. They were similar to those left behind in the Grange and came from Selfridges in London.

In the evenings, she sat alone with her memories, listening to the closeness of the sea. With the rushing tide she heard water thrashing about on the rocks below. When the wind blew it whistled through the cottage like the sound of a rocket firework being launched. At first Maggie was afraid as the property creaked sporadically, but after a while she hardly noticed it.

Bailey liked the cottage where it was always cosy and warm. She spent most of her time close to Maggie, as she sensed her mistress was lonely. Bailey was more of a comfort each day and a loving friendship developed between them.

Maggie knew it was moving day and could not wait to see Jimmy. She dreamed of living with him in Hemsley Grange. However, in the short term, there were bridges to build; she would do anything to gain the Jacksons' favour.

'What's she doing here, Jess?' asked Giles.

He pointed to Maggie through the window. She was seated on a bench in front of the house.

'You must have noticed at Eddie's wake, she spent ages chatting to Mr Jackson, her eyes were all over him.'

'I didn't want to mention it,' he said.

'Mark my words Giles, Maggie is a scheming bitch; there's going to be trouble around here.'

It was mid-afternoon when a taxi made its way up the drive. It was a long journey from the East End of London and Sarah was tired. The van containing the family's possessions was travelling a little slower and lagged behind.

The sunshine disappeared and rain clouds gathered. Small spots of moisture were falling as the Jacksons approached the house under a darkened sky.

Sarah pointed ahead of them.

'Look, Jimmy! Three members of staff and Maggie are waiting for us outside the house.'

'Why's Maggie there?' asked Jimmy.

'I could take a good guess, but I'm more concerned about the others. They're getting drenched, it's ridiculous.'

'I assume it's their usual procedure. I expect there'll be lots of things we won't like, Sarah. We'll deal with all of them in good time, but for now we need to smile and shake hands.'

Jimmy ushered everyone out of the inclement weather and in to the Grange.

'I don't know where all the rain came from, it was a lovely day when we left London this morning,' said Sarah.

'This is what it's like on the coast, you can't trust the weather forecast,' said Maggie.

'You wait till the east wind blows in the winter. The cold really gets into your bones,' said Jess.

Standing in the hall, Sarah, Jimmy and Emily shook hands with the staff and thanked them for their warm welcome.

Giles was nervous. Sarah noticed he was breathing heavily and scratching his face with a fingernail. She drew his mannerisms to Jimmy's attention, with a tug of his jacket.

'I think we need to get to know each other. We'll have a meeting in the sitting room tomorrow, as soon as Jess arrives for work. It'll give each of you an opportunity to ask me and Mrs Jackson questions,' said Jimmy.

Sarah watched Maggie's eyes follow his movements. With her bright pink lipstick gleaming, she smiled at him at every opportunity. Jimmy pretended not to notice.

'Is everything okay, Giles?" asked Sarah.

Giles nodded and disappeared into the dining room.

'Is Giles really all right, Jess?'

'He's been a nightmare today, Mrs Jackson. Forgive me ma'am, but Maggie made him so panicky when she resided here. While laying the table for this evening's meal he dropped two glasses onto the floor. They both broke into several pieces. I also needed to tell him he had mistakenly put out dessert forks for the main course. He's always been nervous, but I think he's got worse.'

When Jess left the Grange and Emily was looking around, Sarah whispered 'I hope Maggie isn't going to be a nuisance, Jimmy.'

'I don't think so; but remember we've asked for her help and she'll be needed for a while. There's so much to learn about our property, the village and what is expected of us.'

The family went into the sitting room where Giles entered with a tray containing tea and biscuits.

'Have we got the right cups and saucers?' asked Jimmy.

Giles was on his way out of the room. He immediately turned around with a look of fear on his face, but Jimmy was smiling.

'I'm only kidding Giles, don't worry, I'm not Maggie, everything's fine.'

'You shouldn't tease him, Jimmy; you know what Jess said. Didn't you see? His hands were shaking, poor man.'

'Yes, most of my tea is in the saucer.'

Jimmy chuckled.

The removal van arrived outside the house and the family chattels were unloaded. There were mutterings amongst the staff about there being so few possessions.

Sarah was in the hall and listened to the conversation.

'Blimey, there's not much is there? I wonder where they lived before,' said Joseph.

'It's none of our business,' replied Jess.

Joseph also lived in the property and occupied two rooms in the basement. He was a short, tubby, middle-aged man who disguised his lack of hair with his well-worn, cloth cap.

Sarah and Emily explored the property together.

'I love this place, Mum.'

Sarah opened doors and cupboards. The luxurious furniture, exquisite porcelain ornaments, fine china plates and beautiful pottery all drew her attention.

'We've spent so little time in Hemsley Grange, I don't think your dad and me have any idea what we've inherited.'

Sarah adored the sweeping staircase and was anxious to show Emily her bedroom. She opened the solid oak door and cried instantly.

'Oh Mum, I love it!' she said, hugging her.

Sarah had arranged for it to be redecorated. Beautiful pink velvet curtains draped the large window which looked out towards the old windmill and the sea. Emily ran her fingers down the smooth material and rubbed it against her face.

On the floor there was a fitted light blue carpet. Sarah watched Emily take her shoes off and let its softness tickle her toes. Her feet snuggled into the thick pile. The bed was large and covered with a soft white eiderdown and matching pillowcases. The wallpaper was of bunches of pink flowers tied with blue ribbons.

When Emily spotted her dressing table she cried again. 'Oh, Mum, I can't believe it's mine.'

Emily sat in her satin-covered armchair and touched her large, gold edged, oval mirror. There was also a brush and comb with her name inscribed on both of them. On the far side of the room there were two large wardrobes and a couch in front of the window.

Emily was used to sharing a small room with her brother, where she slept on a narrow bed. Most of her clothes had hung on a rail attached to a wall.

The rain stopped and Sarah decided to stretch her legs. The air was fresh and scented as Joseph escorted her around the back garden. He told her about the spring flowers and the variety of shrubs on display.

Sarah wanted to know their names and growing habits. Joseph was delighted. He had worked at the Grange for over forty years and tending the garden was his passion. Eddie and Maggie had not taken any interest in his work and rarely spoke to him unless they wanted something. For the first time in his employment he felt appreciated.

On Sarah's return to the house, Jess came out of the kitchen.

'Is there anything you'd like for your dinner this evening, ma'am?'

'Surprise us, Jess.'

'I was going to grill some steak, will that be okay?'

'Sounds very nice.'

'Good, I've a chocolate cake for pudding,' Jess replied with her wide infectious smile.

*

When the staff assembled in the sitting room the following day, Sarah and Jimmy were waiting.

'Let me say straight away, we aren't getting rid of anyone. We've a lot to learn and need all of you,' said Jimmy.

Expressions of concern turned to smiles and relief on the faces of the staff.

'Will you still want me to do the cooking, ma'am?'

'I'm used to doing it, Jess, but I'm told I won't have time.'

'Maggie used to tell me what to cook the day before, ma'am.'

'I'll make sure you know at least a couple of days before and I'll be asking you, not telling you.'

Jimmy interrupted the conversation.

'Look! It's inevitable as time goes by, we'll want to make some adjustments to your routines. We'll have another meeting this time next week and discuss everything then. You never know, we might be underpaying you.'

'Maggie didn't think we worked hard enough. All I can say is I'm always on my feet,' said Jess.

'She isn't lady of the house anymore. She'll be around for a while, but she's not your boss; you can ignore her,' said Sarah.

There were more smiles from the staff.

'Oh, there'll be an extra five pounds added to your wages next time. These last few days have been stressful for all of you. This is to say thank you for your help,' said Jimmy.

At the end of the discussion, Giles' hands were shaking again. He sat on them hoping Sarah and Jimmy would not see his movement, but Sarah noticed the man's distress.

'Stop worrying about everything,' she said.

Giles nodded.

The next day Emily started at her new school in Sheringham. Moving one hundred miles from the only home she knew was a massive wrench for a young girl. Sarah worried how the upheaval was going to affect her.

'I feel so guilty, Jimmy. We've taken Emily away from all her friends, what if she doesn't settle in?'

'I know Sarah, but there was no alternative. I'm sure it'll work out for the best.'

'Not everything is about us, Jimmy.'

'No! But as parents we sometimes have to make difficult decisions in the best interests of the family.'

There were only two years of schooling left for Emily, who was to journey by taxi to Cleybourne station and then make the eight-minute train journey to Sheringham along the Norfolk coast.

Sarah's mind was on edge, wondering what her daughter was doing. When Emily left the house that morning, she was unusually quiet and Sarah sensed a slight resistance in her daughter's arms when she hugged her.

Sarah did not eat all day and spent most of her time walking around the estate. She needed a distraction, but Emily was never far from her mind.

The end of the school day did not come soon enough and Sarah was at the station to greet Emily on her arrival back in Cleybourne. She was dreading seeing her step off the train and when the engine stopped she breathed heavily, as she waited for the carriage doors to open. Emily exited her compartment behind a man carrying a brown sack.

As soon as she saw her mother, she ran towards her.

'I love the school, Mum!' she shouted.

Sarah hugged Emily tightly and all her anxiety ebbed away.

For the next few days the telephone did not stop ringing. Callers were introducing themselves, enquiring about the Jacksons' wellbeing and wanting to nose into their affairs.

Maggie was assisting Sarah when she found time, but life was chaotic in the Grange and Sarah was unable to cope.

'Would you be able to come down to the Grange every weekday?' asked Sarah.

Letting Maggie get more involved in the Jacksons' affairs was the last thing Sarah wanted, but there was no one else to turn to. Maggie did not refuse; she would do anything that might help her get her claws into Jimmy.

'I thought it might be too much for you. If you'd like me to help, of course I will,' she said.

Maggie spent time going through the Grange diary in detail with Sarah, explaining her responsibilities. The workload was enormous and she gave mixed messages. 'It'll be easily manageable once you get into a routine,' and 'It's much too stressful for one person to handle,' were two of her favourite lines.

As much as Maggie wanted her life back in the Grange, she was pleased not to attend the monthly village hall committee meetings.

'Now you're lady of the house, I'm sure they'll want you to be in the chair, Sarah.'

'That's not necessary.'

'Oh, believe me it is. I'll be pleased to get out of it. It's like nursing a lot of kids; it's full of people with tiny minds.'

Maggie told Sarah about other meetings held in the Grange and charity events including the annual fete.

'Why am I involved in the fete?'

'Because it's held on your land. Remember you own the village green.'

'Oh yes, silly me, it seems everything revolves around the Grange.'

'Pretty much, oh the locals play bingo in the village hall on Tuesday evenings. Miss Ward arranges that.'

Sarah was also responsible for the Grange's accounts and she was shown the books. Fortunately, Emily was excellent at mathematics and her help was enlisted for some pocket money.

One of the telephone calls to the Grange was from Sir Donald Scott. He wanted to welcome Jimmy to the village.

'Please tell him I'm not here, Giles.'

'You should join something in the community, it'll be expected of you,' said Sarah.

'I don't want to get involved with him. I've been told Eddie donated funds to help run the bowls club where Sir Donald is president. I know he wants me to join for that reason. Do you remember he was at my father's funeral, the man who was sweating, with smelly feet?'

'Oh him, a very irritating man and a bit of a snob. He might have a title, but if he's touting you, he must have few assets.'

'I'll get involved in something, Sarah, but remember my disability does restrict what I can do.'

Chapter Sixteen

At the next meeting of the Cleybourne Women's Institute, Sarah was the special guest in her own home. The ladies gathered in the sitting room around a large table which, as usual, Giles had draped in a Union Jack flag. Jess provided pots of tea and homemade cakes.

Sarah was expected to be a major supporter of the Institute. She had already met two of the members, as they were on the village hall committee. The other ladies were keen to talk to her, but this was one meeting she was not expected to chair. This responsibility was undertaken by Sir Donald Scott's wife, Geraldine. She was seventy-two and her face was covered in moles.

Geraldine was always last to arrive and spoke to her gathering with unnerving penetrating eyes, as if she were teaching a class at high school. Her first glances around the table commanded the members' attention and they dreaded her opening remarks.

'Mrs Benson, your mauve sandals hardly match your red skirt. I've told you about your clothes before.'

'I'm sorry, Mrs Scott, it won't happen again.'

'I should think so, we have standards.'

Other ladies examined their dress attire to make sure they were colour coordinated, but nobody dared question Geraldine. Her long unkempt hair was hanging over a distasteful low-cut blouse.

Sarah was wearing some old brown trousers and a green woollen jumper, but she was not challenged. She thought, 'It must be because the members are assembled in my house.'

Agendas were always provided for the meetings, but they were rarely followed. Geraldine was known for going off on a tangent and the first discussion about flower arranging was not even listed.

'I can't see flowers mentioned on the handout,' said Sarah.

'Please raise your hand if you want to speak,' Geraldine replied, while rustling paper in front of her.

She was not used to being questioned or giving explanations.

'My neighbour, Florence, asked me to raise the matter, as Mrs Dangle broke her leg and is unable to decorate St John's Church. The displays are not being changed and the spring blooms are dying.'

'Gosh! How did she do that?' asked Sarah.

Geraldine did not answer. She glared at her for speaking out again as the other members immediately whispered amongst themselves.

'It'll be at least ten weeks before she's able to return to her duties. We need a volunteer or volunteers to help out while she's indisposed,' Geraldine replied.

While the matter was being discussed, Miss Jewson moved towards Sarah. She was sitting behind her and wanted to gossip. Miss Jewson wore a straw hat and people called her the scarecrow. She disliked Geraldine because she did not have a kind word to say about anybody and was delighted to tell Sarah the worst-kept secret in Cleybourne.

'Mrs Dangle is a bit frisky, if you know what I mean. She fancies a member of the church choir and apparently chased him up the steps to the pulpit. I don't know why, he's the ugliest man I've ever seen. His face looks like it's been hit with a brick. Anyway, they were enjoying a passionate embrace when her foot slipped and she fell down. Mrs Fiddy was cleaning the organ, out of sight, and watched the incident. She said there was a lot of heavy breathing, followed by a crack, like the snapping of a stick of celery. Apparently, she let out shrieks of pain, as she tried to do up her blouse.'

'Poor woman; what's that got to do with Geraldine?'

'That's the funny part, Geraldine won't talk about it because Mrs Dangle is her sister.'

'Oh, I see.'

'They don't speak now, because a few years ago Mrs Dangle went after Geraldine's husband. They enjoyed a bit of a whirl together, if you know what I mean.'

There were more mutterings amongst the members and Geraldine realised she was the butt of the conversation.

'Is there anyone who's prepared to help out?' she enquired loudly, bringing the meeting back to order.

'I will, if you'll assist me,' said Sarah bluntly.

The ladies were stunned and a synchronised intake of breath was heard in the room. Geraldine was a talker, not a doer and they eagerly awaited her response.

Geraldine stared at Sarah. Her eyes were puffed and piercing.

'As long as we decorate the church on Friday afternoons, and it's *you* who assists *me*.'

'Okay, that's settled then, Friday it is.'

Sarah's head was in a spin as the list of responsibilities attached to the Grange became known. With so many demands on her time, she was hardly able to take stock. Her duties were unrelenting, even in the evenings and at weekends.

Sarah and Jimmy needed to assess the house contents. There were many precious items lying around and some cupboards had still not been opened because nobody could find the keys.

'I think we need everything in this house valued, Sarah; we may not be fully insured.'

'There're a lot of things I don't like; perhaps we can get rid of them,' she said.

'Yes! The stag's head in the hall can go for starters; I'm sure its eyes follow me around.'

'I have that feeling too, Jimmy, it's very unnerving. The suit of armour can go as well, sometimes I imagine breathing noises and think there's someone in it. Oh, that reminds me, do you think there are any ghosts in the Grange?'

'We can ask Maggie, but she'll probably delight in saying yes even if it isn't true.'

With all the committee meetings and other gatherings, such as parties, luncheons and guest of honour appearances, it put a strain on Sarah and Jimmy's marriage. Circumstances dictated they spent a lot of time apart. They imagined it was why Eddie and Maggie eventually became like strangers.

On one of Sarah's quieter days, she assisted Mrs Piper, Emily's art teacher, on a school trip. She had taught children for thirty years and was well known in Sheringham.

Mrs Piper wore her wavy hair down to the small of her back. She was a chain smoker and often left her class for short periods to satisfy her addiction. Her clothes and breath smelt of stale tobacco and she was in the habit of drawing air and saliva between the gaps in her teeth every time she spoke.

Mrs Piper, together with Sarah and other helpers, walked the children for about half a mile into Sheringham Park. The undergrowth in the wonderful woodland was dominated by clusters of rhododendrons and azaleas. With the sunlight piercing through the trees, their colours dazzled, showing off the beauty of nature's creation in full bloom.

Carrying their painting equipment, the pupils strolled down a narrow path and out into a large grassed field. After walking a little further, Mrs Piper instructed her class to settle on a flat piece of ground and assemble their easels. The only sounds around them came from the birds and the insects as the girls and boys prepared for work.

'Look around children, what can you see? I don't mean the trees, flowers, the grass or even the sky.'

The children were not sure what they should be focusing on and Sarah was also intrigued.

'I want you to search beyond your eyes and let your imagination run wild. I'd like you to paint something that will inspire people. It can be anything you like, but there has to be a reason. You need to tell me why you're doing it, who'd be invigorated by it and why,' said Mrs Piper.

The children were enthralled by this teacher. She spoke with emotion in her voice and used her hands to bring the environment alive. Emily sometimes came home believing she could paint anything.

'What are you going to do, Emily?' asked Sarah.

Emily was enthusiastic. She was already laying out her brushes.

'I have an idea, Mum. I wonder what our windmill was like when it was working. It looks so sad now and I'm going to paint it with four sails and try and make it look like they are moving.'

Sarah watched Emily at work creating the colours she imagined in her mind.

'What are you going to do about the top, Emily?'

'It's difficult, Mum, but I know they're usually dome shaped. I'll see what I can do.'

Carefully and concisely Emily used the skills she learned to bring her panting to life. Mrs Piper loved it and when Emily revealed it was the windmill in Cleybourne, it stirred memories from her past.

'That's wonderful, Emily. I remember seeing it when the sails were attached. When my husband was alive, we used to walk past it on our way to Sheringham. It brightened the Norfolk coast landscape and you've managed to capture its past beauty.'

The school day was nearly over and Sarah helped Emily pack up her art equipment. They wanted to get home as soon as possible as the sky was darkening. The air was heavy and a storm was on its way.

It was now three days to the end of the term and Sarah was longing to see Robert and welcome him into the family home. She made the trip down to the East End of London on Saturday morning, to thank Debbie and John for Robert's lodgings and to accompany him on his journey.

Sarah missed Robert and was overcome with emotion. She loved her handsome boy, with his short sandy blonde hair and long blonde eyelashes. Tears streamed down her face as she wrapped both arms around him. Then she stood back and eyed him up and down.

'You're a lot taller, Robert.'

'It's only been two months, Mum. I can't have grown that much.'

They hugged again and this time Sarah kissed Robert on his cheeks. He was embarrassed, as Debbie, John and some school friends were laughing.

'Don't fuss, Mum,' he said.

Sarah and Robert said their goodbyes and waved as their taxi was driven away. Sarah knew Robert was excited about moving, but his face was glum. She understood his feelings were tinged with sadness, as his life would never be the same again.

'Is Dad working hard on the estate, Mum?'

'There's lots to do, but Joseph's a great help.'

'What about you? I suppose with a servant and a cook you've time to yourself.'

Sarah laughed.

'I'm very busy, Robert. The community relies on Hemsley Grange. I'm pulled in many directions and am worn out most days.'

'I can't wait to help Dad, I wonder what I'll be doing tomorrow.'

With so many questions the journey passed quickly. Once they were in Norfolk, the roads were quieter and eventually they were in Cleybourne. The taxi turned into Hemsley Grange drive and Robert got his first glimpse of the house.

'Wow! Is that our home?'

'Yes, but there's a lot more to the estate.'

As soon as Robert stepped out of the taxi he wanted to go exploring.

'Where's Dad?'

'Your father has gone into town with Emily, they're not expecting us to arrive so early.'

Robert ran around to the back of the property. He left Giles to collect his bags. A little later, Robert gave his mum a rundown on jobs that needed to be done.

'There are broken gates and fences, window frames in need of renovation, a cracked stone path and piles of old machinery everywhere.'

'I told you there's a lot to do, Robert.'

'How about the windmill? I wanted to look inside, but the surrounding area is fenced off and its entrance is boarded up. I don't think anyone has inspected it for a long time.'

'I think it's dangerous in there, Robert,' said Sarah as a vehicle was heard outside.

Jimmy and Emily stepped out of a taxi and Robert was ready to greet them.

'Your taller, Son,' said Jimmy, shaking his hand.

'That's what I told him,' said Sarah.

Robert was skinny and stood five feet nine inches tall.

Sarah was pleased to see him hug Emily. Although they were always there for one another, there was never any physical contact between them. However, this was a special moment and Emily responded by briefly putting her arms around his neck.

'I can't wait to help on the estate, Dad,' said Robert.

'I think we need to work out a plan first, but there isn't any rush,' said Jimmy.

At seven o'clock, they sat down to a supper of local fish and fresh vegetables. Jess also made a jam sponge pudding which she served with lashings of cream.

'Do we eat like this every night, Mum?' asked Robert.

'Yes, pretty much.'

On hearing this, Jess put her head through the serving hatch. She was a little tipsy and slurred her words.

'It doesn't matter about me slaving away in a hot kitchen, you can have whatever you like.'

When she wheeled in the food trolley she was drinking red wine and Sarah was astonished.

'Jess, I think you should stick to the cooking,' said Jimmy sternly.

Robert and Emily were laughing and then they heard Jess burp and went into hysterics.

'We really can't have this, Sarah, especially in front of the children.'

'Don't scold her, not tonight. She's been waiting to cook for the whole family and has got carried away with the excitement. She can have a drink, can't she?'

'In a glass, perhaps,' said Jimmy.

Giles was appalled with Jess. Sarah watched him snatch the bottle away from her.

'I'm sorry,' she said and then giggled and burped again as she returned to the kitchen.

The following morning Robert came to the breakfast table holding a painting.

'That's mine! Looking in my bag, were you?' asked Emily sternly.

'It was on the floor outside your room. I accidentally knocked it over and the artwork fell out.'

'Look, Jimmy, it's the windmill painting I told you about,' said Sarah.

'It's very good, Emily; you paint very well,' he said.

'Do you realise what it is, Dad?' asked Robert.

'It's a windmill.'

'It's not just any windmill, it's our windmill. Look at the old window frame laying against the tower and the disused tractor wheel by the entrance,' said Robert.

Emily did not know what all the fuss was about.

'I told you, Jimmy, she painted it in Sheringham Park,' said Sarah.

'What of it?' said Emily, shrugging her shoulders.

Jimmy looked at his daughter's creation again, but still did not understand why Robert was making such a fuss about it.

'Imagine if we restored it to a working windmill, like in Emily's painting, Dad!'

'The windmill is in a terrible state. It would need a great deal of work; it's impossible.'

Emily was bored with the conversation and interrupted.

'Never mind the windmill, now the school holidays are here, when am I going to get my horse?'

'I'm sorry Emily, but there're too many important jobs to do around here, maybe next year.'

'I knew you'd be like this. You promised me.'

Emily's bottom lip protruded slightly and she burst into tears. Sarah did not like her children upset; their plans were both rejected inside half an hour.

'You could make the stable your first job, Jimmy.'

'Emily always thinks turning on the tears will get her what she wants. I'm sorry, Sarah, but there're lots of things that need doing on the estate.'

Sarah sensed her children's frustration. They had moved to a strange place without much resistance or resentment and needed something to interest them.

'Jimmy, do you remember when I told the children we didn't have the money to go to the circus and then you said they could?'

'Yes, Sarah, but this is different.'

'No, it isn't. Do you remember the reason?'

Jimmy was very hesitant. He was not sure what Sarah was getting at.

'I think I said they were good kids and deserved a treat.'

'That's exactly it and the same applies now. We've completely changed their lives, and give or take a couple of Emily-style tantrums, they've gone along with our wishes.'

'Only little tantrums,' said Emily.

'A horse wouldn't be such a bad thing for a young girl and we did promise her, Jimmy. If it's okay with you, I'll go with Emily to see Maggie tomorrow. I detest the woman, but she might know something about horses.'

'Please, Dad!' said Emily.

'Perhaps Robert can go to the library in Sheringham and see what he can learn about windmills,' said Sarah.

Jimmy was outnumbered, but Sarah's suggestions made sense.

'Alright, but I'm not discussing a horse or a working windmill again until we know far more about them.'

Emily rushed around the table to hug him, but Sarah worried because she had undermined Jimmy's authority.

'I'm sorry I bullied you, and in front of the children.'

'It's done now. You might be right anyway, but I thought you and Maggie only tolerated one another.'

'Maggie isn't so bitter lately. I don't think she'll mind helping Emily if she can.'

Chapter Seventeen

Maggie used her time in the Grange wisely. When assisting Sarah, she always found excuses to talk to Jimmy if he was close by. She fluttered her eyes at every opportunity and he responded with winks and grins.

She was at home when Sarah and Emily walked up her garden path. 'What do they want? I spend enough of my time fussing over these nobodies,' she thought.

Maggie was mindful, however, that her local standing could be destroyed with a few damaging words in the wrong places. Reluctantly she opened her creaky door and invited them in with a withered smile.

Emily grinned and there was excitement in her voice, but when Sarah asked Maggie about horses she drew breath and opened her eyes wide. Momentarily she was speechless, then broke into tears. Bailey was lying in front of the fire, her legs stretched out and paws open. She got to her feet and brushed her face against her mistress's legs.

Sarah was shocked and realised she must have touched a nerve.

'I'm sorry, it's not you,' said Maggie.

She wiped her eyes with a tissue she pulled out from under her sleeve.

'Would you like us to leave?' Sarah asked.

'No, it's okay, I think I'll be all right in a minute; please sit down.'

Maggie dried her eyes and took a little while to compose herself. Coincidentally, Sarah and Emily decided to call on this day, but it gave Maggie the opportunity to talk about a tragedy in her past still festering in her mind.

Maggie sighed a little and her lips receded. Sitting up straight she spread her fingers on her knees.

'Two years ago today, I was riding Parsnip. She was my friend Gemma's horse,' said Maggie as more tears streamed down her face.

Sarah and Emily watched uncomfortably, as she held her head in her hands, but a good cry made her feel better.

Maggie got up and took a wooden frame off her mantelpiece. It contained a photo of her with Gemma and two horses. The ladies were smiling and standing either side of the animals as they held onto their reins.

'That's Parsnip, on the right.'

Maggie pointed to a chestnut coloured horse.

'The other one is Daisy and they were both stabled in High Kelling, where Gemma lives. The horses were sisters and we often took them down to Holkham beach in her trailer. We spent ages trotting and cantering down by the sea. I loved Parsnip. She always pricked up her ears when I arrived at Gemma's stables and I think she loved me too.'

Maggie paused again, but held her tears in check and Sarah guessed something bad must have happened.

'I think we should go, this is clearly upsetting you,' she said, but there was no stopping Maggie now.

'It was a beautiful clear day. I remember it was very warm but the sea was unusually choppy. A small fishing boat was rocking on the water as if it was going to capsize at any moment.'

'Really, Maggie, you don't have to do this,' said Sarah, believing she would break down again at any moment.

Maggie continued with tissues at the ready. She was getting intense and squeezed her fingers together. Her face was red and sweaty, and Sarah wished she had stayed at home.

'We arrived at about ten o'clock and Gemma was particularly happy, as Charlie, her ginger tom cat, had returned home after disappearing for three weeks. We walked the horses the best part of half a mile over the mudflats and sand down to the sea. Everything was perfect and as usual, we rode along the beach.'

Maggie's body was twitchy and Sarah was fearful of what she was going to say.

'There was a sudden jolt and Parsnip shrieked in agony!'

Emily gasped.

'Her front right leg went down into the soft sand and she buckled under her own weight. I fell off and hurt my back, but I was more concerned about the horse.'

'Oh no! Was Parsnip all right?' asked Emily.

Sarah realised this was a very serious incident.

'Did you manage to get her out, Maggie?'

'Eventually we did and Parsnip didn't panic at all, bless her. We comforted her, as she lay on the beach, until the emergency services and a vet arrived. Despite her massive discomfort, she hardly made a sound. Unfortunately, she broke her leg and it was necessary to end her life. I haven't ridden since that day.'

Maggie's face was solemn and she was silently crying. She had not displayed any genuine heartfelt emotion in Sarah's presence before and she wondered if she had misjudged her.

It was only for a fleeting moment. Sarah quickly remembered the cold and callous way Maggie dealt with

Eddie's death and her disgraceful behaviour at the reading of his will.

Emily was also in tears, but in a few seconds, Maggie composed herself again. In telling the story a great weight seemed to lift from her shoulders.

'So, who wants to ride then?' she asked.

'It's me,' said Emily.

'We can come back tomorrow, Maggie,' said Sarah.

'Nonsense! We're not going to disappoint this young lady. I bet you didn't know there's a stable on the estate, did you?'

'No, we didn't, where is it?' Sarah asked.

'Eddie wouldn't let me have a horse, so it wasn't used, but he was quite happy to host the annual fox hunt for his high-class friends. It's behind the machine shed. I think Joseph keeps his lawn mower and tools in there now. I'm sure there's somewhere else he could use.'

Emily's tears dried up and her face was beaming, prompting Maggie to take hold of her hands.

'They're not toys, Emily. They're hard work and need a lot of tender loving care. They get bored easily and need to be outside as much as possible. Otherwise they walk around in circles or gnaw stable doors. It's not good for them.'

Emily giggled.

'Listen to Maggie,' said Sarah.

'They also need cleaning out every day; I assume that'll be your job?'

'It certainly will. If Emily wants a horse, she's got to look after it,' said Sarah.

'I will, Mum. I'll do everything, I promise.'

'There is of course the small matter of deciding what to buy. I'd suggest a one to two-year-old filly. A younger horse isn't a good idea as you'll need to have it trained. They can be quite aggressive.'

'What's a filly?' asked Emily.

'It's a female horse. I'll have a word with Gemma and see if she can help.'

When Sarah and Emily arrived back at the Grange, Jimmy was chatting to Jess.

'Maggie has told me and Mum all about horses,' said Emily, interrupting the conversation.

'You're being rude, your dad's talking,' said Sarah.

Emily was not listening and excitedly continued, bombarding him with information.

'Maggie's going to talk to her friend Gemma. I can have a horse, can't I, Dad?'

Emily overpowered her dad with enthusiasm. She was like a clown with a bucket of water.

'It can go in the old stable Joseph uses,' said Sarah.

'Please, Dad, it means so much to me!' Emily pleaded.

'If I agree to this, I don't want anything to do with it.'

'Yes, Dad, I'll do everything, you won't even know the horse is here.'

'I doubt that, Emily, but if it becomes a nuisance it'll have to go, is that understood?'

'Yes, Dad, Mum said I can have lessons too.'

'Did she?'

'We can't teach her ourselves!' said Sarah.

'It seems everything's sorted out. You better get yourself a horse, Emily.'

Jimmy smiled at his daughter and she planted kisses all over his cheeks, like a dancing butterfly.

When Robert arrived home from the library, he too was exuberant and eager to talk. He found his mother and father in the conservatory.

'I didn't expect to find much reading material, but when I perused the section on Norfolk, amazingly I found this. I spotted it straightaway.'

He showed Sarah and Jimmy a book published in 1903 entitled *Hemsley Windmill*. Its photo filled most of the front cover and the name was printed in large black capital letters at the top and on its bright red spine.

'There's lots of detailed information about the windmill's design, its engineering and its past relevance in the community. The windmill was built in 1851. You won't believe it, but up until 1865, every resident in the community received a bag of flour on the day of the fete.'

Robert talked so fast. It was impossible for him to contain his enthusiasm. He was unable to keep his hands still.

'I can see you're excited, please calm down, Son,' said Sarah.

Jimmy listened attentively, while hardly moving a muscle.

'Fact finds are always interesting,' he said.

'Why is it so important?' asked Sarah.

'Don't you see, 1965 is two years away. We can renovate the windmill and give everyone a bag of flour at our fete for the first time in a hundred years. It would be amazing. Can you imagine our own windmill in motion?'

Robert's face was illuminated, but as much as he tried, he was unable to stir any positive emotion in his dad.

'I'm not convinced, Robert, this is a massive project and would take up most of our time. I don't think we'd be able to handle it. There's also the expense.'

Robert was visibly disappointed and slumped sadly back in his chair. He did not cry, but his withered face told his father his whole world had collapsed around him.

Sarah stayed silent throughout the discussion, but she did not want Robert disappointed.

'Isn't there any way the windmill can be restored? With Robert here, you've an extra pair of hands.'

'I have my horse, why can't Robert have his windmill?' Emily asked.

'I've nothing else to say,' said Sarah.

There was disappointment in her face. Her creased mouth and watery eyes were evident and Jimmy hated seeing Sarah upset. After further consideration, he changed his mind.

'Perhaps I'm being too hasty, Robert, your mother obviously thinks so. I'll read the book and we'll see where we go from there.'

The following day Maggie telephoned Gemma. The two ladies first met at a council meeting soon after Maggie moved to the Grange. They used to be good friends but had not spoken since Parsnip's death. Maggie believed Gemma blamed her for the accident and did not suggest riding with her again. It seemed an appropriate time to end their relationship.

Gemma was a rich woman who owned a large stud farm. She was highly respected in Norfolk for her horse-breeding and attracted buyers from all over the country. Maggie missed her friend and when her call was answered, she held her breath. Gemma also missed Maggie and they chatted freely, but Parsnip was not mentioned.

'You send the little lady down to me and I'll see what I can do. We must go riding again, Maggie; it's been a long time since I've seen you.'

Maggie thought, 'It's a strange thing to happen, but the Jackson family has brought me and Gemma back together.'

Sitting up in bed that evening, Jimmy finished the book. Like Robert, he was surprised by its contents.

'I can see now why he's so interested in the windmill. I've changed my mind, Sarah, I think our son has a great idea. To think the old beast on our estate was once used to make flour for bread and feed for horses and cattle. This is a wonderful opportunity.'

'Oh Jimmy, I prayed you'd want to do it. This year's fete is in four weeks' time. We can tell the local people about Robert's plan. I think they'll go mad for it.'

'Oh yes, I meant to talk to you about the fete. I really don't like it taking place in our front garden. The area to the left of our drive has been cordoned off for a few days now. People have been meticulously measuring areas of ground and securing them with poles and ropes. I get the impression our property is going to be completely taken over.'

'I think you're exaggerating, Maggie told me the fete has always been held on the Grange estate without incident.'

'I'm not convinced. If it's wet, people will be in the house and we'll be left with mud everywhere. What about toilet facilities?'

'There will be mobile units supplied by a company called 'At Your Convenience'.'

'Seriously, Sarah, or are you winding me up?'

'It's true, although I'm told a lot of the men go in the bushes, behind the entertainment area.'

'Lovely!'

'I'm delighted I don't have any fete duties, Jimmy. All I have to do is help Jess serve teas and cakes.'

'I suppose it's the old bat, Geraldine Scott, who's in charge?'

'Actually, it's not. The fete has been run for the last twenty-four years by Bummsy.'

'Bummsy! I know that name, he was mentioned in the golf club only last week.'

'He's the village eccentric. His real name is Danny Bumm. He's only about five feet two and has a very large bottom. That's why he's called Bummsy.'

'Poor fella, I bet he's taken some stick over the years!'

'He does do weird things, Jimmy. Last week, he was in the high street wearing a Nelson hat, cleaning his bicycle with a bright green feather duster.'

'Oh yes, I remember the conversation now. Apparently, every time someone looked at him, he burst into laughter. So this is the man in charge of the fete, God help us!'

While Sarah and Emily had gone to see Gemma, Robert was helping Joseph remove his tools and other belongings from the stable. Maggie knew Jimmy was alone and decided to go and see him. With mischief on her mind, she approached the Grange wearing a low-cut blue lace blouse and a wavy bottomed white skirt. Maggie usually tied her hair back in a ponytail, but left it flowing in the wind. She still possessed a door key and unnerved Giles on her entrance.

'Where's Jimmy?'

'He's upstairs, My Lady, if you'd like to go into the sitting room, I'll tell him you're here.'

'Mmm! I think I'll surprise him!' Maggie said, smiling mischievously.

Giles was appalled; his face was ashen with worry.

While climbing the staircase, she heard him moving about in the master bedroom. The floorboards squeaked, a sound she was familiar with. She stopped briefly to undo the top two buttons on her blouse and hoisted up her skirt to reveal more of her legs. She looked at herself in a wall mirror and lifted her bra.

Maggie smiled as she crept along the landing, holding her sandals. She longed for a moment like this. Jimmy was unaware of her presence, until she pushed the door open. He was startled to see her.

'What are you doing? You shouldn't be up here, Maggie.'

She entered the room and stood up straight with her hands on her hips. Then she lifted her golden hair above her head and let every strand slip between her fingers. Jimmy did not take his eyes off her.

'Go away, Maggie,' he pleaded.

'I've seen you staring at me, Jimmy. Every time we're in the same room, I can feel your eyes exploring my body.'

'Stop it, Maggie!'

'Do you know how many times I've slept there, Jimmy?' The bed was beside them.

'I said stop it! You have to go. Giles is downstairs.'

Maggie was not listening.

'My soft, smooth, naked body lying between those silky sheets, all aroused thinking of you.'

Jimmy watched, as she sat on the bed and slowly ran her legs over the lustrous sheets.

'Stop it, Maggie. You know I'm married, and I know you tend to the needs of other men in the village.'

'It's only sex with the others, it's you I desire. I have done since the first day I met you.'

She was cupping and squeezing her breasts as she ran her tongue along her lips.

'Please get out, before you're seen.'

'Tell me you haven't thought about it, Jimmy. Tell me you don't want me.'

Maggie lay back; her skirt riding, showing her black lace panties.

She knew she was arousing him, from the increasing bulge in his trousers.

'Don't you want to make love to me?'

She pushed her breasts forward, tightening her blouse.

'Don't do this Maggie, you know I can't, even if I want to.'

Jimmy walked out of the room.

'You won't reject me forever!' she shouted.

Maggie followed Jimmy downstairs and out of the Grange. 'I know he wants me. Sarah will never satisfy him like I can,' she thought.

Away from the Grange, Gemma took an instant liking to Emily on her visit to the stud with Sarah. Gemma was a slim lady in her early thirties and had ridden horses since she was seven. She only trained committed riders and was keen to make sure Emily would be able to look after a horse. She repeated what Maggie said to her.

'Unfortunately, I don't have a filly suitable for you, but my friend Jenny owns Kelling Hills Stables. It's only down the road, next to the large thatched cottage.'

'Oh yes, I know where it is, but will she be able to help us?' asked Sarah.

'She's actually a trainer and instructor, but she has a horse for sale called Lottie. It's about two years old. I haven't seen it, but she told me it came from good stock and has a placid temperament. Shame it isn't mine.'

As Emily and Sarah were on their way to Kelling Hills, Emily said, 'Gemma has very large buck teeth!'

'Yes, it's a shame. She's a little horsey.'

Emily giggled.

'She smells too, Mum.'

'I think living on a farm it's the kind of pong you get used to. It was very rude of you to hold your nose in front of her.'

Jenny was cleaning out Lottie's stable when Sarah and Emily arrived.

Sarah witnessed Emily falling in love with Lottie at first sight. Her face was illuminated, as she stood next to the beautiful animal and talked to her like an old friend. The horse was black with long pointed ears and a thick mane.

Jenny put a riding hat on Emily and helped her into the saddle.

'Hold on to the reins!' she said.

'Hold tightly!' said Sarah.

Emily was nervous. 'I think I'm going to fall off.'

'Put your feet in there, Emily,' said Jenny. She pointed to the stirrups and steadied Lottie with a strong arm.

Jenny's face was large and round. Her bony hands were as rough as a doormat and she wore rings on each finger. Sarah watched Emily, as Jenny walked Lottie around the yard outside her stable. Emily gained in confidence with every slow gait and after she was helped to dismount, Jenny gave her a carrot to give to Lottie. The horse and Emily were very comfortable with each other.

'They seem well suited, Jenny,' said Sarah.

On Jenny's recommendation, Sarah bought the horse. This was subject to the satisfactory completion of the Royal College of Veterinary Surgeons and the British Veterinary Associations vetting process.

'It seems such a fuss when I am buying the horse from you,' said Sarah.

'It has to be done for you to get a certificate for the insurance company. It will take about two and a half hours, but at least the process can be completed at Kelling Stables and you will have peace of mind knowing Lottie's in perfect health.'

Emily could not wait to tell her dad about Lottie. When she got home he was trying to repair an old tractor in the yard.

'She's so beautiful, Dad, I will love her forever,' she said with her face beaming.

'Lottie will need a paddock so she can stay outside on her own,' said Sarah.

Jimmy raised his head away from the engine and he was angry.

'I thought it was agreed I'd have nothing to with it,' he said loudly.

'I know Jimmy, but Lottie has got to be looked after. The stable will have to be prepared at least. All the exposed areas need to be covered in metal to prevent the horse from chewing.'

'Please Dad, you will love Lottie so much when you see her.'

Emily looked at him with her sorrowful eyes. She was desperate for his help but his face was glum.

'I'll do everything else Jimmy, I promise,' said Sarah.

Jimmy knew Emily was about to burst into tears and Sarah's eyes were demanding his approval.

'I'll prepare the stable for Lottie's arrival, but the paddock will have to wait until next month. Is that understood?'

Emily jumped up and down with joy whilst Sarah was relieved. She would have kissed him but his overalls were covered in oil and dirt.

'You wouldn't believe how much horses drink. They urinate a lot and together with manure they produce about forty pounds of waste a day. I've got to purchase large supplies of sawdust, shavings and wood pellets to help with the soak away,' said Sarah.

'What are you going to do with the manure?'

'I don't know, perhaps we can sell it, but if not, we have plenty of room to keep it. There's enough other muck around here.'

On the day of Lottie's arrival, Sarah reminded Emily to cover the stable floor with hay, as horses naturally graze with their heads down. Sarah placed grain in a manger.

'What's the time, Mum?'

'Five minutes later than when you asked me last time.'

'Gemma said after picking up Lottie from Kelling Hills, she expected to arrive at the Grange around ten o'clock, Mum.'

'It's only twenty past nine, Emily.'

'Do you think there's enough hay, Mum?'

'Lottie won't be able to get into the stable if you put any more in, Emily,'

Gemma was early. 'Thank goodness,' Sarah thought when she saw the horsebox coming up the drive.

'Emily! Lottie's here!' she called out.

Mother and daughter stood outside the Grange and as Gemma approached, Sarah encouraged her to drive around the left side of the house.

Prior to Lottie's arrival, Emily visited her each day and she sensed Emily's presence. Lottie whinnied and stomped.

'Keep quiet, Emily. I'm sure Lottie needs to stay calm,' whispered Sarah.

The horsebox doors were opened and seeing the animal on the Grange estate, Sarah understood the scale of the responsibility being undertaken. Lottie was young and zestful, and Sarah realised the warning given by Maggie was not exaggerated. 'The horse is going to take up a lot of time,' she thought.

Soon after, Maggie arrived to see Gemma. The two ladies hugged and there were smiles of relief as they put the death of Parsnip behind them.

'Would you like to see Lottie?' asked Emily.

'It would be good to have a look at her.'

Sarah opened the stable door and she ventured inside. Maggie ran her hand over Lottie's face. It was the first time she had touched a horse since the terrible accident on the beach.

'You're beautiful, aren't you?'

It was rare for Sarah to pay Maggie a compliment, but through her introduction to Gemma, she made Emily very happy.

'I'm pleased we consulted with you,' she said.

'If you like, I can exercise Lottie during the day, until Emily is trained and while she's at school.'

Sarah did not expect such an offer from Maggie and she was still wary of her. 'Nevertheless, this arrangement would take a great weight off my shoulders,' she thought.

'Thank you, that's brilliant.'

Maggie was privately elated. Her assistance was now required less and less by Sarah, but by helping Emily, she was able to keep visiting the Grange and continue her pursuit of Jimmy.

Chapter Eighteen

The day before the fete, a large number of people amassed at the Grange. They arrived in various modes of transport including a tractor and a horse and cart. Some of them brought tents to sell their local produce in. Others came with tables and stalls to be set up for games and other frivolities, to include tombola, splat the rat and a guess the weight of the cake competition.

The largest lorry to arrive carried all the necessary parts to build a temporary stage for music and dancing. While they were unloading, a van arrived containing sound and lighting equipment.

Bummsy arranged to meet Sarah at the fete entrance at ten o'clock. He arrived on his bicycle, wearing a bright pink knitted jumper which came down to his knees, over his red trousers. He liked being in charge and took delight in being pernickety.

As a newcomer, Sarah wanted Bummsy to escort her around the arena and she soon witnessed the stallholder's irritation.

'Err, your tent's an inch outside the fete parameter. We can't have that, Mr Dixon?' he called out.

'No, we can't have that, the whole world will end.'

Sarah was surprised by Bummsy's unfriendly approach to the volunteers, but when they reached the coconut shy she was shocked.

Bummsy studied the fruit and compared it to the size of the wooden balls which would be thrown. Mr Wills watched him, as he held a coconut in one hand and a ball in the other. Sarah thought Bummsy was checking the weight and smiled when the nut fell out of his hand and dropped onto his foot. Bummsy was wearing sandals and winced when it bounced off his big toe.

'That must be painful!' she said.

There was no reply. Trying to hide his discomfort, Bummsy calmly picked up the coconut and handed it back to Mr Wills.

'Err, the coconuts are too big; we don't want to make it too easy, do we? It's all for charity.'

'They were the only size I could get.'

'Err, you'll have to make the balls smaller then.'

Mr Wills was very angry, as Bummsy always found something to moan about.

'I'd like to make your balls smaller,' he uttered under his breath.

Along with the stallholders, Sarah found Bummsy to be pedantic and his habit of saying, 'Err' before every sentence was annoying.

The following morning, while in the Grange, Sarah heard noises coming from the crowd of people waiting to enter the arena. She walked down her drive to the entrance gate and saw Bummsy climbing up a ladder to his wooden panelled hut. It was from there he was to direct proceedings, starting at eleven o'clock.

His girlfriend, Lucy, was standing down below. She was a large woman, always heavily made up and was wearing a flimsy white blouse tucked into a very short tight green mini skirt. A red ribbon was tied in her curly auburn hair.

Sarah heard people discussing Lucy, as she waited for her instruction to open the gate.

'What does she look like?' said Miss Norris.

'She looks better than last year. Do you remember the feathered dress she fell out of?' said Julie Tucker.

'Oh yes I do, people kept plucking her.'

Sarah felt sorry for Lucy, but she too thought her dress sense was appalling.

It was now 10.56. The crowd was getting bigger and people were becoming impatient and were shouting at Bummsy. He antagonised them by holding out his arm and pointing to his watch. At 10.59, he waved his flag and Lucy walked across a patch of grass to open the gate.

'Come on girl, hurry up!' called out a woman wearing a pink plastic hat.

Lucy moved across the grass and slipped on the wet surface. Her legs went forward and she fell backwards onto her bottom, soaking her skirt and underwear. She also sustained a nasty cut on her face and an injury to her ankle from a rusty piece of metal protruding from the ground. When she got to her feet, there was mud in places she had not seen for years.

In agony, Lucy limped towards the entrance. It was now 11.03, as she unlocked the catch and released the gate. The crowd surged forward and Sarah quickly made her way back to the Grange forecourt, where Jess set up the cake stall.

Bummsy welcomed everyone to the fete through his loudhailer and everyone was shocked to hear him remind Miss Coot of her misdemeanour the previous year.

'Err, I hope no one is going to get food poisoning this time. I think we all know it was the chicken last year!' he remarked.

'That's terrible, Jess,' said Sarah.

'You wouldn't say that if you'd eaten one of her sandwiches! My stomach ached for days,' remarked Joan Withers, who worked in the flower shop and wore carnations in her hair.

'Well if that's all you've got to complain about, you were lucky, I had the shits for nearly a fortnight. My backside was like a red-hot poker. I'll never eat that woman's food again!' said Mr Clayton.

He was a farmer with enormous eyebrows and a loud voice. His legs were like tree trunks and his hands were greasy from working with tractors and other machinery.

Listening to these comments, Sarah was worried about the food displayed in the heat of the sun. She was also concerned about Jess, who appeared to be a little tipsy. She was slurring her words and needed to constantly steady herself against the cake table.

'Have you been drinking?' asked Sarah.

'Maggie brought me a couple of bottles of wine down this morning.'

When Maggie was living in the Grange there was an uneasy relationship between her and Jess, but with Eddie out so often, they had enjoyed the occasional drink together.

Maggie had made mischief, but Sarah thought Jess was hilarious; cracking jokes and imitating Bummsy. She heard her say, 'Err, I think the darts are too pointed, they need blunting Mr Childs' and 'Err, Miss Coot, your chicken's foul.'

Geraldine Scott came up to the stall. She sampled some lemon curd tarts, before asking for two finger biscuits to enjoy with a cup of tea.

Jess put her glass down on an uneven surface, causing the wine to spill over a salmon sandwich.

'You're not sober, Jess, I think you should lie down,' said Geraldine, in her usual commanding way.

'You can't tell me what to do: I'm not one of your WI flock. If I was, I'd have flown far away from you.'

Sarah laughed and Jess burped as Geraldine walked away.

'I bet that's not the first time you've received two fingers!' Jess called out.

Jess went too far and Geraldine momentarily stopped in her tracks. The villagers standing close by drew breath; they did not believe what they heard. Sarah thought, 'How am I going to face her at the next Women's Institute meeting?'

Laughing out loud, Jess found it difficult to stand. Some villagers got a cake in a cup while others got tea on a plate. Sarah sent her home and Emily helped out for the rest of the day.

While serving, Sarah spoke to villagers about the windmill and the giving of flour. Generally, people liked the idea, but Bummsy was not so sure.

'Err, I want people spending their money and not wasting time in a windmill.'

'There's nothing to stop you asking for donations for the flour. I'm sure you can persuade them to part with their money,' Sarah replied.

Bummsy only took a moment to consider this opportunity.

'Err, we'll make them two shillings per bag.'

Chapter Nineteen

Sarah was now more comfortable in the community and warming to her position as lady of the Grange. She was respected for listening to the villagers' views and, using her gentle powers of persuasion, she got things done.

Sarah and Jimmy's time was precious, but they dined together whenever they could. One evening Jimmy was quieter than usual. He did not respond to Sarah's chatter and his smile had deserted him. She was worried.

'What's the matter, you're not your usual jovial self?' she asked.

'It's this damn leg. It won't do what I want it to.'

'I know it's a struggle, Jimmy, I wish I could help.'

'It's restrictive, not prohibitive, so I can get most things done, but we are so busy with the windmill and sometimes I have to ask Robert for help.'

'What are you doing at the moment, Jimmy?'

'We're concentrating on the surrounding area of the tower. It's been a dumping ground and now, after years of decay, it's dangerous.'

'You be careful Jimmy.'

'Every day there are new challenges, but at least we've managed to finish the paddock.'

'Yes, now Emily wants to spend even more time with her beloved horse. I often worry about her neglecting her studies.'

With time on her hands, Maggie was constantly thinking about Jimmy. She was willing him and Sarah to drift apart, as their respective activities took them in different directions. 'It's like me and Eddie, having less and less time for one another,' she thought.

On one of Maggie's visits to the Grange to exercise Lottie, she noticed Jimmy sitting in the conservatory. Sarah was at a church meeting, Robert was in the windmill and Giles was on an errand in Sheringham.

Maggie was dressed for riding, in old slacks and a woollen jumper. 'Damn, what an opportunity and I'm not even wearing makeup,' she thought.

Jimmy was studying the windmill renovation drawings when Maggie opened the door from the garden and came inside.

'Hello handsome!' she said, standing with her hands on her hips.

'I don't think you should be in here, please go, you're supposed to be tending to the horse.'

Taking no notice, Maggie sidled up to him and caressed his face with her hand. Jimmy walked away, but she followed him and blocked his exit.

'No you don't, not this time; I know you want me.'

Jimmy was open-mouthed. The desire in her eyes was absorbing, but he tried to push past her. Maggie grabbed hold of him and put her arms around his shoulders. Jimmy was speechless, as she ran her fingers down his back and he did not resist her. She kissed his neck and moved closer. Maggie felt his breath racing on her skin and her heart was pounding. Their lips met, their tongues mingled and they were locked in a tight embrace.

Jimmy's resistance had gone. He removed Maggie's arms so her upper body was free. Then, holding her tightly, they kissed again. Maggie forced herself upon him, but now Jimmy was in control. She used all her strength to stay upright, as he explored her mouth, and when their lips parted they were panting.

Maggie smiled; she believed she had caged her tiger.

'It's me you love, tell me you want me.'

To her dismay Jimmy's response was not instant. 'What if I've misjudged him? Is he still going to reject me?' she thought.

Maggie's aims were two-fold. She wanted Jimmy, but more than anything, she dreamed of returning to the Grange. She was relentless in her search for an answer, while their faces were only three inches apart and their eyes were longing and expectant.

'Please Jimmy! Tell me you want me. I can't go on like this.'

Maggie was desperate.

'Okay, I'll leave Sarah,' said Jimmy.

They kissed again, but Maggie was not convinced. There was no excitement in Jimmy's voice and the warmth in his arms receded. His face was drawn and solemn, as if he already regretted his words.

'Are you sure, Jimmy?'

'I've said so, haven't I?'

'When will you leave Sarah?'

'I can't tell her now; the time has got to be right.'

'The time will never be right, do it today, Jimmy.'

Maggie ran her hands down his arms. Eagerly she awaited his further response.

'I'll do it when the windmill is restored.'

'That's two years away, I can't wait that long.'

Maggie lowered her hands and unbuckled the belt on his trousers.

'What are you doing? Someone might come in here.' Jimmy pushed her away.

'I need you!' she replied.

Her sunken face was saddened and frustrated.

'It'll be easier then, the children will be older and Sarah will be more settled in Cleybourne,' said Jimmy.

'I wish Sarah was dead,' thought Maggie. 'Okay, my darling, but I want you now,' she said aloud.

At that moment the front door banged and it startled them both.

'Is that Sarah?' asked Maggie.

'I don't think so, it's probably Jess, she's been arriving early for work lately. You'd better go, Maggie, I don't want her finding us together.'

Maggie thought she got everything she wanted. The man she desired was in waiting and it was her ticket back into the Grange. She did not give a fig about Sarah and smiled as she sneaked away down the path to her cottage. She forgot all about exercising Lottie; only Jimmy was on her mind.

Over the coming months, they stirred each other's bodies with their every touch and kiss. They made love in the stable, the wine cellar, the timber yard and anywhere else the mood took them.

'You'll leave Sarah, won't you, Jimmy?' Maggie asked him over and over again.

'Yes, my love, when the windmill is built. I can't wait to be with you,' he always replied.

One evening, when Jimmy came into the Grange from working on the estate, he sat down with his head in his hands.

'Whatever is the matter?' asked Sarah.

'The windmill was inspected today and its condition is much worse than we envisaged.'

'You knew it was in a bad state, Jimmy.'

'Yes, but some of the parts we thought would be okay need to be replaced, so the renovation will take longer.'

'Is there enough time before the fete?' asked Sarah.

'We'll have to put in more hours; that's for sure.'

'You do enough already, Jimmy.'

'I know, but we have no choice. It was obvious new sails were required and the cap needed replacing. What we didn't know was with the top gaping to the sky, the elements of the weather caused the inside to decay so badly.'

'Oh no! That's terrible.'

'There's so much to do, Sarah. The wooden floors have rotted, much of the ancillary equipment has rusted and it's dangerous to venture up the stairs. The whole mechanism is in need of replacement and making things worse, all the parts have got to be made to order.'

'How long will it take, Jimmy?'

'I don't know, but it includes the wooden windshaft. It's a massive thing that connects the sails to the brake wheel.'

'What are you going to do now?'

'Tomorrow we'll cover the top with some raised tarpaulin to stop the rain causing further damage. Then we can get on with carpentry and metal work inside. There're also other jobs that need doing around the estate.'

*

August 1964

The sheep farmer's lease on the Jackson's land was due for renewal. As expected, Sarah received a letter confirming the option for a further period was not to be taken up. The tenant, John Jenkins, aged seventy-five, was now retired and living in Cromer.

'The occupancy ends on the thirtieth of September, Jimmy.'

'I suppose we should have guessed Jenkins wouldn't renew his agreement. His body is riddled with arthritis and there haven't been any sheep on the estate for months.'

'Do you want me to seek a further tenant, Jimmy?'

'Not now, but perhaps eventually we can find an arable farmer. The land must be fertile; it's laced with manure.'

'Walking down the lane, there were some strange smells wafting around. I don't think they can be healthy,' said Sarah.

'They're coming from containers on the leasehold land which look like they've been leaking chemicals for years. We'll have to get rid of them. We also need to repair fences, dispose of the sheep pens and old rusting machinery.'

Emily's relationship with Lottie was blossoming. She was now able to ride her comfortably, even though she only trotted. Sarah was delighted with her development but did not think she was proficient enough to ride Lottie without Jenny's presence.

Emily dismissed her mother's concern and when the family was together at a mealtime she showed her frustration.

'It's not fair, I'm not a child. I want to ride my horse alone.'

Emily threw her napkin across the table.

'Actually, you are still a child and you're certainly acting like one. You can ride alone when Jenny says you can and not before.'

'It's hard, Mum. Now the railway line is closed I have to go to school by bus. I get home later and spend less time with Lottie when I want to spend more!' she cried.

'It won't always be like this,' said Sarah.

Emily challenged authority more often as she got older, hating it when she did not get her own way.

'Maggie says I'm all right to ride Lottie now!' she shouted. Emily leant forward and planted her elbows on the table.

'Does she? Well Maggie can mind her own business! If she keeps interfering I'll stop her riding as well.'

'Lottie has to be exercised, Mum. If Maggie doesn't do it, who will?'

'She's not doing us any favours. She rides for her own pleasure. I'm sure someone in the village would like to take her place. I can't wait to get rid of her.'

Emily huffed and puffed, but Sarah took no notice.

'Jenny thinks you'll be okay in the spring. Then you can have Lottie out in the paddock on school nights and ride her on the estate during the weekends.'

Having spoken with authority, Sarah carried on eating. Emily did not finish her dinner. She stormed out of the room and went upstairs.

'You handled that very well, my love. I thought you might cave in after Emily's little tantrum,' said Jimmy.

'I might have done in the past, but my social duties and having to stand up to Maggie have toughened me up. I'm used to saying no when needs be.'

Sarah was now enjoying life in Cleybourne so much, she was getting even more involved in local affairs. She liked all the attention paid to her, and often came up with ideas to raise money for charity.

To Sarah's dismay, Bummsy was accepted onto the village hall committee. Whilst never doubting his enthusiasm, she witnessed his strange mannerisms and felt his presence was a hindrance. Sarah kept rejecting his money-making ideas with the support of the other members.

Sarah was spending more time away from the Grange and when the property was empty, Jimmy and Maggie exploited the situation. They made use of the library, the walk-in larder and the kitchen, before Jess arrived for work. However, as the weeks went by, Maggie sensed Jimmy was getting tired of their relationship, from his lack of smiles and his loveless arms.

'You do love me, don't you Jimmy? We're going to be together, aren't we?' she asked, while they lay naked in the hayloft.

'Yes, my darling, you know how much I need you,' murmured Jimmy.

Chapter Twenty

December 1964

The new windmill machinery and cap arrived. They were very cumbersome items and were transported separately in two lorries. Sarah watched as the heavy pieces of precision equipment were moved from the vehicles by crane to their final locations. The old windmill parts had already been removed and taken away.

Sarah was worried when the cap was lifted out of the vehicle. The chain cradle was dirty and rusty. It creaked and jangled, as it was raised high in the air before being swung over the windmill. Seeing the cap dangling, she screamed when there was a sudden jolt.

'Oh my God! I thought the machinery was going to collapse on top of you!' she called out to Jimmy and Robert.

They were standing underneath the crane and laughed off her concern.

'It would hold up an elephant!' said Jimmy.

The cap was eased down at a snail's pace onto its housing. It was designed and built so it would turn automatically, so that the sails would benefit from any wind direction. The movement was achieved by using a winch from the fifth floor.

'Everything is now falling into place, Sarah. Now we can get on with replacing the old timbers and making the floors safe,' said Jimmy.

'Are we back on schedule?'

'Yes, I think we are; the new sails will be delivered in the spring.'

The family was so busy with the windmill and social activities that Sarah and Jimmy were rarely at home. Emily spent more time with Maggie who, after exercising Lottie, was often around when Emily came home from school.

They sat and chatted about Emily's school work, her friends and personal things she should be discussing with her mother. Maggie was fed up playing nursemaid, as she had no interest in the Jackson family, apart from Jimmy.

One afternoon, Emily came home looking sad.

'What's the matter?' Maggie enquired.

'I've been told off for day dreaming.'

'Why's that, Emily?'

'I'm fed up. Life seems so complicated now.'

'What do you mean complicated?'

'Everything has changed. It wasn't long ago my mum and dad struggled for everything, but I didn't realise then how poor we were. Now things are different, but I don't think as a family we're as happy as we used to be. There're so many people involved in our lives, we don't have time for each other.'

'I'm sure your parents love you very much.'

'I'm not sure, some days I don't even see them. Mum and me used to be close, but we don't share much time together now.'

'You must talk to her; perhaps she'll put you in her diary.'

Maggie was purposely being flippant, but she didn't care.

'I don't feel I'm contributing or part of anything,' said Emily.

'You will, once you leave school and get a job.'

Emily found a smile amongst her gloom.

'I want to be a horse jumper.'

'Do you? What have your parents said about it?'

'I haven't told them yet. I'm going to do it this evening after dinner, but I'm worried about it. I don't think my mum and dad ever wanted me to have a horse.'

'I'm sure they only want what's best for you.'

Emily waited until everyone finished their meal. Sarah and Jimmy were in a good mood. They were joking about Geraldine, so it seemed to be a good time for her to mention horse jumping. However, when she broached the idea, the response was negative.

'You know nothing about it, Emily,' said Jimmy.

'That's why I want to learn. Maggie thinks it's a good idea.'

'I'll swing for that woman! Maggie this and Maggie that; I don't know why she won't mind her own business!' said Sarah.

'You have your GCEs to take in two months,' said Jimmy.

'Oh! You've remembered, have you? I can't recall the last time you asked me about my studies. Do either of you actually remember what subjects I'm taking? I never see you these days!' Emily shouted.

Sarah and Jimmy were accused of neglecting their daughter and she was not finished.

'Mum, you spend all of your time on village things and Dad, you're always in the blooming windmill, unless you're with Maggie.'

'Why are you spending time with Maggie? She doesn't have much reason to be around here now,' said Sarah.

Jimmy glared at Emily.

'She still rides Lottie each school day and has always walked around the Grange with her dog. If I happen to see her, we stop and have a chat, that's all,' he replied.

'We won't need her to ride anymore when Emily finishes school, so I suppose you won't see her much after that.'

'I've never really liked the woman, Sarah. You know that, but there's no harm in being sociable.'

Jimmy was feeling guilty and snapped at Emily, 'Have you quite finished, my girl, or is there anything else you want to get off your chest?'

'Yes, Emily, let's have it all out now,' said Sarah.

'Well, don't you think it's about time you or Dad asked me if my studying is going okay, or if I'm bothered about anything? That's what normal parents do isn't it?'

Robert was quiet, watching the argument unfold. Although he never said it, he loved his sister and did not like her upset, so he spoke up in her defence,

'She's right, we've all neglected her and as soon as she asks for something, it's refused. She's as much a part of this family as anyone else.'

Robert got up from his chair, walked over to where Emily was sitting and put his arms on her shoulders.

'I'm sorry, Ems, and I'm sure Mum and Dad are too. Please calm down and we'll try and put this right.'

Sarah was a little tearful. 'I don't know what to say, Emily, I'm truly sorry.'

'It's okay, Mum, all I ask is you don't forget I'm here. Spending most of my time studying or with Lottie I'm busy too, but we need to be busy more with each other.'

'I'm lost for words too, Emily. The windmill has become an obsession. It sounds like a terrible afterthought, but what do you want to do when you leave school?' asked Jimmy.

'I told you. I want to be a horse jumper.'

'Oh no! You're getting a proper job, my girl.'

The conversation got heated again, then Sarah came up with an idea.

'Emily, you want to be a horse jumper and we want you to go to work.'

'Yes.'

'Jimmy, we've plenty of room here to run a business. Suppose she learns to be both a horse rider and a trainer. She'd earn a living and learn to jump.'

Emily stopped sulking; she was smiling and encouraging her dad to agree.

'Please let me do this, it would be perfect.'

'I don't think you've behaved very well, Emily. You've been rude and aggressive. Nevertheless, I do agree we've not supported you very well. Yes, your mum's right, it'll give you a purpose in life.'

Emily hugged her dad as her mother sat watching quietly.

'Excuse me, I'm over here, I think this was my idea,' commented Sarah.

Emily laughed and then walked over to her mum and planted a kiss on her cheek. 'Thank you, Mum.'

'Remember, you still have your exams to worry about.'

'I know, but it'll be perfect, I'm going to tell Maggie tomorrow.'

'You see far too much of that woman,' said Sarah.

'I don't know why you despise her so much; she's been good to me. Anyway, it's only because of the horse.'

Meanwhile Maggie was counting down the days until she and Jimmy would be together. 'I'll be back in the Grange and Sarah will be gone,' she thought.

Over the previous few months Maggie's dog, Bailey, gradually became quite unstable and was having episodes of incontinence. She appeared to be in severe pain in her hips and Maggie made the very difficult decision to end her suffering.

She was behind her cottage, playing with Bailey when Emily arrived. Emily often came in through the side gate into the remaining part of the garden. There had been a rock fall many years ago, leaving about twelve feet of ground at the back. A metal fence was the only barrier between land and sea.

Emily noticed tears in Maggie's eyes, but she was invited in.

They sat down together on a blanket under the old apple tree and Maggie explained the situation. It was heartbreaking for her, but she reminisced about the wonderful times she enjoyed with Bailey.

'She's my best friend, my only friend really,' she said.

Maggie opened a packet of bone chews and Bailey looked at them greedily. Today was no time to worry about how much she ate; it was about giving Bailey a lovely day that Maggie would remember. Bailey ate them all very quickly, as well as a few slices of ham. Then Emily took Bailey's ball and threw it for her last playtime.

'Look at her face, Emily; she's like a grey-haired puppy. I'll never forget this; she's so loving and having so much fun; she's no idea what's going to happen. I'll miss her so much.'

Emily was surprised by Maggie's emotion when the vet arrived. 'Animals are her weakness,' she thought.

'The vet is a kind man who's tended to Bailey all her life; he knows her well, Emily,' said Maggie.

They watched as he spoke to her gently while shaving a small patch on the dog's leg. Then he inserted a needle deep into her vein and as he pushed the syringe, Bailey slowly relaxed. Maggie was surprised to see her fight to stay sitting up, but then her breathing slowed and laboured. Bailey groaned, was gently laid down and became very still. All life ebbed from her and she was now at peace.

The air was still and tears were streaming down the faces of Maggie and Emily. Maggie was surprised how quickly it happened.

'I'm sorry, I'm so sorry, my darling.' She knelt down, embracing Bailey's heavy lifeless head in her lap. 'I feel so guilty.'

However, Emily knew Bailey's quality of life had deteriorated over recent weeks.

'It was a true act of kindness and nobody will blame you. You've done the right thing,' she said.

After a few minutes, the vet took Bailey away, so Maggie and Emily went into the cottage for coffee.

'Why did you come here today?'

'It doesn't matter, we can talk about it another time.'

'I assume it must be something to do with Lottie?'

Emily was hesitant.

'It's not important, really.'

'Come on, whatever it is it'll help take my mind off what I've done today.'

'My mum and dad have agreed I can learn to be a horse trainer and a horse jumper. I'm finishing school this year and it's going to be perfect.'

Maggie thought, 'That'll put paid to me riding Lottie. Can the day get any worse?' Then she smiled, as she realised she wouldn't have to be Emily's after-school stand-in mother anymore.

'I'm pleased for you, but I'll miss Lottie almost as much as Bailey. If you don't mind, I'd like to be on my own now.'

On her way out, Emily noticed a photo on the mantelpiece.

'Is that my grandad?' she asked.

'Yes, that's Eddie.'

'I've heard both Jess and Giles talking about him, but as soon as they see me, they always change the subject. Mum and Dad never mention him at all.'

'Wait a moment.'

Maggie went into her bedroom and returned with a photo in a brown wooden frame, of him with Emily's grandmother Gladys. They were sitting on two striped deckchairs. The back of the photo showed it was taken in July 1934, next to Southend-on-Sea pier. Gladys was wearing a full length black bathing suit and Eddie was bare chested and wearing rolled up trousers. They were both smiling as if something had made them laugh.

'I wish I knew what was funny. I don't know anything about them. What were they like?'

'I didn't meet Gladys, as she died in 1938, but Eddie was a lively man. The trouble was, we wanted different things and disliked each other's friends. Over time we drifted apart, but I've got over his death now. Here, you can have the photo if you like. Now all I want is my home back; I belong in Hemsley Grange.'

'It's my home!' said Emily.

'For now, but nothing is forever!' Maggie replied menacingly.

Chapter Twenty-One

It was now spring and with Jenny's blessing, Sarah allowed Emily to ride Lottie unaided. She exercised her outside the paddock after school.

Maggie was no longer required and found it harder to be alone with Jimmy.

'You'll have to come to the cottage more often,' she said.

'It's difficult; I don't have time during the day. The windmill has to be ready for the fete.'

Maggie did not care. She continued to overwhelm him with passion at every opportunity. Sometimes it was for no more than ten minutes in the gun shed, the greenhouse or even in the pen where the sheep dip used to be.

One evening, while Sarah was out, they were in bed together in the cottage when the wind blew violently. Rain beat against the windows and the old property creaked more than usual. There was a movement below and hearing the thrashing of the waves gave them an uneasy feeling of instability.

The lights flickered on and off as a strong gust of wind moaned eerily around the house.

Maggie drew breath. She held on to Jimmy tightly with her head buried in his chest.

'Are there any ghosts here?' he asked.

'I don't think so, but it's not happened before, at least not while I've been living here.'

Maggie was shivering.

'It's probably a loose wire connection that was somehow agitated by the extreme weather.'

But this incident awoke her guilty conscience about Eddie, and for once, she lost her appetite in bed, so Jimmy got dressed.

'Maybe someone's telling us not to do this Maggie; it's a wake-up call.'

'Don't be silly, it's just a bad storm,' she replied, regaining her composure.

A few days later, the windmill sails were delivered. The cumbersome pieces of machinery were pulled by a horse on a large cart up the drive. They were made in a millwrights' shop in North Walsham.

The size of the sails amazed Sarah.

'I don't know how we're going to bring the mechanism alive on time, the fete is only four months away,' said Jimmy.

'I thought it'd be plain sailing now,' Sarah joked.

'Apart from the windmill, there's a mountain of other jobs including painting, furnishing and preparing the ground outside. It's like a death trap at the moment, with old machinery parts, the remains of the cap and pieces of decaying wood lying around.'

'I'm sure you can do it, Jimmy.'

'I can tell you, Sarah, there've been times when I questioned my decision to restore the windmill. The financial cost has been enormous and the rest of the estate has been neglected.'

When the sails were finally assembled, Sarah knew it was the proudest day in Jimmy and Robert's life.

'They look beautiful!' she said.

'Yes! I think they do. The sails impose themselves on the landscape,' Jimmy replied.

'The windmill is stunning, Mum. With the sea in the background and the sun beaming down from a perfect blue sky, it's like Emily's painting,' said Robert.

Whilst the windmill was being readied in time for the fete, Sarah's estate obligations were still rising. As chairman of the council planning committee, she was heavily involved in discussions for a new village hall. The existing facility was too small and not suitable for the growing population.

The site identified for the building was on part of a farmer's field. It was next to the main road at the bottom of the village. The owner, Mr Winslow, was eighty-six and in poor health. He agreed to sell his land for money and residency in a local care home.

Once the new hall was built, the existing building, in the centre of Cleybourne, was to be knocked down. Sarah was present when arguments raged about this small development at a public meeting in the old village hall.

'If they build down there, before we know it there'll be houses everywhere and we'll have more people from London moving in,' said Mr Clayton.

People clapped.

'He's right you know. Remember what happened after the health centre was built. We have flats there now,' said a gentleman in a red bow tie.

'We need the health centre,' said Wendy Snippets, sitting in the third row. She had recently moved to the village.

Mrs Fiddy snapped! 'It's where the old tennis courts used to be and they've not been replaced.'

Other people frowned at the new resident for daring to speak.

The comments and objections were considerable, but Mr Clayton endorsed the feelings of the older generation. They did not like change and there was concern about the cost to the tax payers.

'I don't want this hall pulled down. Me and my Johnny's wedding reception was here in 1921 after we got married in St. John's Church,' said Maud Denning.

'We need a bigger facility,' Sarah said loudly, to be heard over the muttering.

'It may not mean much to you, Mrs Jackson, but I've lived here all my life and my Johnny died last month. You've only been here since yesterday and think you can do what you like,' Mrs Denning replied. She waved her walking stick at her.

'Why can't we keep this hall as well?' asked Mr Clayton.

There were whispers amongst the council members. Unknown to the villagers, once the hall was demolished, new houses were to be built.

'We don't need two halls Mr Clayton,' Sarah replied.

Amongst the gathering there was some support for the new facility, but sympathy for Mrs Denning.

'Can she have the oil painting of St. John's Church. Look! Over there on the wall by the stage?' asked Mrs Fiddy.

There was a quorum of village hall committee members present and they readily agreed. Mrs Denning was overwhelmed with tears and clutched it to her heart.

*

Emily's exams were getting closer. The Jackson household was under pressure, but Sarah was determined her needs would not be forgotten. Emily was nervous and irritable. She made a constant stream of demands. Every word from Sarah's mouth drew criticism, but she provided all the support her daughter required.

When Sarah walked into the village on a Saturday morning, Bummsy was encouraging interest in the fete. He stood on a small pub table outside the post office, covered in flour, with a wooden garden windmill attached to his head.

'I hope it rains,' said Mr Clayton.

There was a large ugly cloud above that looked ready to dispose of its load and he held out his hand for the tiniest drop of wetness. Local residents laughed at Bummsy, the sky darkening further every second.

Sarah thought they were very unkind, but her eyes turned to Lucy standing beside him, wearing a bright orange revealing tunic that resembled a camisole.

She handed out leaflets and people who did not want them were chased across the post office concourse until they succumbed.

'I don't need a leaflet,' said a stranger to the community wearing a green check shirt. He was on holiday and only came to the village to post a letter. He walked away, but Lucy followed him. He increased his pace, but Lucy would not be deterred and cornered him by the telephone box. He took three leaflets and hurried away. Sarah was appalled.

The rain came, accompanied by a cold breeze, and the flour stuck to Bummsy like glue. He was not discouraged and Lucy continued to harass the people who braved the inclement weather until her leaflet supply was saturated and unusable.

Bummsy and Lucy pestered everybody about the fete, but this year, their unwelcome interference was not necessary. People were interested in the windmill and curious about the free flour.

On Sarah's return to the Grange, Jimmy was working outside the windmill.

'You'd never believe what I've seen this morning.'

'Don't tell me Sarah, it must be something to do with that idiot Bummsy.'

'I think he and Lucy would do anything for the fete. They've warmed to the idea of flour making.'

'I daren't tell people it's not the best for baking. The book on our windmill says it's coarse in nature and better used as a horse and cattle feed,' said Jimmy.

'It doesn't matter, from what I've heard, the villagers like the idea of making a traditional loaf,' Sarah replied.

The day of the fete was hot. At nine o'clock the temperature was already sixty-nine degrees Fahrenheit. The humidity was unusually high and there was not any wind to blow the sails.

'There isn't even a breeze, Sarah,' said Jimmy.

'It's very early, give it time.'

Sarah watched as Jimmy and Robert threw twigs above them, hoping for a sign of movement, but the air was as still as a ship in a bottle. However, there are not many windless days in North Norfolk and inside an hour, the leaves on the trees fluttered. Within minutes, a stiff wind was rushing through the trees and the weather conditions were perfect.

'We're okay, Sarah!' Jimmy called out with glee and relief.

Bummsy waved his flag and the fete opened at eleven o'clock. Sarah was down at the entrance and watched Lucy, wearing a skin tight red dress and yellow shoes, open the gate to a cascade of unsavoury remarks.

'Are you going to a fancy dress party later?' Mr Clayton shouted out.

By the time Sarah arrived back at the Grange, most people were inside the arena. Bummsy made his welcoming address, but the volume on his loudhailer was set too high and everyone put their hands over their ears to reduce the sound level.

'Err, don't forget to spend your money, it's all for good causes.'

'Err, boys and girls, flour and water bombs aren't allowed. Anyone found with one will go into the stocks.'

Then he turned his attention to the cake stall.

'Err, Jess, please keep off the booze. You don't want to upset Geraldine Scott again, do you?'

He chuckled and added, 'Err, let someone else do it this year.'

The fete gathering was enormous. There were more stalls than usual and a record number of dancers and singers entered the stage competitions. Almost everyone, however, wanted to see the moving sails and collect their free bag of flour.

At 11.55am Sarah was nervous as Jimmy made his way into the windmill.

He told Sarah he needed to climb the stairs to the third floor from where he would release the brake using the rope from the verandah. This was attached to the lever in the cap and Jimmy explained it needed a good tug.

Sarah worried about Jimmy, because of his disability, and knew progress would be slow. He was only in the windmill for four minutes, but it seemed much longer. 'Come on Jimmy,' she said to herself.

People gathered outside, waiting to see the large sails turn for the first time in years.

'I'll believe it when I see it,' said Mr Clayton, talking aloud to everyone in earshot.

A creaking sound interrupted his conversation, as the sails burst into life, gathering speed on the wind. The villagers clapped and cheered and Sarah thought, 'I hope Jimmy can hear the applause.'

Emily's school teacher, Mrs Piper, came to the fete specially to see the windmill.

'It's wonderful watching the old girl turning again, Mrs Jackson.'

She was still drawing breath and saliva between her teeth.

'It happened because you inspired your art class on that wonderful day in Sheringham Park, Mrs Piper.'

'Oh no, it's your Emily who deserves the credit, Mrs Jackson.'

When Jimmy came out of the windmill, there was more applause and Sarah hugged him. He was breathing heavily as he acknowledged the amassing crowd.

'I feel so proud, Sarah. To think we've done this because of Emily's painting and Robert's dream.'

Sarah was sombre and tempered her excitement.

'Haven't you got to carry the wheat grain up the stairs to the fifth floor? You need to tip it into the millstone below, don't you?'

'Yes, but not until we need to.'

'You told me the sacks are very heavy Jimmy. How are you going to do it?'

'I'll manage with Robert, I can drag the sacks up behind me.'

'I'm not sure, it's so hot today. The humidity must be intense in the windmill, by the look of the sweat running down your face and soaking the back of your shirt.'

'I'll be all right, Sarah.'

'I'm concerned that's all; with all the physical work you've undertaken in recent months you've lost three stone.'

'Please Sarah, don't fuss.'

'Why can't Giles and Joseph carry the heavy sacks?'

'Because I want to do it myself! Giles and Joseph are to scoop the flour into small bags and lay them out on trestle tables. The local community has a population of 297 people and, to be on the safe side, we're preparing three hundred gifts.'

The fete was soon in full swing and the crowd was enjoying the activities. Stalls selling ice cream and drinks sold out early and the cake stand was as popular as ever.

'I'm going to make the flour,' said Jimmy, after lunch.

He put on white overalls and a pair of white gloves.

'Carry the sacks with Robert, not on your own; they're too heavy for you!' Sarah pleaded.

Jimmy gave her a wry smile and walked away towards the windmill with Robert.

At two o'clock, the first sack of grain was tipped. Sarah was on the ground floor and watched Giles and Joseph filling the bags for collection. The process was working well and Jimmy left Robert in the mill to get some fresh air. He sat on the grass outside and rested his head against the tower.

'You're exhausted Jimmy, you can't go back in there.'

'I'm okay, I just want a breather. Stop worrying, Sarah.'

There was nothing she could do and stood by as a constant stream of people offered their congratulations. By restoring the windmill, Jimmy was a local hero.

News of the event spread far and wide. Both local and national newspapers sent reporters and photographers. Working windmills producing flour were few and far between in England.

In an instant, however, the wind driving the contraption became a tiny breeze and the sails ground to a halt. People sighed as they witnessed the machinery stutter and stop.

'Oh no! Where's the wind?' said Jimmy getting to his feet.

'Have you got any special powers?' said Sarah to Reverend Fiddy.

'I wish I did. I'd ask for a slightly cooler day. This heat is stifling.'

Most people shared Jimmy and Sarah's anxiety, but inevitably there is always a minority who want to delight in someone's misfortune.

'That's buggered you up then!' remarked Mr Green.

'Language please, there are children present!' said the Reverend.

Mr Green was a rather loud man who spoke with a lisp. His hands were enormous. His annoying habit of fiddling with his long fingers made them look spider-like. Sarah remembered him from Eddie's funeral and knew he was a friend of Sir Donald Scott.

In a few minutes the wind blew once more, but it changed from a south westerly to a southerly and the sails remained still.

'Why aren't they turning, Jimmy?'

'I don't know, Sarah. The mechanism is built so the blades automatically alter their direction.'

'The windmill doesn't look that scientific to me,' said Mr Green.

'It's probably a bit technical for you, but it's done with the use of the fantail and a system of cogs moving underneath the cap. There's a row of teeth on top of the brickwork for the cogs to drive the cap around on wheels.'

'I'd better see what's happening,' said Robert as he walked back towards the windmill.

'I'm going back to the house.' said Sarah.

Meanwhile, there was a commotion by the cake stall. Maggie had been screaming and throwing her arms about.

'He won't get away with this; the lying bastard,' she shouted. Her voice ringing out across the fete arena.

Chapter Twenty-Two

As Sarah walked around the left side of the Grange, Maggie came in the opposite direction around the right. Maggie's face was red and forlorn as she pushed herself aggressively through the crowd.

In her haste, a little boy on crutches was knocked to the ground and a man drinking a can of beer was elbowed to one side. Maggie was oblivious to her actions and ready for a fight.

'You bastard, you bloody bastard!' she called out to Jimmy.

He was visibly shocked. His eyes seemed to recede into his face as Maggie stormed up to him. She was shaking with anger and slapped his cheek so hard he widened his stance to stay upright.

The crowd did not believe what they were witnessing. Maggie tried to hit him again, but this time Jimmy ducked and held her arms. She struggled, pushing and pulling, until he released them and she sobbed in front of him.

'What's this all about, Maggie? What's the matter with you?'

'Oh, please don't embarrass yourself. I overheard Jess talking to Mrs Fiddy.'

Maggie tried to punch Jimmy again and was restrained by Mr Green, who managed to clasp her wrists.

'When were you going to tell me about your cosy holiday with your "butter wouldn't melt in her mouth" wife?'

Jimmy had recently arranged a holiday in France. He was mortified and tongue-tied.

'Don't bother to answer, you're never going to leave that cold bitch, are you?' she shouted.

Whispers amongst the crowd were heard in every direction. People were aghast as they understood what was going on. Maggie was known to be a tart amongst the locals, but Jimmy was respected.

Robert was confused and angry, but ignoring Maggie's continued rantings, he said loudly, 'What are we going to do about the windmill, Dad?'

'I suppose it'll be another 100 years before it works again,' said a man in a white peaked cap.

Maggie had not seen him before and thought he must be a journalist. He was smiling and took pleasure in Jimmy's misfortune.

'It'll be worth waiting for another scene like this,' said Geraldine Scott. She never liked Maggie, but along with other villagers, she was shocked. 'She's not only been riding horses then, Mr Jackson!' she added, with a whiff of self-acclaimed importance.

'Like a bit of gossip do you, Geraldine? If I were you, I'd look closer to home. How's your randy sister?' Jimmy snapped back.

'Come on, Dad, we've got to get the windmill going,' Robert pleaded.

'I'll talk to you later, Maggie.'

Jimmy tried to get away.

'Don't you turn your back on me; talk to me now!' she demanded.

By this time, many more people arrived, including Sarah who had returned from the house. They had heard the commotion coming from behind the Grange and watched as Maggie followed Jimmy back towards the windmill.

'You're not going to get away with it!' she shouted at the top of her voice.

Jimmy disappeared inside and as he climbed the stairs Maggie was close behind him.

'What's happening, Miss Jewson?' Sarah asked.

'It's not for me to say, Mrs Jackson, but I think your Jimmy and Maggie have been more than neighbours, if you know what I mean.'

Sarah had nurtured suspicions, but she did not allow herself to believe them.

Up above, Jimmy was shattered, having climbed up and down the windmill several times during the day. Every step took longer than the one before.

'There's nowhere to go, Jimmy, I want an explanation!' Maggie bellowed at the top of her voice.

She was grabbing at his legs and all his energy was gradually sapped out of him. As they reached the top, there was a shudder.

Maggie screamed.

The mechanism righted itself and the cap lurched to the left. In seconds, sounds were heard of the sails rotating outside. Jimmy was relieved and tried to go back down the stairs, but Maggie blocked his exit.

'You're not going anywhere, until you talk to me.'

Her arms were stretched out wide. They were both perspiring in the immense heat as she continued to demand answers.

'Tell me it's not true! Tell me you're still going to leave Sarah and you want to be with me!'

Maggie's voice was angry and loud and she punched his shoulders, but he didn't speak. She hit him harder, with the stairwell inches behind her.

'You've been using me, you've always been using me!'

Jimmy held her arms down by her sides and with a quick tug, he pulled her away from the stairs. In two steps they were both standing by the shaft in the centre of the floor.

'I'm sorry Maggie, I love being with you, but I can't leave Sarah.'

Maggie was full of hate. Her breathing was erratic and her body was rigid.

'When did you decide this, last week, last month? How long have you lied to me? Come on, be honest for once in your life,' demanded Maggie tearfully.

'I think deep down I've always known.'

Jimmy was calm and sorrowful. Maggie spat in his face, but then in an instant all the anger inside her disappeared. She wiped Jimmy's cheeks with a tissue from inside her bra and put her arms around him.

Once again, he was mesmerised by her eyes, glinting from a streak of sunlight. They kissed passionately and hugged, but the embrace became intense and more like a pursuit as if it was a challenge to hold more and more of each other.

'I knew it was me you loved, Sarah will never fulfil your needs,' said Maggie smiling.

Immediately, Jimmy released his arms from her body.

'No, this is wrong I told you, I can't leave Sarah.'

Maggie's eyes filled with enmity once more.

'I'll not be treated like a piece of meat.'

She pushed Jimmy away and his foot slipped on some loose grain. He fell sideways and because of his disability, he was unable to right himself. His momentum and his lack of balance made him fall over the edge to where the brake wheel and the wallower were married together.

Maggie looked down as Jimmy screamed in agony. His legs were engulfed by the machinery which drew the rest of his body into the mechanism. Piercing shrieks of despair haunted the windmill and, as his cries diminished, the sound of breaking bones became more prominent.

It sent a cold shiver through Maggie's spine, but there were no tears. She stood there silently and motionless as the sails once more came to a halt.

'That bastard will never lie to anyone else!' she shouted.

Maggie felt like a matador who had slayed a bull. She calmly walked down the stairs and out of the windmill. By this time most people had gathered close by.

'Where's Jimmy?' shouted Sarah.

'He is in bits.'

Sarah screamed. 'What do you mean?'

'I told you, he's in pieces. He slipped and fell. He should have been more careful, I'm not his keeper.'

Sarah immediately ran towards the windmill, with Robert chasing after her. Unfortunately, she reached the entrance before him, and not long after a cry of horror rang out.

When Robert caught up with Sarah, she was standing close to the mangled body. She was crying, as he took hold of her arm and tried to pull her away. Sarah did not want to go and stood her ground.

'I don't want to leave my Jimmy, I never want to leave him!'

Robert put his arms around her.

'Come on, Mum, we have to go, you know there's nothing we can do for him now.'

Sarah somehow managed to gaze at Jimmy's body once more and called out, 'I love you Jimmy, no matter what's happened, I love you!'

Getting to her feet, still sobbing, she eventually let Robert lead her out of the windmill. Fete activities came to a swift close and nobody got any flour. Maggie did not have any words of sympathy or comfort. She was always jealous of Sarah, as she stood between her and Jimmy.

'It was me he wanted, Sarah. You weren't able to love him like I did; he told me he was leaving you.'

There was menace in her eyes. Maggie wanted to leave Sarah with nothing, but with their faces close together, Sarah did not flinch.

'You were his dirty bit on the side. Perhaps I didn't give him everything he wanted, but women like you aren't hard to find; you were just convenient.'

'Well, we can't ask him now, can we? Someone should get a shovel and pick him up.'

Sarah sobbed in Robert's arms.

Maggie ignored tirades of abuse from the villagers as she made her way home. Inwardly, however, the incident affected her and she was in shock.

After entering her cottage, she went out into the back garden to the edge of the cliff. Her eyes wandered down to the rocks below. Her world was destroyed and she thought about ending her life there and then. However, the sea air cleared Maggie's mind and now she was feeling differently. She reasoned, 'He lied to me for far too long and deserved all he got.'

Emily was riding with Jenny in Kelling and when she arrived home, emergency vehicles were on the forecourt. Sarah was back in the Grange not knowing how she would tell Emily her father was dead.

Giles opened the door and Emily stormed in.

'What's happened, Mum? Why are there two police cars outside?'

Sarah was in a terrible state and broke down in tears again. Her face was red, her hair was untidy and she was exhausted.

'It's been the most awful day; something terrible has happened!'

'What do you mean? Tell me, Mum!'

'There was a horrific accident in the windmill.'

Emily was frightened as Sarah hugged her tighter than ever before. 'Where's Dad and Robert?'

Sarah was unable to speak. She had experienced much family tragedy in her life, losing her mum, dad and sister. Now, in less than an hour, Jimmy had been taken from her.

Robert came into the house from the back garden. Emily was relieved to see him but worried for her dad even more.

'Where is he?' she asked frantically.

Robert was silent.

'Please, Robert, where is he?' Emily was on her feet, grabbing his arms and demanding an answer.

'Dad fell into the windmill machinery and he's dead.'

'No!!!' Emily yelled.

'It's not possible, I don't believe it!' she shouted.

'Maggie said he slipped on the top floor,' said Robert.

'What was she doing in there? She wasn't making flour surely?'

'We don't know, but trouble seems to follow that woman around,' said Sarah, wiping her eyes and rubbing her face.

'How can this have happened? Everything was perfect this morning. There was such a wonderful day to look forward to. My dad can't be dead!' she exclaimed.

The villagers made their way home and the police declared the area a crime scene. Jimmy's mangled body was removed for examination. Two days later it was released by the coroner for burial.

An immediate investigation followed and, having listened to villagers' comments, the police were keen to visit Maggie. They arrived at her cottage the following morning. She was expecting them.

'All I can remember is an argument which led us into the windmill, then Jimmy slipped and fell. He was an invalid, you know, and it was difficult for him to keep his balance.'

'What were you arguing about?' said DCI Housley.

He already knew the answer from interviewing other people but wanted to hear it from Maggie.

'I was upset because he deceived me; that's all.'

'Wasn't it because you found out Jimmy wasn't going to leave his wife for you, Miss MacArdle? You must have been in quite a rage.'

'I told you there was an argument and he fell.'

'How convenient, like the death of Eddie Jackson, that was convenient too wasn't it?'

This accusation shook Maggie and she responded immediately.

'How dare you accuse me! Charge me or get out of my cottage!'

'If I've any more questions, you'll be coming down to the station,' said DCI Housley.

He was hoping for a quick confession, but Maggie was adamant it was an accident and there were no other witnesses. Many more questions were asked of the family and local residents. Time and time again, the police were told Maggie was not liked by some villagers and was both a flirt and a snob. However, although people harboured their suspicions, no one possessed any evidence to suggest she might be capable of murder.

Chapter Twenty-Three

Relations between the Jacksons and Maggie, already strained, were now at rock bottom. Maggie was not allowed to walk on the estate. She was told to keep to the road and footpath that were the rights of way to her cottage.

Sarah was filled with hate. She thought, 'Whatever really happened in the windmill, Jimmy would still be alive if Maggie had stayed outside.'

'The only good thing that's come out of this catastrophe, is we are free of that bloody woman. She's been a curse on this family and I'd prefer it if you didn't talk to her,' she said to Emily and Robert.

'You needn't worry about me, Mum, I'll not go near her,' said Robert.

Sarah was pleased Emily was not at home when her dad died and did not witness Maggie's rant, but it meant her eyes were still blinkered.

'Maggie might have done some awful things, Mum, but she's been very good to me. I don't think she's capable of murder,' she said.

'I think she's capable of anything!' said Sarah.

'This is my fault! If only I hadn't persuaded Dad to renovate the windmill, Mum,' said Robert.

'If I hadn't painted the damn thing, it'd still be a ruin,' said Emily.

Robert got to his feet and Sarah saw the anger exploding in his eyes.

'I can't bear seeing you both suffer any longer,' he said.

Robert stormed out of the house, leaving the door wide open.

'Where are you going?' Sarah called out.

'Where I should have gone a long time ago, she's not going to get away with it!' he shouted back.

Sarah watched him run down the path towards the windmill and the cottage.

'I'm frightened Emily, Robert might harm Maggie,' sobbed Sarah, fraught with worry.

'I'll go after him, Mum,' said Emily, putting her shoes on in haste.

Sarah knew her daughter was a faster runner and watched her gain ground on him from her window. The siblings reached the cottage at the same time and Robert banged violently on the door with his hand.

Maggie had expected a confrontation with the children at some point. She heard Emily shouting at Robert outside and opened the door. Robert pushed his way past her and Emily followed him into the kitchen.

'It was your fault, all your fault!' shouted Robert.

'What do you mean, Jimmy's death or him loving me?' Maggie calmly asked.

She was smiling nonchalantly, as if she did not have a care in the world.

'I don't know why our dad went near you, but there must have been a reason.'

'I think you need to look closer to home. If Sarah had been a better wife, he wouldn't have needed me.'

'What do you mean a better wife?' asked Emily.

'I think you know what I mean, I gave him all the love he needed.'

Emily cried and Robert went to strike Maggie, but she raised her arm and stopped him.

'Go home, Robert, and you too, Emily.'

Sarah waited frantically, until Emily and Robert were seen walking back to the house. She had endured enough heartache and was relieved there had been no more than an argument.

'Maggie was placid about it all, as if Dad's death didn't matter. There wasn't any remorse,' said Emily tearfully.

'Perhaps at last you've seen Maggie's dark side,' Sarah replied.

The tragedy reminded Sarah she was living her dream in the country, but she thought, 'I knew something bad would occur. That's what happens to ordinary people; the good things in life come at a price.'

Listening to her children's conversation, she was saddened they were so upset.

'We shouldn't have come to Norfolk, Mum,' said Robert.

'It's easy to play the "what if" game. If we'd stayed in London, who knows what our lives would've been like, but you wouldn't have worked with Dad and Emily you wouldn't be riding Lottie.'

'I wish I'd been at the fete when Dad died. I didn't get the chance to say goodbye. I'll never forgive myself for going riding.'

Sitting down next to Emily, Sarah held her close. She knew what happened was far too much for her to take in.

'Please don't torment yourself. Although Dad didn't often show it, he loved you very much. You sometimes quarrelled, but in many ways you were too much alike. Both a little bit stubborn and believing you were always right, but he knew you loved him too.'

Sarah stayed strong for her children, but she missed Jimmy every day. In the small hours it was her time to grieve. She lay awake staring at a photo taken at the fete the previous year. It was in a metal frame standing on her bedside cabinet.

Jimmy was smiling, having locked Bummsy in his hut. She remembered he had mistakenly left his key in the door. It was a silly thing to do, but there was much laughter. The memory warmed Sarah's heart. However, she kept thinking about his body crushed in the windmill. How she wished her final memory of Jimmy was different.

The responsibilities attached to Hemsley Grange were enormous and Sarah decided to carry on as normal as possible. She did not cancel or postpone any meetings and visited both the village hall and the local shops. She instructed her children to do the same and people quickly rallied around and offered their sympathy and support. Fifty-seven bereavement cards were received at the Grange.

On the day of the funeral, an envelope was pushed through the letter box. Everyone forgot about Emily's GCE results, but they were now lying on the floor in the hall. The envelope was brought to the breakfast table by Giles and placed in front of the young lady. Emily stared at it, but on this day, her results were immaterial and she continued eating.

'Open it, Emily,' said Sarah.

'I can't, I don't want to think about anything else today but Dad.'

'I think he'd want you to; he's probably watching right now,' said Robert.

'Go on, we all want to know your results,' said Sarah.

'I certainly do,' remarked Giles as he cleared some plates away.

Giles rarely said a word unless he was spoken to, but he was fond of the girl. She always treated him with respect.

Emily slid her finger under the flap. The envelope was not sealed very well and quickly opened. Taking out a folded piece of paper she immediately beamed and announced excellent results. This was the first time she smiled since her father's death.

'I wish Dad was here,' said Emily.

She cried and Sarah took hold of her hands.

'I know, we all do, but this is good news; it's what the family needed. Dad would have been very proud of you, let's give him the send-off he deserves.'

The day was sunny and warm. Sarah ordered enough flowers to completely decorate the hearse in the colours of navy blue and white. Sarah wanted to ride alone with Jimmy in the hearse. The children followed behind in a second funeral car.

After Sarah entered St John's Church, the coffin was laid at the front of the aisle. The pews were packed for the remembrance service. Reverend Fiddy was about to commence proceedings when Sarah got up from her seat. She was dressed in a smart black pleated skirt and black blouse.

'What are you doing?' whispered Emily.

She did not notice her mum was carrying a large bag.

Sarah walked out in front of the congregation and took out a photo of Jimmy. She kissed the frame and stood it on top of the coffin. Sarah stepped back and, at her lowest ebb, she burst into tears. Up until now she had controlled her emotions. Her two children joined her in solidarity. Standing each side, they held her arms and bowed together in honour of the man they loved.

After retaking their seats, Reverend Fiddy addressed the congregation and invited everyone to stand and sing 'All Things Bright and Beautiful'.

Emily gave a reading. Holding back the tears, she talked about God always walking beside people. She said when people needed help, sometimes they worried because they did not feel him next to them, but in truth it was because they were being carried by him.

Then to everyone's surprise, Sarah stood up again. She made up her mind the people of Cleybourne were going to know more about Jimmy even though it would intrude into her private life.

'I can tell you it was tough during the war in London. We didn't know if we'd survive from one day to the next.'

Along with the other mourners, Emily and Robert were amazed by the stories. They tried to imagine their parent's chance meeting at Bank tube station during a bombing raid, and the stigma attached to their dad's invalidity upset them. They were warmed however by happy memories of their childhood.

'Like us, most people didn't have any money.' Sarah paused and added, 'It was just as well, because with rationing, there was nothing to spend it on anyway.'

The congregation laughed and then Sarah cried. Emily was about to step forward with a tissue.

'It's all right,' said Sarah.

She wiped her eyes with her fingers.

'I want you all to know, I feel incredibly proud to have been Jimmy's wife and lucky to live such a luxurious life. I was not born with a silver spoon in my mouth. At the moment it's not easy for me, but the Grange estate and I will support the community as we've always done.'

Sarah left the pulpit in silence and then there was a ripple of applause at the back of the church. Most of the people in Cleybourne respected Sarah and they were sympathetic for her loss. By the time she sat down, everyone was clapping and Emily clasped her hand.

After the ceremony Jimmy was buried in bright sunshine next to his dad. It was close to an old oak tree and a large number of people gathered around the plot to pay their last respects. Sarah and Emily sobbed throughout the proceedings as Reverend Fiddy committed Jimmy's body to Christ.

Sarah had made her mark in Cleybourne, but there were mixed feelings for Jimmy. He was liked by his friends, largely of the male gentry, but the women now generally despised his memory. Revelations of his affair with Maggie appalled them.

After the ceremony and when the crowd moved away, the Jackson family stayed on their own. Silently they stood by the grave still wondering how the tragedy happened. It seemed inconceivable they would never see Jimmy again.

Maggie did not attend the funeral. Not only because her presence would unsettle proceedings, but also because she believed Jimmy had let her down and she was not going to grieve for him.

Chapter Twenty-Four

The burial of Jimmy gave rise to the reading of his will, two days later. Like his father, he appointed Mr Barker as his executor and the solicitor asked for Sarah, Emily and Robert to attend. They all assembled in the sitting room, where Giles served tea.

With solemn and yet expectant faces in front of him, Mr Barker opened his brief case and took out a long brown envelope. He removed the will and placed it on a table in front of him.

'Jimmy listed the smaller provisions first; £1000 is left to each of your staff, Giles, Jess and Joseph.'

There were smiles from the family, because the servants were hardworking people. They would never forget how Jess and Giles in particular went out of their way to help them settle into the Grange after Eddie's death.

'I now come to the main beneficiaries. The remaining assets of Jimmy's estate are to be shared equally between you, Mrs Jackson, and your children.'

Sarah was shocked and disappointed. She never envisaged being in this position, believing any monies going to Robert and Emily would be her decision. She was unsure of Jimmy's motives.

'It's me who runs the estate; what was Jimmy thinking of?' she calmly asked Mr Barker.

'He didn't confide in me, Mrs Jackson.'

Emily and Robert were also amazed. Their faces were beaming but Sarah sensed some anxiety in Mr Barker's delivery.

'There are conditions,' he said.

'What conditions?' asked Sarah, feeling irate and folding her arms.

She felt let down by her late husband and was anxious to know what other surprises Jimmy was going to spring on her.

'Hemsley Grange can't be sold, unless all the main beneficiaries agree.'

'It's our home, that's a very strange thing for him to say,' Sarah replied.

'I don't think any of us would want to sell it,' said Robert.

'I want to stay here forever,' said Emily.

'When I said the assets are to be shared equally, I have to tell you there are four people listed in the will.'

Sarah's facial expression changed. Her body tensed up and she pushed her fingers hard into the fabric of her chair. The children were shocked, seeing their mother's anxiety. Along with the solicitor, they waited for her to speak. Sarah did not imagine she would ever have this conversation. She was not prepared and there was nowhere to hide.

'It's Mary, isn't it?' said Sarah, and she sobbed.

Emily comforted her, but along with her brother, she wanted more information.

'Who's Mary, Mum? Did you have children with someone else before you married Dad?'

Robert was equally inquisitive and waited for an answer but it did not come.

'Do you know where she is, Mrs Jackson?' asked the solicitor.

'No,' she replied.

The children were amazed. The existence of a sibling changed everything in the Jackson household.

'How did you keep such a secret for so long?' asked Robert.

The children were upset; they had been cheated and deceived.

'You didn't mention Mary at the funeral service!' shouted Emily angrily.

'Sit down, Emily; it's nothing like you think. Jimmy is her father, but it's complicated,' sighed Sarah.

Mr Barker, listening to the conversation and witnessing all the family emotions, wanted to finish his business. His briefcase was already closed and he was about to leave. Interrupting the children's grilling of their mother, there was one more thing he wanted to say.

'The provisions to Emily, Robert and Mary will be held in trust until they reach the age of twenty-one, with the exception of a monthly allowance of fifty pounds.'

Emily and Robert smiled again.

Finally, Mr Barker gave a letter to Sarah from Jimmy. She snatched it out of his hand as if somehow he was responsible for her husband's last wishes. Giles escorted him out of the house and the moment the door was closed, the children continued the interrogation of their mother. They demanded an explanation.

'Why haven't we been told about her before? Is there something wrong with her?' asked Emily.

'I don't think we're going to get any answers at the moment, but we have a sister,' said Robert.

'I gathered that much.'

There were so many questions and the children were impatient and unrelenting in their search for answers. Sarah was still sobbing; she did not believe Jimmy would do this to her. Her eye make-up mixed with her tears, making a mess of her face. Ignoring the barrage of questions, she left the sitting room and made her way upstairs.

Robert and Emily followed her close behind.

'You have to tell us what this is all about, Mum.'

Sarah stayed silent. She had not seen Mary for twenty years; Emily and Robert had been deprived of a sister and Mary did not know her real family. These things always troubled Sarah greatly, but they were secrets she had intended to take to her grave.

Both the children were getting more annoyed and, ignoring their mother's tears, Emily snapped as they reached the landing.

'We've a right to know!' she shouted out.

After closing her bedroom door, Sarah collapsed on her bed. Her children were outside and she heard them whispering.

'Don't you dare come in!' she loudly commanded.

'Then talk to us, Mum,' pleaded Emily.

Lifting her head off the pillow she called out, 'Robert told you, Mary's your sister, so now you know.'

There was anger and grief in her voice.

'Where is she then? How old is she? Why has she never been mentioned?' Robert enquired.

Sarah knew she would have to face the truth and provide answers.

'I can't talk about it now. Please don't try and make me. We can discuss it later.'

Lying on her bed, Sarah wiped away her tears and opened Jimmy's letter. His writing was normally scruffy, and she remembered telling him it was like a worm out of control. It made her smile, as surprisingly, in this prose all his words were neat and clear. 'Bless him, it must have taken ages,' she thought. Holding it aloft with both hands she read:

I obviously don't know when you'll read this. If I out live you, I guess you never will. We were married a long time and as the years went by I came to realise how lucky I was to have you in my life. Sometimes I wished we'd never left the East End. We were poor, but we were together all the time and there weren't any outside pressures interfering with our lives. I'm sorry if I've let you down.

Before reading on, Sarah placed the letter next to her heart. She had already forgiven Jimmy for his philandering with Maggie, but it was a special moment and reminded her of all the good times they spent together. There were a few more tears, but this time they were tears of comfort.

Composing herself again, she raised the letter in her hands once more and read:

We both know our marriage has been incomplete. Mary was rarely mentioned and yet I suspect a day hasn't gone by without you remembering her, as I did. Sarah my love, you'll never be at peace until Mary is found. I pray she'll be re-united with you and her brother and sister.

For the next two hours, Sarah laid thinking about her long-lost daughter. She read the letter over and over again. Finding Mary was Jimmy's wish, but she was not sure how she would cope with his legacy.

She thought, 'Jimmy's right, all my life I've wondered about Mary. I've longed to know if she's safe and happy. Now there may be a chance to find out, I'm petrified. I don't think I can face her.'

Sarah bathed and changed her clothes. She combed her hair and made her way downstairs. The children having calmed down were more amenable. They still wanted answers and Sarah was now ready to provide them, although she was not prepared to tell them the whole truth.

'Mary is your sister. She was born on 8 May 1945, the day the war was over. It was very sad, but we decided not to keep her. We didn't have much money and lived in a tiny flat. Remember what I told you and the congregation at Dad's funeral.'

'Wasn't it like that for most people, they didn't all give up their children, did they?' asked Robert.

Sarah was not sure how to answer, but she was determined to protect Jimmy.

'There was an opportunity to give Mary a better life. I can tell you, giving up a child is the hardest sacrifice a mother can make and I'll never forget the moment she was taken from me.'

This admission caused Sarah to burst into tears again and Emily, now more sympathetic, put her arms around her.

'Where is she?' she asked softly.

'I told the solicitor – I don't know, Emily.'

Their mother was overwrought, so they decided not to ask any more questions for the time being. Mr Barker said he would make all the necessary enquiries to try to find their sister and they were prepared to be patient.

The solicitor visited the Grange the following week. He wanted information about Mary's adoption. Sarah decided to ignore Jimmy's wishes, as she did not want her found, but she did mention Mary's large egg-like birthmark on her left arm. She kept Cotland Home a secret and said the baby was taken from her in the Hackney Mothers' Hospital.

Chapter Twenty-Five

A few days later the police concluded their enquiries. They did not uncover any evidence to suggest murder or manslaughter and Jimmy's death was recorded as an accident.

Sarah, although grieving, was worried about Robert. He was working every daylight hour.

'Please take a break!' she said regularly.

Robert only stopped long enough to eat a sandwich.

'I need to keep busy, Mum; the estate has been neglected for too long. There are fences to repair, silt-filled ditches to dig out, gutters to clear and worn out machinery needs to be replaced.'

Sarah knew Robert missed his dad. He had worked with him closely for two years. She believed he was out, every daylight hour, to try and keep his mind active and not dwell on the past.

'You need a rest, Robert,' she said.

Robert broke down in tears and Sarah hugged him, but it was not comfort he required.

'I want to knock the windmill down brick by brick. Wherever I am it always seems to be in my eyeline. I'll never be free of this monster. It killed Dad and will haunt me forever.'

Nothing Sarah said consoled him. All she could do was to wait for the pain inside him to go away.

Emily spent most of her time on her own, bottling up her grief and Sarah thought it was time for her to pick up her life.

'Don't you think I should enquire about horse training courses, Emily?'

'I don't feel like doing anything, Mum.'

'Dad wouldn't want you moping around.'

The telephone rang.

'It's Mr Barker, Mrs Jackson,' said Giles.

The solicitor arranged a meeting for the following morning to discuss his initial enquiries about Mary.

The next day, Mr Barker reported back on his investigation.

'I hadn't been to the East End of London before and knew it was going to be a difficult task. I went to the Hackney Mothers' Hospital, as you suggested, but my enquiry wasn't welcome. As soon as I mentioned adoption, I was met with a brick-wall response. I was told quite aggressively the hospital didn't have any record of Mary's birth and wouldn't share it if it did.'

'I imagined there'd be something on file, in case of emergencies,' said Robert.

'It was a long time ago,' replied Sarah.

'I went to the local library and obtained a list of all the media publications in the East End. I posted a large advert in each. I also placed postcards in shop windows wherever they were allowed, across the vast area.'

'Do you think they'll do any good, Mr Barker?' asked Emily.

'To be frank, I don't. Without any photos and only the name Mary and her birthmark to go on, the chances of finding her are slim. We don't even know if she's still in the area. All we can do is to wait and see.'

'Mr Barker is doing all he can,' said Sarah.

In the afternoon, Robert was in Splashets, the local newsagents in Cleybourne, with his friend Sam. He was Joseph's nephew and sometimes helped out on the estate. Sam was seventeen and wanted to join the police force but was not accepted as his thought process was a little slow and he stuttered.

Maggie came into the shop and was browsing some books and magazines. Out of their sight, behind a two-sided bookcase, she eavesdropped.

'You'd not believe it, Sam, but I've a sister called Mary.'

'You're having me on, Robert.'

'No, seriously, a solicitor is trying to find her, she was given up for adoption back in the 1940s. I think she'd be about twenty now.'

Maggie was shocked and upset, as Jimmy had not mentioned her, and listened further.

'Blimey, Robert, how do you feel about that?'

'Not sure, Sam, but I'd like to meet her. The trouble is the solicitor doesn't believe there's much chance of finding her.'

'I wonder if Mary knows anything about you and your family?'

'Yes, that's what I've been thinking. If the solicitor can't locate her, I'm going to London to try and find her myself, once I've learned how to drive. I'm already taking lessons.'

The boys walked out of the shop leaving Maggie to ponder. 'This might open a can of worms,' she thought.

After a few weeks, all Mr Barker's lines of enquiry reached dead ends and the Jackson family was no nearer finding Mary.

'I'm going to try a different approach, Mrs Jackson,' said Mr Barker.

'I don't know what else you can do,' said Sarah, showing little interest in further enquiries.

'I'm going to mention the inheritance in the media.'

The response was substantial, with a long line of 'Marys' making contact. It was very sad, as many women sought parents, albeit not their own, when money was involved. One by one they were removed from the list, when they failed the egg birthmark test.

Maggie now rarely crossed paths with the Jackson family, although they lived in close proximity. Along with many local people, they did not want to talk to her. However, Jess's unlikely friendship with Maggie continued, even though in the past she was treated more like a skivvy than a cook and cleaner.

Sometimes, when the family was out, Maggie visited the Grange for afternoon tea. Giles frowned at seeing her in the house, but as Jess often helped him out when his nerves took hold, he said nothing to Sarah.

When Maggie told Jess about Mary, she was only half surprised.

'I heard the name mentioned last week. Emily was talking to Robert about her, but as soon as I got close to them they finished the conversation. That's a turn up for the book isn't it?'

'Damn right it is, Jess.'

These meetings reinforced Maggie's love affair with the Grange. She strolled around as if she was still lady of the house. Maggie believed it was where she was meant to be, but needed a new plan to fulfil her ambition. The existence of Mary pleased her. 'At least there's one member of the Jackson family who doesn't hate me. Maybe she'll be found. I'd like to know more about her,' she thought.

Sarah went to Kelling Hills to discuss Emily working with horses.

'Do you think it'd be a good career path for her, Jenny?'

'Yes, I'll be pleased to train her to become both an instructor and a jumper. As you know, I enter events and it'd be fun if we eventually entered competitions together.'

'I think that's a long way off, Jenny.'

'You might be surprised. Emily's already a proficient rider and Lottie is five years old. The horse's bone structure is well developed; she's very strong and in good physical condition.'

Sarah looked around Jenny's trophy room. Colourful rosettes decorated the walls and awards spanning many years filled a large mahogany cabinet. They were made of bronze, pewter and some were silver plated. She spent some time reading the inscriptions.

*

Mr Barker requested another meeting with the Jackson family.

'I've done everything I can to try to locate Mary. It now seems inconceivable she'll ever be found.'

'It's not been long enough, she might still turn up,' said Robert.

'The trouble is, we've so little information about Mary and her name may have been changed,' said Mr Barker.

Sarah thought to herself, 'Thank goodness, now we can put Mary to bed forever.'

'I'm here out of courtesy to inform you I now intend to apply for probate. When the formalities are completed, the inheritance will be distributed amongst the remaining beneficiaries.'

Robert was not happy and raised his voice to the solicitor.

'This is our family, not yours, Mary must be given more time.'

However, Sarah agreed with the solicitor.

'Have you listened to Mr Barker? He's explained he's done all he can.'

'I'll try and find Mary. I'll go to London myself.'

Robert was now a qualified driver and, with his mother's cash, was the proud owner of a brand-new Ford Anglia motor car.

'There's no point, we don't have enough information. How are you going to find her?' Sarah asked.

'Mum's right, you don't know London and have nothing to go on,' said Emily sadly.

'I have to try, she's our sister Ems; Mary must be somewhere.'

'Perhaps Mary doesn't want to be found,' said Sarah.

Robert wouldn't be deterred.

'Please, Mr Barker, can we have a little more time?' he pleaded, with his hands together.

The solicitor deliberated. He was moved by Robert's sorrowful face.

'I'll not be making any further enquiries, but I'll delay probate for a final period of six months.'

Mr Barker left the Grange.

'I'll come with you, Robert,' said Sarah.

Emily and Robert were shocked.

'I didn't think you wanted her,' said Emily.

'All you've done is dismiss Mary, as if she doesn't matter,' said Robert.

'It's been a terrible shock. I've wanted Mary all my life, but when I considered her being found, it scared me. What will I say to her? How do I make up for all the lost years?'

'What's changed your mind, Mum?' asked Emily.

'The desire you both have to see your sister. Also, I've realised this is not all about me, Mary might be desperate to find her family.'

'We still haven't got any new clues,' said Emily.

'I told Mr Barker that Mary was born in the Hackney Mothers' Hospital, which is true, but I didn't tell him where I nursed my baby until the adoption. It was in Cotland Home, Amhurst Park in Stamford Hill.'

Chapter Twenty-Six

The journey from Cleybourne to Stamford Hill is over 130 miles. Robert mapped out the route to be undertaken in midwinter and they left home on a clear crisp morning at eight o'clock.

A heavy blanket of frost covered the fields and the ungritted roads were icy and treacherous. Sarah worried as Robert lacked driving experience. She was concerned he might not be able to handle the conditions.

'This is the first time you've travelled back to London since we moved, Robert.'

'So much has happened, Mum, it seems like years ago now.'

As Robert drove south, the amount of traffic increased; there were fewer crop fields and less farm animals seen. The urban landscape was dingy with smoke bellowing from factory chimneys and there were rows of terraced houses with tiny gardens.

After around four hours, they were nearly there. Sarah felt nervous as she considered visiting Cotland. 'I don't want to see the awful place again,' she thought.

Robert drove along Seven Sisters Road and turned the corner into Amhurst Park. Sarah expected the maternity home to be ahead, but it had been demolished.

'Perhaps it was bombed in the war, Mum,' said Robert.

'No! I told you, Mary was born on VE day and we came back here before moving to Norfolk.'

They both got out of the car and stood on the pavement next to a wire fence which secured the empty space.

'Cotland was our only clue,' said Robert.

Tears crept out of his eyes and Sarah put a comforting arm around his shoulder.

'Perhaps it wasn't meant to be.'

Robert pushed her arm away and snapped, 'You never wanted Mary found, Mum, I suppose you knew about this and that's the reason you mentioned Cotland.'

'No, I told you, the thought of seeing Mary scared me, but I was being selfish, I really want to find her.'

Sarah stopped an elderly man passing by.

'Do you know what happened to Cotland Home?'

'It was there!' he said.

The man pointed to a few piles of bricks that remained on the property site.

'Good riddance is what I say. If it wasn't for the charity, most of the women who were in there, would've been in the gutter where they belong.'

Sarah, somewhat shocked, kept calm. She did not know the home had been ridiculed in this way, but reasoned, 'If it was true, no wonder it was pulled down.'

'Do you know what happened to the home? Did it relocate anywhere else?'

'Sorry, not a clue!'

Robert and Sarah asked other passers-by, but their responses were negative. They were feeling dejected and sat in Robert's car.

'Why were you in that terrible home, Mum?'

'The women in Cotland were there for various reasons. Most were poor unmarried mothers in desperate need. The man was right about the charity, without it, babies would have died on the streets. It was different for me, as your father provided support.'

Robert racked his brains for what to do next.

'Somebody must know what happened to the home. There's the police station, the library and the council office. Let's try them all.'

Their enquiries failed to provide any new information and Sarah thought they were wasting their time.

'There's really nothing else we can do, Robert.'

'Wait a minute; Mr Barker said he went to the Hackney Mothers' Hospital. That's where Mary was born wasn't it, Mum?'

'Yes, but his visit wasn't welcome.'

'I know he was rejected, but perhaps someone might at least be prepared to tell us what happened to Cotland. Can you remember where it is?'

'No, I was only there for Mary's birth and on a quick visit prior to leaving the East End.'

'So, Hackney's all we've got to go on, I might drive around for hours, Mum, without finding the home.'

They were at a dead end until Sarah remembered a scrappy yellow piece of card on the car dashboard.

'Where's the note Emily left us? She scribbled down Mr Barker's telephone number, but it's missing. I'm sure he'd tell us how to get there.'

They both searched on the floor and Sarah found it under her seat.

'Look! There's a telephone box across the road,' said Sarah.

They walked over the busy street. Sarah and Robert waited as a tall lady in a blue overcoat was in an intense discussion. She was talking so loudly they heard every word.

The conversation went on for several minutes as she continued to insert money from her purse into the payment slot. She was seemingly oblivious to their presence. Robert became impatient, listening to her chatter about cat litters and banged on the cracked door window.

'Will you hurry up, please!' he said, pointing to his watch.

The woman glared at him and turned her back. She continued talking until her supply of coins ran out.

When Sarah called Mr Barker's office she was saddened further.

'He's out with a client and not expected back until late afternoon,' said his secretary.

Barriers appeared to be lining up against her and Robert, one after the other. They did not know what to do next and were about to drive home when Sarah squeezed her son's hand.

'I've another idea. I don't know why I didn't think of it before, we can hire a taxi.'

Leaving Robert's vehicle in a car parking area, they walked down Amhurst Park. Robert waved his arms in the air and was irritated as several cabs passed him by.

'Robert, don't hold your hand up if the front light isn't on. It means passengers are inside, or the driver is not doing business.'

Amhurst Park, however, is a busy street and it was only a short while before an empty taxi that Sarah beckoned pulled up beside them.

'Hackney Mothers' Hosptial, please,' she said.

As soon as they got inside, the driver sped away causing them to fall back on the seat. They arrived at their destination within eight minutes and Sarah realised he probably wanted a larger fare. Nevertheless, the cabby was ill-mannered and she did not give him a tip.

The Hackney Mothers' Hospital was an imposing building that breathed authority and respect. It occupied a prominent frontage in Lower Clapton Road with a pillared entrance gate and two distinctive arches leading to the main entrance.

Inside, Sarah spoke to a small, slim lady with a mass of blonde curls. She was seated behind a desk surrounded by filing cabinets.

'We're trying to find out what happened to someone in Cotland Home, can you help us please?'

'Sorry, but no I can't,' she said forcibly, while playing with her pearl necklace.

She held it in one hand and flicked the beads with her other fingers. The lady spoke with a high pitched, bird-like voice.

'We only want to know what happened to the home, we're not asking for personal records,' said Sarah.

'Why didn't you say so? There seems to be a never-ending line of people who come here thinking we can undo family secrets. I'll see what I can find.'

Sarah and Robert waited while the contents of a drawer were searched. There was not a sound to be heard in the building apart from the rustling of paper between her fingers.

'How many homes can there be?' Sarah whispered to Robert as the drawer was closed.

'I think I've the information you require; it seems the home moved to 13 Laura Place in Hackney. It's called Crossways, but I don't think they'll be able to help you.'

At last Sarah and Robert were getting somewhere. After leaving the mothers' home they took a further short cab ride to their destination.

The driver was friendly and chatty. He talked continuously throughout the journey. In a few minutes Sarah and Robert knew the names of his wife and children, his sister suffered from piles and his brother was in prison for what he described as burglary with menaces.

The cabby also wanted to know Sarah's life story. In different circumstances she might have told him, but only Mary was on her mind.

Getting out of the vehicle, Sarah looked up at the building and thought, 'What another dreary place this is.'

Large open black doors led to a reception area, where a lady with short brown hair was seated. Her name was Miss Davis, as indicated by a wooden plaque on her polished oak desk. Sarah stood in front of her, but she did not raise her head. She was too busy typing to acknowledge her presence.

Sarah coughed loudly.

'Excuse me!' she said.

Miss Davis, jolted and grunted.

'Yes! What is it?' she asked impatiently.

'I'd like to make an enquiry about an adopted child.'

'So would a lot of people, but it isn't possible.'

Sarah tried hard to sweet-talk her.

'This home must have been a comfort and support to so many ladies over the years,' she said.

Miss Davis was not moved and kept pounding her keys.

Sarah did not like her attitude. She thought Miss Davis was rude, and frustration came out in her voice.

'I don't think you're taking my enquiry seriously. I have a name, date of birth and a birthmark. I know it's not much to go on, but I thought you might at least try and help me.'

Miss Davis was unmoved and stayed silent; she did not seem in the slightest bit interested.

Sarah lost her patience. 'Do you get pleasure in your work? Do you enjoy distressing families?'

Sarah's conversation was loud and the door opened behind Miss Davis' desk. A lady with a red face, about fifty-five years old, walked into the reception area. She was small, with broad shoulders, had a double chin, and wore large-framed glasses. Her name badge said Mrs Priest, and she stood in front of Sarah and Robert with her arms folded and her lips puckered.

'This woman seems to delight in ignoring people. I know you have rules and regulations, but surely an adopted child would want to find their parents,' said Sarah.

Mrs Priest calmly replied, 'Not necessarily.'

Sarah wouldn't be deterred.

'Don't you think the adoptees should be asked?'

'It's complicated; what about the adoptive parents?'

'It's a child's right to know their own mother and father.'

'Is it? Well that's not what the law says.'

Sarah felt she was banging her head against a wall. She realised that without any help from Mrs Priest, finding Mary would be impossible. In a last attempt to obtain information she told her about the inheritance.

'Mary is to receive a very substantial part of her father's estate and he was a very wealthy man.'

Mrs Priest listened and seemed surprised. It was not every day an inheritance was mentioned in the home, but she maintained her stance.

'I'm sorry, there aren't any circumstances which allow me to breach the law; there's nothing here for you.'

Sarah took out a notebook and pencil. She scribbled down some information and asked Mrs Priest to keep it on file in case of need.

Mrs Priest did not want to take it.

'It's not appropriate, Mrs Jackson.'

'Please, Mrs Priest!' pleaded Sarah, placing the note in the centre of her hand.

Visiting Crossways had not provided any answers and Sarah and Robert were exasperated. They did not even know if the home held any information that would help them.

After taking another taxi back to Stamford Hill, they embarked on their long journey home. As Robert drove towards Norfolk, Sarah noticed his anger. He was gripping and un-gripping the steering wheel and rubbing his eyes. On a winding road a large red deer jumped out in front of the car.

'Look out!' Sarah shouted and covered her face.

It stood in front of the car, staring at Robert, who put his foot on the brake. The vehicle skidded and Sarah expected the worst, but at the last moment the beast jumped out of the way. Robert regained control of his car as he swerved towards a ditch. He stopped by the side of the road and Sarah breathed heavily.

The incident disturbed them and as the journey continued, Sarah worried about Robert.

'Are you okay?' she kept asking him.

Fortunately, the frightening ordeal with the lone dear provided him with enough adrenaline to stay awake until they reached home.

'I keep thinking about the windmill. If only I'd not wanted it renovated. I wouldn't have known about my sister, but Dad would still be alive. If we find Mary, I might feel differently, but for all we know she might be dead too.'

Robert was angry and his face was boiling. When they arrived back home Robert went straight around the back of the Grange. Sarah was scared.

'Where are you going?' she called out.

Sarah knew Robert's mind was unstable and she was frantic with worry.

'To do something I should've done straight after the funeral.'

Sarah followed Robert to the machinery shed. It was locked and he forced it open with the end of a pickaxe lying on the ground. He came out holding a can and some matches. Sarah was terrified.

'What are you doing?' she asked.

Making his way back out into the yard, it was almost dark. There was still frost on the ground from the morning, as he hastily walked in the dim moonlight towards the windmill, with Sarah lagging behind.

'This monster isn't going to torment me any longer, and I don't deserve to be alive,' he replied with desperation in his voice.

'Please no, Robert! Come back to the Grange!' Sarah shouted.

On reaching the windmill she grabbed his arm, but he pushed her away. He wrenched the heavy door open with his bare hands and made his way inside.

Sarah ran back to the house to get Giles or Joseph, but only Emily was at home.

'I think Robert's going to set fire to the windmill and I don't know what to do.'

Sarah was crying in fear.

'Oh no! What about Lottie? Anything might happen, I must get her out of the stable and take her around the other side of the house,' said Emily.

She rushed off to look after her horse.

'Please don't go, I need you!' Sarah shouted out, terror-struck.

Sarah returned to the windmill alone and stepped inside. It was dark and there was a musty smell. The polluted air had got into Robert's throat. She heard him clanging about on the floorboards above. He was retching and being sick.

'I'm so sorry, Dad!' he called out, over and over again.

Then she heard him coming down the stairs and the sound of trickling liquid. 'Oh my God, that's petrol,' she said to herself, smelling the fumes.

Robert had not been in the windmill since the day his father died. He was sobbing, but laughing out loud until the pungent petrol odour made him cough violently.

'Please, Robert, don't do this, I love you!' she pleaded once more.

When he reached the bottom, Robert was wheezing and Sarah watched as he emptied the remains of the can on the ground floor. With the moon still shining through the door, she saw his feet were sodden.

Oblivious to Sarah's pleas he shouted, 'It's over! I'll not be tortured by you ever again!'

Robert took the matches from his pocket, but Sarah snatched them out of his hand and ran out of the mill. Robert chased her back into the machinery shed and picked up another box, lying on the bench. With a large garden post, he wedged the door closed with Sarah inside and returned to the windmill.

Joseph arrived home and heard Sarah screaming. Accompanied by Emily, who had tethered Lottie to a tree, they let Sarah out as a whooshing sound unnerved them. In seconds the windmill was alight and in three minutes the building was an inferno.

'Oh no! Please no! Robert's in there!' Sarah screamed.

The howling wind, blowing in their faces, was hot and spiteful. The flaming sails increased in speed and resembled a large Catherine wheel, until they released themselves from their axle housing and crashed to the ground.

Sarah was scared the fire might reach the house, as bits of burning timber littered the night air. There were large bangs as paint tins stored inside the mill exploded.

'Where are you, Robert?' Sarah shouted over and over again.

She was in tears as she continued her search with Emily and Joseph. There was then a shuddering noise, as the remains of the cap collapsed inside the tower, causing Sarah to scream again.

Walking slowly in the semi darkness around the back of the windmill, Sarah made up her mind Robert was dead.

'He wouldn't survive this horror!' she said and wept.

'I think he wanted to die in the mill; he's hated himself every day since the incident,' said Emily.

She held her mother tightly.

'I know, but I never thought it would come to this.'

Then in the distance, the smoke momentarily cleared from Sarah's view. She reined in her tears as a ghost-like figure appeared in front of them.

Someone was sitting on an old barrel, watching the blaze and Sarah thought it must be Robert. She ran towards him, with the sound of fire engines approaching the Grange behind her. He was silent and there was no reaction when Sarah put her arms around him.

'Thank God you're safe!' she said.

Robert was mesmerised. The flickering flames played tricks on his eyes and he was motionless. Sarah kissed him all over his face while clasping her arms around his body and gradually he came out of his trance.

'We thought you were dead; what an earth were you thinking of?' Sarah asked.

'I couldn't stand it any longer, Mum.'

As the firemen extinguished the blaze, Sarah walked back to the house with her son and daughter. She hoped Robert had removed some demons from his mind, but Mary was still missing and Emily needed to be told.

Maggie was on her way home having visited a friend. As she approached the Grange drive she was shocked to see the fire scene in front of her. Fearing the house was in danger, she raced along the road. Maggie did not care about the occupants or her cottage. All her thoughts centred on the Grange. Seeing it standing undamaged was a relief as she watched the Jacksons arriving home in the moonlight.

Chapter Twenty-Seven

Many people witnessed the fire from their homes. Flames and smoke filled the night sky. Windows were closed to stop the stench of burning entering their properties.

When Sarah visited the village the following morning, she encountered mixed reactions. Some people were shocked when they heard the windmill had burnt down and offered their sympathy, but others were less supportive. She accidentally overheard the villagers talking about her.

'Ever since the Jacksons moved here there's been trouble,' said Mr Clayton, outside the village hall. 'People from East London are a pain in the arse and think they can take over the place. We'd be better off without them.'

'I know what you mean, the Jacksons do seem fated, but we have to feel sorry for them,' replied Mr Ruffles.

He was the baker and still managed to work despite losing his left arm in the war.

'Sorry for them! They probably set fire to the windmill on purpose. I wish we could pack them off to where they came from.'

'I'm not sure about that, the Grange is important in our community. Mrs Jackson has worked hard for us despite her personal tragedy. I can't imagine what she's gone through.'

'Poor Mrs Jackson? You didn't believe all that crap she mouthed at Jimmy's funeral did you Mr Ruffles? I didn't mourn for her.'

Mr Clayton went too far. He spilt his unkind and unjust words in a public place and Sarah was not going to let him get away with it. She had been quiet and unnoticed until she stepped forward.

'You've not got a good word to say about anyone. Do you thrive on upsetting people or do you like the sound of your voice?'

Mr Clayton did not look at her and whispers amongst the other villagers ceased.

'What's the matter, have you nothing else to rant about? I'm here now, why don't you tell me to my face?' said Sarah.

There was no response.

'You're a very bitter man, Mr Clayton, and I suspect you wouldn't be missed if you left the village.'

The other villagers were shocked. They had not seen Sarah berate anyone before and finally Mr Clayton was stirred. He gritted his teeth and shouted loudly, 'I'm not going to make room for any more of your kind!'

Mr Clayton pushed past people to get away.

'That bloody woman can go to hell!' he bellowed.

*

Sarah and Jimmy had not thought about insuring the windmill, so the incident did not give rise to a claim. The fire service, however, was keen to carry out a thorough examination of the building.

Sarah was determined the cause of the blaze would not be discovered. She instructed Joseph to remove the empty petrol can from the remains of the windmill and to make sure there was nothing left that might be attributed to the fire. She wanted Robert protected from any media attention and idle gossip.

'If anybody asks questions, you must refer them to me!'
she told Emily and the staff.

Sarah knew Robert was still grieving for his father and
angry that Mary had not been found. She realised he was
under unbearable stress and that setting fire to the windmill
was his cry for help.

He would not leave his bedroom, so Sarah took meals to
him on trays, but he hardly ate. She found him sitting away
from the window, out of sight of the monster he tamed.

'Come downstairs, Robert, we're worried about you,' she
said, time and time again, but he did not answer.

Robert's absence from the estate put a heavy burden on
Joseph. Jobs that should have been done before the windmill
was completed, were piling up.

'I can't go on like this, Mrs Jackson, I need help.'

'I know, Joseph, I hope it won't be for too long. Please
do the best you can.'

With each passing day there was no improvement. Sarah
noticed Robert's cheeks were pale and he had lost weight.
She was getting worried about his health and confided in
Jess.

'I don't know what I'm going to do.'

'I've tried to fatten him up with food he particularly
likes, but I don't think he wants to eat,' replied Jess.

'Yes, I know, but to be honest it's his mental state that
bothers me. I think that's why he's not eating.'

'I should have said this before. I've a cousin who lives in
Holt who's a private medical councillor. His name is Colin
Jameson.'

'Do you think he'll see Robert?'

'He'll definitely see him, but it won't be cheap, Mrs
Jackson.'

Sarah eventually persuaded Robert to accept help, and she was present as the mental health specialist explored all of Robert's anxieties. Over a period of five weeks Sarah saw him gradually come to terms with the loss of his father. He was now talking freely about him.

'I don't mind telling you, Jess, I thought he might try to commit suicide.'

'Well his appetite has certainly returned, Mrs Jackson, he ate three pieces of apple pie last night.'

Day by day, new milestones were reached. With the specialist still on board and Sarah's gentle care, Robert's confidence improved and he was soon ready to resume work.

The village hall was completed and, with Sarah in charge, a large range of events were organised. They included film shows, dances and a five-a-side football competition.

Sarah instigated projects to raise money for the construction of a bandstand and a memorial garden. She also encouraged local railway enthusiasts to use the hall as their headquarters to direct procedures for the restoration of the line between Sheringham and Holt, which had been dismantled in 1964.

A little while later, Emily embarked on her chosen career to be a British Horse Society instructor. Sarah supported her as she completed stages one and two of her exam modules and saw her competence improve as she worked towards her goal. Sarah thought Emily was likely to qualify by the age of twenty-two.

Jenny was also teaching Emily horse jumping. Sarah arranged for a field on the Grange estate to be laid out with fences of various make-ups and sizes. There was even a water jump over two oak logs about eleven feet wide. Emily and Lottie spent every spare moment practising and Sarah watched them whenever she was at home.

'Lottie loves jumping as much as Emily, Mrs Jackson. I think they might be able to compete in a gymkhana next year,' said Jenny, during a visit to the Grange.

'That would be wonderful, but I don't think we should tell her yet.'

'I agree, Mrs Jackson, Emily has lots of training to do. I don't want her becoming complacent.'

Jenny's confidence in Emily reminded Sarah of the need for a larger stable at the Grange. Jenny suggested a facility for eight horses and an extended paddock, in anticipation of Emily's business requirements after she qualified.

The Jackson household was buzzing. There were endless activities and engagements for Sarah to organise, but she did not let people down. However, she was concerned about her family and insisted they spend time together. They tried to gather for breakfast and for evening meals, when they took an interest in each other's lives.

One morning, Giles answered the telephone in the hall and came into the sitting room.

'It's a lady by the name of Mrs Priest. She's asking to speak to you, Mrs Jackson.'

Sarah was astonished and intrigued; she did not expect to speak to her again.

'Hello Mrs Priest, this is a surprise. Why are you telephoning me?'

'Mrs Jackson, subsequent to our meeting some time ago I found myself with a lot of thinking to do. I was placed in a very difficult position, as the law makes enquiries such as yours very difficult to deal with.'

'Yes, I think you made it abundantly clear you couldn't or wouldn't help me.'

'Hmm, rules and laws are made for good reasons. In normal circumstances I wouldn't assist you, but these aren't normal circumstances.'

'What do you mean, not normal?'

Mrs Priest took a moment to compose herself. 'Mrs Jackson, you weren't the only person who contacted Crossways about your family; Mary did as well.'

Sarah was flabbergasted.

'Why on earth didn't you tell me when I came into the home?' she demanded to know.

'There was no reason to tie both visits up, Mrs Jackson. I didn't know she was your daughter.'

Sarah was angry.

'So how did you find out? I assume Mary had a wasted journey to Crossways too,' asked Sarah.

'Yes, I told her I was unable to help.'

'How did she find out about Crossways?'

'Mary said after her adoptive parents died, she found some papers in their bedroom. Amongst them was a document referring to her, which contained the address of Cotland Home and her enquiries led her to Stamford Hill.'

'I suppose she's lost again now?'

'She was wearing a sleeveless green top, but what I remember most was the distinctive egg birthmark on her left arm. I am very sorry, but it was not until three weeks after you left I opened the note you placed in my hand. Then I realised it was the same person.'

'What prompted you to look at it, Mrs Priest?'

'I don't know, but I suppose some things are meant to happen. Mary's adoptive parents died in a car crash and I happened to remember the incident. It occurred in Forest Road, near to where I live in Walthamstow. Their car was hit by an oil tanker. It was parked by the public toilets and was crushed against a wall.'

'That's awful.'

'Yes, the driver had been drinking and was arrested. I read he was heavily intoxicated and lost control of his vehicle.'

'How did Mary survive?'

'She was pulled out seconds before the tanker burst into flames. Apart from a few bruises she was miraculously unharmed. I was mortified at the time. In my job I'm used to people pleading for information, receiving sad news or having to provide comfort and support. This is different, as Mary lost both her blood parents and her adoptive parents. It's the worst tragedy I've known since the war. So, I had a real dilemma and thought, "Should I abide by the law, or let my heart rule my head"?'

'You made it clear to me you always play by the rules.'

'As I said it was a very difficult decision.'

'You've no idea what stress our family has been under since we left Crossways empty-handed,' Sarah remarked bluntly.

'I'm truly sorry, but this is an exceptional case. When I saw Mary, her face was drawn, she was dirty and clearly undernourished. I wasn't able to stop worrying about her.'

'You are making me feel very sad,' said Sarah.

'When I read your note and realised you were looking for the same person, my conscience got the better of me. I delved into the closed files and by chance came across a newspaper photo of Crossways when it first opened.'

'Is this relevant, Mrs Priest?'

'This little piece of history made me wonder if a local newspaper might have recorded the names of Mary's adopted parents, after the accident, and a telephone call to the Walthamstow Guardian brought immediate success.'

'Do we really need to know all this?'

'The receptionist confirmed the deceased's name was Heard. She remembered the incident too, as she witnessed it while riding her bicycle close by. I was shocked, as by coincidence, I met the Heard family years ago and it confirmed my thoughts that finding Mary was meant to be. The Heard family were friends of my sister, before she immigrated to Australia. I recalled them having two daughters and was sure one of them was adopted.'

'I still don't understand why you're telling me.'

'Mary hasn't enjoyed a good life and if I bring you together, I think you need to know what she's been through.'

'What do you mean, not a good life, Mrs Priest?'

'I got an inkling when I visited her family's old address. A woman with a long scar on her right cheek opened her door. She was wearing a metal necklace, and jutted her face out of the door in an aggressive manner. I felt intimated and smelling her cigarette stained breath I almost retched. When I asked to see Mary, she was very rude, but pointed to a tower block of flats in the distance. I was told Mary was on the top floor.'

Sarah was shocked but listened further.

'I didn't believe my eyes when I got to the tower. Outside, old furniture, worn-out tyres and litter were strewn everywhere. The building's glass entry door was smashed and inside there was unsavoury graffiti on the walls. A single lift served the eleven floors, but chalk writing on its double metal doors said it was out of order.'

'What did you do, you said Mary was on the top floor?'

'I climbed the stairs, Mrs Jackson. They were tainted with unpleasant smells and ugly stains. At the top of one walkway there was a decaying mattress, crawling with maggots. It was in my path and I was only wearing a knee-length skirt.'

'Goodness! To think Mary copes with this every day.'

'I held my breath and took three quick strides. My feet sank into the mattress with each step. Afterwards I kept rubbing my legs, imagining the grubs were on me. I still do sometimes.'

'Why didn't you give up, Mrs Priest?'

'I told you, Mrs Jackson, there is a family friend connection and I thought Mary was in need. When I reached the top of the stairs and opened the door it was dark and gloomy. I didn't know in which one of sixteen flats Mary lived, but, fortunately, a lady came out of her home. When I mentioned the large birthmark, I was told she lived at the far end of the corridor. It's a horrible place, Mrs Jackson, with dogs barking, music blaring out and the smells were so foul I put my hands over my nose and mouth.'

'I didn't know such places existed, Mrs Priest. I used to be poor, but it was never like this.'

'When Mary opened her door, her face was drawn and her hair was matted. She was wearing a stained red jumper and a torn black skirt. She was shocked to see me and resisted my entry, but I persuaded her to let me inside. The smell of body odour hit me and the kitchen diner was a mess with utensils piled up in the sink. There was a stench of damp coming from fungus on the walls.'

Sarah cried and Mrs Priest paused for a moment.

'This is my daughter, I can't believe what's happened. I'm going to look after her.'

'I've not seen anyone living in such bad conditions and when I asked Mary if she was all right, I got an understanding of what she'd been through. Gillian, her sister, if you can call her that, threw her out and the council gave her this grotty flat. She used to do the night shift in the Edith Spires Care Home in Stratford but the bus was often late. She was sacked two weeks ago.'

'She can't stay in that disgusting flat.'

'Don't worry, Mrs Jackson, I didn't leave her like that. Mary has a large frame, but she was all skin and bones. She hadn't eaten for two days and there was no food in the cupboards, so I decided to take her home with me. She's safe and warm now.'

'Does Mary know about her family?'

'Yes, I explained you tried to find her and that she has a brother and a sister. I also told her about the death of her real father. Although she didn't know him, this revelation brought tears to her eyes.'

Sarah sobbed again.

'When I told Mary about her inheritance, including part of the Hemsley Grange estate she was staggered.'

'So, what happens now? Does Mary want to meet her family?'

'Sadly, Mary only wants to see Emily and Robert. I have to tell you, although it was twenty years ago, she still hasn't got over being given up for adoption. The thought of any kind of reconciliation with you troubles her at the moment. Hopefully in the fullness of time, she'll feel differently.'

Sarah was clearly distressed by Mary's decision. Tears came easily to her, but, while sobbing, she agreed arrangements for the three children to meet in a public house called The Standard in Walthamstow, close to where Mrs Priest lived.

When Sarah informed Emily and Robert that Mary had been found they were excited and wanted to know all about her. Sarah told them her adoptive parents had died, but she was reluctant to mention the squalid conditions she lived in. She reasoned it was a private matter for Mary.

After a while, the enthusiasm in Robert's voice mellowed.

'I wonder how Mary will change our lives?'

'What's going to change?' asked Emily.

'If she's going to live here, what will she be like? She's not used to living like we do, is she.'

'Have you forgotten Robert, you came from East London too?' said Sarah.

'You sound a bit snobby, Robert. We've found our sister, that's all that matters,' said Emily.

'Where's Walthamstow?' he asked.

'Don't you remember; it's where the road is with the eels shop called Manze's. The eels wriggled about outside in a large tray with ice in it. I used to point to the ones I wanted and a man chopped their heads off and cut them up,' said Sarah.

'Oh yes, I hated the smell when you cooked them in milk, Mum; it was rank,' said Robert.

'I remember my doll, Susie, was mended in the shop on the other side of the road,' said Emily.

'Do you realise our sister may not have been living very far away. She might have gone to the same school. Perhaps we were close to her every day without knowing it. We might have spoken to her,' said Robert.

'I don't remember anyone by the name of Mary, except Mary Shields and it definitely wasn't her, because she has a twin sister.'

Sarah advised Mr Barker that Mary had been found and he wrote to her, care of Mrs Priest's home, with details of her inheritance. He also enclosed photos of the Jackson family.

*

Wednesday 18th April 1966

It was an ordinary day for most people, but for the Jackson family it was to mark a turning point in their lives. Emily and Robert were to meet Mary for the first time and Sarah was petrified. She worried what Mary might say about her and the impact her presence might have on the family.

Sarah carried out her village duties in a whirl, taking little interest in the people around her. She glanced at her watch regularly and thought about the lunch her children were to share. The day passed slowly until finally Robert and Emily arrived home.

'Don't worry, Giles, I'll go to the door,' said Sarah.

She was desperate for information and asked Emily and Robert to join her in the sitting room.

'What's Mary like?'

'She's not like us, Mum,' said Emily.

'What do you mean?'

'When we met, it was all hugs and smiles. Mary wanted to know everything we remembered about our lives.' she said.

'We found out we lived close to one another. Mary was in Church Road and went to Sybourn Street Junior School. I joked about Miss Blythe the headmistress and Mary described her as a witch,' said Robert.

'She used to make us sit in the hall and listen to classical music,' said Emily.

'You liked the Christmas plays though. Each class entertained for ten minutes on the stage while everyone else watched,' said Sarah.

'I reminded Emily and Mary about Saturday morning pictures at the Odeon Cinema. The manager sometimes stopped the films and pleaded with the children to behave,' said Robert.

'It was the boys with pea shooters who caused all the trouble. As soon as the lights went out, all hell broke loose and within ten minutes no one would be sitting in the middle stalls,' Emily replied.

'That's terrible,' said Sarah.

'I know, Mum, but it was funny.' said Emily.

'The girls screamed when the peas hit them,' said Robert

'It seems like you got on well together,' said Sarah.

'As I said, we did when we first met. It was fun chatting about being kids and we also told Mary what happened to Dad and about her grandfather,' said Emily.

'I told Mary about Maggie too, as she'll find out anyway,' said Robert.

'What did Mary say about her?'

'I painted an unpleasant picture, but it seemed to excite her and she wants to meet Maggie.'

'Oh well, I suppose she'll have to find out for herself.'

'The strange thing is, every time we tried to talk about you, Mary changed the conversation,' said Robert.

'Didn't she want to know anything about me?'

'When I asked her the exact same question she told us finding her blood family was a massive shock and she'd prefer to have a conversation about you another time,' said Emily.

'We did try and find out more about Mary. We wanted to know what it was like as an adoptee. However, she was evasive, other than to say she was well cared for and worked as a sales manager in a shop. I think it was called Stokes in Hackney,' said Robert.

'She gave the impression she enjoyed life to the full, but her voice was guarded; I'm not sure she told the truth,' said Emily.

Sarah knew it was all lies.

'Then we were astounded when Mary informed us bluntly, she wanted her inheritance as soon as possible and asked when Hemsley Grange would be sold,' said Robert.

'When we told her it wasn't possible, she became angry and shouted out, "I want my share and I don't care if it messes up your perfect lives",' said Emily.

Sarah blamed herself for Mary's outburst. She thought, 'I should never have abandoned her and now my worst fears are coming true.'

'I got really upset, Mum, and told her it was our father's wish to prohibit the sale of Hemsley Grange,' said Robert.

'I said, I think he did this to make sure we come together as a family,' said Emily.

Mary drew breath.

'She got angry and yelled, "The Grange doesn't mean anything to me, I wouldn't care if it burnt down"!' said Robert.

'With the conversation turning bitter, there was nothing more to say, Mum. We parted without hugs and kisses, but reluctantly agreed for Mary to visit the Grange next Wednesday, so she can see the estate and possibly meet you,' said Robert.

'I'm glad it's over, Mum, Mary made us feel very uncomfortable and her attitude towards the Grange was outrageous. I'm not looking forward to seeing her again,' said Emily.

Sarah was furious.

'How dare you arrange a meeting without asking me first! I'm a busy woman and might not be here. I'm not sure she really wants to meet me anyway.'

'Mum, I know from our meeting it's going to be hard, but you have to do it sometime. You've been in a dreadful state lately,' Emily replied.

Sarah was more apprehensive each day as she tried to prepare her mind. It adversely affected her community work, she was forgetful, indecisive and her usual good timekeeping deteriorated.

While Sarah was out, Jess chatted to Maggie. She had overheard the conversation about Mary's visit.

'The long-lost daughter has been found and she's coming here next week,' she said.

Chapter Twenty-Eight

On the day of Mary's arrival, Sarah told her children she was going to the village to see a friend, but she really wanted some quiet time alone. Sarah was dreading meeting Mary and wandered down to the sea. She thought, 'Emily and Robert told me Mary is unforgiving and revengeful, so what can I possibly say that'll placate her?'

Maggie had been to the post office and when arriving home, she noticed Sarah by the cliff edge. She was sitting on a small strip of grass about eighty yards away from the cottage. With the noise of the waves, Sarah did not hear her car. Maggie crept up behind and startled her.

'Thinking of throwing yourself over, Sarah? I can understand why you'd want to; with all that guilt inside crawling through your veins. I'll give you a little push if you like.'

'Go away, you're an evil conniving bitch!'

Maggie noticed Sarah was shaking. Looking down, she saw a photo of mother and baby on the grass beside her.

'So that's who you gave up, like a bag of potato peelings?'

Sarah's face was solemn. Today she was seeking the strength to confront Mary and did not welcome Maggie's intrusion.

'How did you know?'

'I heard your precious son talking in the newsagents and you know how people gossip. I'd be surprised if there's anyone in Cleybourne who doesn't know you were blessed with three children.'

'Why do you get so much pleasure out of hurting our family?'

'Because you stand between me and Hemsley Grange. How long have you been sitting here?'

Sarah ignored her.

'You don't know how you're going to face Mary, do you? If I was her, I'd give you a hard slap. To think you gave up an innocent child; you're a heartless woman.'

Sarah cried.

'Don't turn on the tears, although your good at it, aren't you? The slightest word said and the taps run like Niagara Falls.' Maggie loved teasing and taunting. 'Three young children too much for you to handle, were they?'

She was standing over Sarah menacingly, with her hands on her hips.

'At least I've got children and I don't go around after other women's husbands! Mind you, everyone knows you're the village mattress and most of them won't go near you.' Sarah retorted.

Maggie laughed.

'I've always kept my men happy, including your Jimmy. You never satisfied him.'

'I knew what he was doing, but he always came home. He was never going to leave me for a slag like you. Who've you got your grubby hands on now?'

Maggie laughed again and bated Sarah further.

'Did he ever tell you what we did in your bed, between your lovely silk sheets?'

Maggie was not seeking an answer, but Sarah was brought to tears again and the grief of losing Jimmy returned. She was raging inside and jumped up to strike Maggie.

Maggie ducked and grabbed Sarah's arm tightly as they stood close to the edge of the cliff. There was evil intent in Maggie's eyes and Sarah was scared. 'Maggie's going to kill me!' she thought.

Believing it to be her last act of defiance she said forcibly, 'Hemsley Grange is my home, it will never be yours!'

Maggie pushed Sarah and laughed as she slipped on the grass. Sarah screamed as she fell on the edge of the precipice. She was on her stomach, her hands gripping the earth and her legs dangling.

Maggie looked down with a sadistic smile.

'Go on, do it. I must be the next member of the Jackson family on your death list!' said Sarah.

She was scared to move and Maggie trod on her fingers. Sarah screamed in pain.

'I don't think so, there've been too many accidents on the estate. People might get suspicious. I think I'd sooner see Mary despise you and get her revenge for the childhood you took away.'

Maggie walked back to her cottage, leaving Sarah sobbing. She had never been so frightened in her life. Fortunately, the earth was dry and she eased herself up inch by inch until she was on safe ground. Making her way home, she felt anxious, tearful and shivery.

Sarah decided not to tell Emily and Robert about the incident, but her clothes were badly soiled. She entered the Grange through the conservatory and managed to creep into the house and up the staircase unseen. She lay on her bed gathering her thoughts, dreading the hours ahead.

As expected, around quarter past three a taxi arrived at the house entrance. The family waited outside, as the vehicle door opened and Sarah and Mary got their first glimpse of each other.

There was an uneasy silence and Emily broke the ice by greeting Mary with a kiss on her cheek. She tried to forget the events of the previous meeting and Mary responded with a tiny smile from her thin lips.

'Hello, Mary,' said Sarah.

She held out her arm for a limp handshake.

'Mother!' Mary replied.

From her fiery eyes it was obvious she was wound up and ready for a fight, but Sarah hated confrontation. She was determined to calm her down.

'I know we need to have a long chat, but would you like a bath or a rest after your journey?'

'No, let's get on with it!' she replied.

Sarah escorted Mary into the sitting room and said, 'I don't know what to say to you.'

'Tell me where you've been all my life. Do you have any idea what the consequences are of what you did?'

Mary was leaning forward and clamping her fingers on the edge of a table.

'Mrs Priest told me what your life was like when she found you. Was it always like that?'

'What does it matter? You didn't care about me then and I don't suppose you care about me now.'

'I know I can't make up for the past, but I do care, Mary.'

'Why didn't you come looking for me? Even if things were different when I was born, you still brought up two other children. Why was I left behind?'

'Nothing I can say will console you, Mary, but every day since I let you go, I hoped you were enjoying a good life.'

'So, you want me to ease your conscience. Well I can't and you'll have to live with it for the rest of your life.'

Sarah watched Mary as her anger stirred inside her. Her face was red and her voice was loud.

'Everything was okay until I was twelve. My adopted parents told me I wasn't their flesh and blood on my birthday, I think they planned it for some time. I suppose I needed to know, but it changed everything.'

'I'm sorry, Mary.'

Sarah's eyes welled up.

'I don't want your sympathy, it's too late. I'm telling you because I want your guilt to eat your guts out. Gillian, my sister who was eleven, found out at the same time and her attitude towards me changed. We were like normal sisters, going out, dressing up in each other's clothes and having fun. I assumed we'd always be close. Things, however, were never the same after the revelation.'

'Why ever not, Mary?'

'Oh, don't worry, Mum, I'll tell you; I want you to know every last detail. Gillian thought she should be treated better than me because she was 'real family' as she used to say. She was strong-willed and always got her own way. Our parents, wanting an easy life, used me like a skivvy. I did the washing, cleaning, shopping and even made all the beds. Before long, I felt more like a home help than a daughter. My list of jobs was always increasing, while Gillian spent her time away from her school work lying around reading and playing records.'

'Mrs Priest said Gillian was a bit intimidating.'

'Intimidating! She got worse as she got older and became aggressive. After my adoptive parents died, she threw me out and I rented a grotty council flat.'

Sarah wanted to hug Mary, but she daren't go near her. However, having vented her feelings, Mary was much calmer.

'I needed you so much after I knew I was adopted. I often wondered what we'd be doing. I thought about going shopping, helping you cook and you being there when I came home from school. I longed for your affection. Why now, after all this time, did you want to find me?'

'I'm not going to lie, Mary, your father left a letter when he passed on. It was his dying wish and without it, I wouldn't have searched for you.'

'So, I was right, you never wanted me, and you don't want me now.'

'It was complicated, Mary.'

'How about Emily and Robert, you kept them?'

Sarah was unable to find any words of comfort and Mary lowered her head.

'Are you going to stay here?' asked Sarah.

'Too right I am, this my home. If it's not going to be sold, I'm going to live in it and to the full. Now I'd like to go to my room.'

The following day, Maggie and Mary met by chance on the coastal path by the windmill.

'You must be the village hussy,' said Mary.

'I'll take that as a compliment. Someone's got to look after the hot-blooded men around here. I assume you're the long-lost daughter.'

Mary liked Maggie instantly and listened to her criticising the Jackson family. She told Mary how she had lost her home and the suspicion placed upon her after both Eddie's and Jimmy's deaths.

'The Jacksons have turned the whole village against me. Now all I've left is my cottage by the sea. That can't be fair, can it?'

'What are you going to do about it?'

'I don't know yet, but somehow I'll get back into the Grange.'

'That's my home now,' said Mary.

'I know it is,' said Maggie with a sly smile.

They both laughed.

'I want to know why my mother gave me up. I can't get a reasonable explanation.'

Maggie told Mary to visit her cottage whenever she liked and a friendship, frowned upon by Sarah, blossomed. On a rare occasion, when the Jacksons and the staff were occupied elsewhere, Maggie decided to visit the Grange. She gained entry using the key she kept after vacating the property.

Once inside she made her way up the staircase to Sarah's bedroom. She remembered, when surprising Jimmy, that there was a pink diary on her bedside cabinet and thought it might contain information about Mary and provide a clue to why she was given up.

In Sarah's bedroom everything was tidy. Pillows were neatly arranged on the bed and ornaments were placed exactly the same distance from each other on the windowsill. Sarah even lined up her hair brush and comb on her dressing table in front of her mirror.

'Where's the diary?' Maggie said to herself. Only Eddie's photo, a lamp on a small wooden stand and a clock radio sat on top of Sarah's cabinet.

One by one she searched each of its four drawers, trying not to disturb the various items inside. Sadly, the diary was missing and Maggie walked around the room looking for places in which it might be hidden. Standing by Sarah's wardrobe, she opened up its double doors. Underneath clothes hanging on the left she found a large green box on the floor. She lifted it out and placed it on the bed. On inspection it contained two watches, some old tarnished beaded necklaces, three rings and a bracelet.

There was also a small brown paper parcel. Maggie was curious about its contents and carefully unwrapped it. Inside there was a beautiful brooch. She remembered Sarah receiving it from her grandmother at her wedding. Maggie returned the box to the wardrobe with all the contents replaced exactly how she found them.

'Where is it? It must be in this room somewhere,' Maggie thought, as she searched a shelving unit on the right-hand side of the wardrobe. It was packed with books and old mementoes. Maggie rummaged through Sarah's things and in the top compartment she felt something like a book.

It was the pink diary, but it was locked and required a tiny key to open it. 'That's that then, she's probably got it in her bag,' Maggie thought, sitting down on the bed.

She examined the catch that secured the pages of the diary and remembered a key in the bottom bedside cabinet drawer. It was quickly located and it fitted the lock. This was the ultimate intrusion into Sarah's life, but Maggie was determined to find out more about Mary.

The key was turned. It was stiff, but with a little finger pressure there was a click and the catch released. Inside the diary's back page there were lots of little handwritten notes. She thought they must have been important at the time and made sure they were not disturbed.

Maggie opened the diary in the middle; it was December 1941. She flicked through the pages until she reached September 1943 when Sarah and Jimmy got married. Maggie was irritated as Sarah had written that she thought Maggie was a snob and a flirt.

Reading on, Maggie was surprised to find out about Jimmy's violent behaviour. Sarah was explicit about being raped and Maggie was astounded. She never witnessed any aggression from Jimmy. 'I can't believe it!' she said to herself.

From some of the comments, Maggie knew Sarah was very distressed at the time, but she was now armed with the information she wanted.

*

In the weeks that followed, arguments raged in Hemsley Grange as Mary settled in to her new home. Everything her mother, brother and sister did was challenged and to the staff she was like a rabid dog compared to Maggie.

'Why do you have to be so demanding; sometimes you treat the staff like slaves?' asked Sarah.

'I own a full share of this property and I'll do as I please. That reminds me, I want your bedroom, Emily.'

'What?'

'I'm the senior sibling and I want your room. If you don't let me have it, I'll make your life hell.'

'Let her have it, there are two nice rooms at the front of the house,' said Sarah

'Mum!'

'I can't bear all the aggravation, Emily.'

'Pack your things up tomorrow. I'm going shopping,' said Mary.

Emily was brought to tears.

'Why are you being like this, Mary; what have we done to you?'

'It's all very well you turning on the waterworks, but how would you feel? Our mother gave me away over twenty years ago and still doesn't want me.'

'How do you know that's true?' asked Robert.

'Ask her! She didn't make any effort to contact me after I met you in Walthamstow. That's hardly the act of a loving parent.'

Sarah nodded reluctantly. She thought she had let Mary down and went along with all her ridiculous demands.

Giles and Jess complained.

'We can't go on like this, Mrs Jackson. Mary wants her meals served on hot plates at the same temperature each evening and her bread rolls have to be sliced exactly down the middle. You know I always do my best for your family, but she has to be reasonable,' said Jess.

'Yesterday she moaned about dust she found on top of the crystal chandelier above her bed. She is even finding hairline creases in pillowcases.'

'Last week Joseph was told not to mow the lawn when she's having an afternoon nap,' said Giles.

'She loathes the smell of coffee too. Forgive me, but I purposely put a fresh pot on every afternoon when she's home,' said Jess.

The following day, Sarah helped Emily move rooms. They took everything out, including the curtains. Mary arrived home in a taxi, with enough clothes to fit out a wedding party.

Mary realised that if she were to establish herself in the local community, she would have to get involved in Grange activities. Sarah welcomed some weight taken off her shoulders and decided to introduce her to Geraldine Scott and the Women's Institute. 'That will be a challenge for her,' she thought.

'Thank goodness Mary doesn't want to get involved in my horse jumping business,' said Emily.

'I don't think she knows what she wants, but I did hear her say she doesn't like horses,' said Sarah.

The relationship between Sarah and Mary was now bearable, but after taking over some of Sarah's work load, she made excuses for not attending meetings.

'You said you wanted to get involved, so you have to get your hands dirty. There's no room for shirkers in our small community,' said Sarah.

This was the first time she criticised Mary since she arrived.

'We do too much around here, it won't hurt if we miss the odd meeting, what are they going to do about it?'

'It's our reputation, Mary.'

'It might be yours, but it's not mine. I'm going to see Maggie, where I'm wanted.'

She went to the cottage most evenings and with their relationship growing, Maggie wanted to talk to Mary about her father. She was concerned the history between her and Jimmy might disturb her.

'I've something important to tell you. I should have mentioned it a long time ago,' she said, taking hold of Mary's hands.

Mary smiled.

'It's okay; I know about you and my dad. Jess told me. I have this feeling she thought it would upset me.'

'You don't mind?'

'My mum's never done anything for me; let's not talk about it.'

This was a relief to Maggie. If there was any chance of her moving back into the Grange, it was important they were good friends.

During their get-togethers, Mary was told about the people who attended meetings, other activities and who she would cross paths with in the community. Geraldine Scott often popped up in their conversations.

'She's a bit of an old battle axe and thinks she's a cut above the rest. She runs the Women's Institute like a school classroom. She doesn't care what she says, even in the Grange, and woe betide anyone who's late.'

'Sarah's told me about her and wants me to attend the next meeting. I'm sure I can find things to annoy her with.'

'I noticed in the house diary there's a fete mentioned in August. What's that all about?'

'It happens every year, Mary, and is run completely by Bummsy and his friend Lucy. They're a right pair I can tell you. The least said about the woman the better and Bummsy's clock only strikes eleven.'

'There was a man walking down the high street in flippers, wearing a fez and carrying a dead chicken yesterday. That wouldn't be him I suppose?'

There were shrills of laughter from Maggie.

'Oh yes, that's definitely him!'

'Hmm, how strange; what's the fete got to do with the Grange?'

Maggie remembered when Sarah and Jimmy asked her the same question.

'It's on your land, that's all, but as I said, it will be taken care of by Bummsy and Lucy. They are laughing stocks, but somehow the fete works and they make loads of money for charity.'

Over the next few months, with Maggie's influence, Mary drifted further away from her family.

'We never see her, these days,' said Emily.

'Thank heavens for small mercies!' Robert replied.

'She hates us and doesn't want to be a part of this family. I wish things were different, but I think she would like to destroy us all,' said Sarah.

Chapter Twenty-Nine

Summer 1967

On a bright Monday morning Sarah was surprised to see Jenny on the Grange forecourt. When she stepped out of her Range Rover, her face was illuminated and Sarah knew there was something important on her mind.

'I've been doing a lot of thinking about Emily over the weekend. She's now completed further stages towards her horse coaching qualification, and for several months I've been training her for show jumping.'

'Yes, I watch her practice at home whenever I can and I've noticed how much she's improved.'

'She has a good understanding with Lottie and I think they're both ready for competition.'

'Are you sure, Jenny, it's a big step for her?'

'Yes, the time is right.'

Emily came out of the stables while her mum and Jenny were in conversation.

'What are you doing Saturday week?' Jenny asked.

'You've got nothing planned have you, Emily?' said Sarah.

'I'm normally training with you, Jenny. Do you want to go to the beach?'

'I'm going to enter you into a competition at Swaffham.'

Emily froze. It was one thing to jump alone in a field, but to expose herself in front of other people was something completely different.

'It's all right Emily, Jenny tells me you're ready,' said Sarah.

'Why didn't you mention it before, Jenny?'

'I needed to speak to your mum first and I knew how you'd react. I remember the first time I was asked to enter an event. I was the same age as you when I was encouraged to jump at Holkham. I know it feels scary, but you're ready.'

'Swaffham is a big venue, there'll be lots of riders who are much more experienced than me.'

'You've been working hard for a long time, Emily. Jenny says you're as well-equipped now as you'll ever be. I think you should trust her judgement,' said Sarah.

'Jumping competitively is what you've been training for.' said Jenny.

'Yes, but the event is only twelve days away.'

'What's the worst thing that can happen?' asked Sarah.

'If I knock down all the fences and everyone laughs.'

'There're eleven jumps, including a double and a water tray. Do you think you can do that?' asked Jenny, putting an arm around her shoulder.

'Yes, Lottie likes jumping so much; she can clear them all without any help from me.'

This is exactly what Jenny thought she'd say, prompting a further response.

'I hate the thought of people watching me, but I knew it'd happen sometime. Okay, it'll be fun I think, let's do it.'

'Everything will be fine, but we need to go shopping,' said Jenny.

'Shopping!' Emily exclaimed.

'You need some proper clothes, you can't enter a competition in jeans, my girl. There's a shop in Sheringham called 'Stirrups and Saddles' which sells everything required in connection with horses. We might as well go there now.'

At the shop, Sarah watched Jenny help her daughter make the right selections. Emily chose navy coloured breeches, a purple shirt, a tie and a navy jacket.

'You must try on every item of clothing, to make sure they fit perfectly,' said Sarah.

'It's all happened so quickly, Mum. I was a trainee this morning and now I'm an eventer. I wish Dad was alive.'

'So do I, Emily, we have to believe he's watching over us.'

That evening was one of the rare occasions when all three siblings and their mother were together for a meal. The chatter around the table was limited, but while they were eating, as usual, an argument broke out.

'Do you really have to see so much of Maggie?' Robert asked Mary.

'She's the only person who understands me. She knows I don't pretend to be something I'm not, like our mother.'

'That's a terrible thing to say, she helps all sorts of charities and organisations in the community,' said Emily.

'No! The truth is our mother swans around in posh clothes and can't keep her nose out of other people business.'

Sarah had been silent, but lost her patience. She promised Maggie her past would not be revealed, but the lies she was telling Mary about the Jackson family were relentless. Also there was the frightening ordeal on the cliff edge, when Maggie might have killed her.

'There's no one more pretentious around here than Maggie. She's a gravedigger's daughter. Ask her about her family in Stockport and how she paralysed her sister.'

'I think you'd say anything to destroy our relationship,' said Mary.

'Maggie's only sidling up to you to get at us. She's a ruthless, conniving snob and will cast you aside like a sweet wrapper when you're no longer of any use to her,' said Sarah.

'I don't believe you, Maggie said the Jackson family destroyed her,' Mary retorted.

'If it hadn't been for that woman, our father would still be alive,' said Robert.

'Yes, you heard what happened in the windmill?' said Emily.

'Nothing was proven and anyway Maggie's not the real reason you're upset. It's because I'm here – that's what really bugs you.'

'You might be in Cleybourne because of Dad's death, but Mum never wanted to find you. She even tried to stop us looking for you,' said Emily.

'Stop it!' said Sarah.

Emily wouldn't keep quiet.

'You were unwanted, a rejected child who was shunned from the day you were born.'

Anger built up inside Mary. Her face was red and she banged her hands on the table. Emily continued to goad her with unsavoury comments until Mary stood up. Emily's confident assault on her sister stopped, when Mary pushed her chair away with the backs of her legs. Emily was scared, as Mary walked slowly around the table and grabbed her hair.

Emily shrieked.

'Let go, you're hurting me, Mary!'

'Take your hands off her!' demanded Sarah in a loud voice.

Mary wasn't listening and pulled so hard Emily was dragged from her seat and she screamed again. Using all her strength, she managed to punch Mary in the face, before Robert was able to separate them. He squeezed Mary's arm hard, forcing her to let go, and Emily ran upstairs to her room.

'Why don't you go back to London? You're not wanted here!' said Robert.

'Sell the Grange and I'll go!'

'That's what you've wanted all along, isn't it?' said Sarah.

There was now an impasse between Mary and the rest of the family. They refused to speak to one another and any communication between them was through Giles and Jess.

Maggie exploited the situation and told Mary more lies, while she spent time in her cottage.

'My family want to get rid of me,' said Mary.

'The Jacksons want me out of the way too. They also want to poison our friendship, but they're the real villains. Jess told me it was Robert who burnt down the windmill.'

'No! Really? Are you serious?'

'I wasn't surprised, Mary. There's been the odd fire on the estate; I think he's a bit of a pyromaniac. There's something else. Your excuse for a mother takes bribes for her support in the community.'

'How do you know, Maggie?'

'I still have a few friends in the village. She took money for persuading the council planning committee to approve the building of the new village hall.'

'Who gave her the money?'

'It was the farmer who wanted to sell his land.'

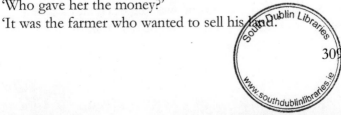

Mary was staggered and Maggie's lies cemented their relationship further.

Estate duties continued to be neglected by Mary, but Sarah was pleased she was out of the way. Robert and Joseph got on with agricultural activities and Emily made final preparations for her show jumping.

On the day of the competition, Sarah woke Emily as soon as the sun made its presence in a cloudless sky. She was excited for her daughter and had not slept a wink.

'I don't think I can face any breakfast, Mum, I feel so nervous.'

'I think you should have something, Emily. Toast and orange juice will give you a bit of energy before we go.'

'I didn't realise you were coming with me, Mum.'

'I wouldn't miss your first event for the world, Emily.'

Sarah was crying.

'Are you okay, Mum?'

Emily followed her into the kitchen. Sarah tried to hide her tears. It was a release of happiness for her little girl, taking a big step in her life.

'What's the matter, Mum? I know you're sad sometimes. You've been through a lot, what with losing Dad, dealing with Maggie and now Mary.'

'I have to stay strong for all of us, Emily. It's tough, but I have you and Robert. I still hope things will get better with Mary. She's not all bad.'

'You always see the good in everyone, Mum.'

Sarah looked at her watch.

'Have you seen the time?'

'Goodness! Jenny will be here soon. I've got the stable to muck out and Lottie to attend to,' said Emily.

Sarah watched as Lottie was exercised and cleaned. Emily was combing Lottie's mane when Jenny drove up to the Grange at nine-thirty. The horse was in pristine condition, wearing her travelling boots and a green blanket ready for the journey, as Emily led her around to the front of the house.

Lottie was used to this environment from her visits down to the sea at Holkham, but Sarah was concerned she might be lonely.

'Has Lottie been in a horsebox on her own before?' she asked.

Jenny and Emily were stunned.

'Not since the day she arrived,' said Emily.

'I hope she doesn't refuse,' said Sarah.

'I'm sure she'll be okay,' said Jenny.

Lottie was the most placid of horses and entered the box with Jenny holding her reins. It was as if she sensed she would be jumping in a competition.

On arriving at Swaffham, it was wet. Unlike in Cleybourne, there had been a thunderstorm early in the morning and there were large puddles inside and outside the arena.

'Oh Mum, there's water everywhere. I can't see the event going ahead.'

Sarah was worried, as Emily had summoned up all her courage to get this far. She thought the competition might be postponed, but Jenny was more positive.

'It's very hot, Emily. The sky's cleared and with the event over two hours away, the riding arena will dry up,' she said.

Jenny drove into the lorry park where Lottie was unloaded. While she was having a drink and stretching her legs, Sarah went to see the show secretary to collect Emily's competitor number. They were all laid out on a table in front of her and Emily was given number seven.

Lottie was then temporarily put back in the horsebox so Jenny and Emily could inspect the show ring. Sarah walked the course with them while they noted the sequence of the jumps. She also watched them pace the distances between the fences so they knew how many strides Lottie would need to take between each one.

'The lorry park is getting packed; most of the competitors must have arrived,' said Sarah.

They were eating their lunch when a jeep was driven up next to them. It was pulling a bright green horsebox and a teenage boy pushed open his door and got out.

'Hurry up!' he said impatiently to the girl in the passenger seat.

He was beckoning her with his right hand when his foot slipped and he fell onto the muddy ground. When he got up his jumper and trousers were badly soiled. He used his hands to remove the dirt that was stuck to him and realised there were eyes upon him when Emily laughed.

'Where's my camera when I need it?'

The boy was not amused, but without saying a word, he walked to the tent with the girl to register her attendance.

'You were very rude,' said Sarah.

'I was a bit, wasn't I? He was very nice. I guess he won't talk to me now.'

'You're not here to flirt with boys, Emily, and he's with a girl anyway.'

'You've got to remain focused on the competition,' Jenny said sternly.

There were to be three jumping competitions and two races that day. A large gathering assembled around the show ring and to keep people well fed and amused there were refreshment stalls and fair attractions.

Sarah was pleased Emily was in the first event. She was surprised by the morning storm, but the forecast for later in the day was atrocious. Very wet and wild weather accompanied by an abnormal spring tide was to invade Norfolk and already a gentle breeze was sweeping across the arena.

After watching Emily putting on her competition dress and tacking up Lottie, Sarah accompanied her daughter to the warm-up ring where the horse went through a sequence of exercises. It involved practicing jumping at gradually increasing heights.

Sarah knew from Emily's number she was positioned seventh in the line-up and there were twelve entrants who were all girls.

'I feel a little scared, Mum, most of the competitors seem to know one another.'

They were chatting amongst themselves and nobody made an effort to talk to her.

'Don't let it worry you, Emily. I'm here for you,' said Sarah.

One by one, the competitors took to the arena and prior to Emily's turn, no one performed a clear round. Two girls knocked over one fence and the other four dismantled three.

It was Emily's turn and Sarah hugged her.

'Good luck!' she said.

'Lottie is in her best condition and she loves to jump, Mum. All I have to do is keep her calm and ride her like I do at home.'

Emily entered to a warm applause from the spectators. She trotted around the arena and waited for the bell. When it sounded she was off cantering towards the first fence, but for some reason Lottie stopped.

'Why didn't Lottie jump?' asked Sarah.

'I don't know, Mrs Jackson. It's not happened before, let's see what happens this time.'

Emily trotted around in a circle and tried again, but Lottie refused once more and Sarah was frantic with worry.

'What's happening, Jenny?'

'I'm not sure if it's the fence or the wind, but Lottie hasn't experienced such conditions before,' said Jenny.

The third time the horse's resistance caused Emily to fall off. Sarah screamed and wanted to run into the arena, but Jenny stopped her.

'I think she's okay, Mrs Jackson, she's already getting up.'

Fortunately, Emily landed on a soft muddy patch of ground and only suffered a few bruises, but her riding outfit was badly soiled, especially her jacket. It was muddy on her back and right arm. Emily remounted Lottie and continued to the next obstacle which she jumped with ease along with the other fences until she completed the course.

When she finished, Emily trotted over to Sarah and Jenny.

'I don't think I ever want to ride again!' she said and burst into tears.

'You will, Emily, it's only because Lottie refused the fence. Something unnerved her and we need to find out what it was,' said Jenny.

'Has the fall shaken you up, Emily?' asked Sarah.

'I'm okay, no broken bones.'

The refusal and subsequent time faults weighed heavily against Emily as three of the remaining entrants enjoyed clear rounds. Jenny took a photograph of the fence which had two blue panels and a red pole on top. It was similar to an obstacle Emily practised on at home that Lottie cleared with ease.

Sarah was disappointed with Emily. She was sulky and wanted to go straight home.

'You've got to help Lottie cool off,' said Jenny.

Emily was very quiet. Sarah watched, as reluctantly she got her horse doing some stretching exercises and then washed her down before taking her for a bite of grass prior to going home.

When preparing for their departure, the boy in the jeep approached Emily. His girlfriend was entered into the third competition, so he saw Emily compete.

'Didn't you realise you have to jump all the fences?' he asked sarcastically.

Emily ignored him.

'The boy's talking to you,' said Sarah.

He was intent on getting a reaction and laughed.

'It's not so funny when it's you in the mud is it? I hope my sister provides as much entertainment as you, but preferably on her horse.'

Emily remained silent as she got into Jenny's Range Rover.

'Serves you right, Emily. It's hard for me to find sympathy for you. You behaved badly and who knows how it affected Lottie,' said Sarah.

'I'm so sorry. Do you think Lottie's refusal was my fault?'

'We'll never know, but horses are sensitive animals and your mind was not properly prepared for the competition. Perhaps next time you'll be more focused,' said Jenny.

It was two o'clock and the weather was worsening fast. The promised rain clouds were moving at pace and merging to further darken the threatening sky.

Emily was quiet for the rest of the journey and tears intermittently ran down her face. On arrival at the Grange,

Lottie was returned to her stable. While providing her with fresh hay Sarah reflected on the competition.

'It was your first time in a show arena and despite the upset, I thought you coped very well.'

'Jenny doesn't think so. I behaved badly and let you both down. I'm sorry Mum.'

Chapter Thirty

Walking back into the Grange, Sarah and Emily heard Mary arguing with Robert in the sitting room. Emily needed to bath and change her clothes and Sarah went to see Jess.

'How did it go, Mrs Jackson?'

'It was a bit of a disaster. Lottie wouldn't jump, but I think Emily's state of mind was responsible. She wasn't right from the moment she got up this morning and has been acting out of character all day. She even chatted up a boy whose horsebox was parked next to us.'

'Really! That's not like her at all.'

'Never mind, she can try again, if Jenny hasn't lost her patience with her.'

Mary was speaking with a loud voice and Sarah heard her name mentioned. She went into the sitting room.

'What trouble are you bringing to the house today?' she asked.

'I told Giles that unless he stops slouching, I'll sack him. He can't do his cleaning jobs properly.'

'You know he has a back problem, Mary, and so Jess does the work he's unable to do.'

'Jess has been complaining about it. If he can't do his job, he's got to go!'

Jess heard the conversation from the kitchen and called out,

'Oh no I haven't, Mrs Jackson!'

'You're a servant; don't speak unless you're spoken to. You say too much in this house!' said Mary.

'What do you mean, too much?' asked Jess.

'I know it was you who told Maggie that Robert burnt down the windmill.'

'I haven't told a soul, Mrs Jackson. Someone must have overheard a conversation.'

Mary was intent in causing trouble at every opportunity. She was relentless in her mission to force her family to sell the Grange. Sarah's relationship with her was unbearable and she was mortified that Mary's friendship with Maggie was growing ever closer.

'Mum!' Emily shouted out from the landing.

She sounded panicky and was crying.

'What is it? What's the matter?'

'My window was open and a gust of wind has blown it off its hinges. It was so scary. I'm frightened.'

'Come down here Emily, Joseph will deal with it,' said Sarah.

For a few moments Mary's latest tirade was stopped in its tracks, but her mood was increasingly bitter and distressed. For over two hours she criticised everything she could think of.

Getting to her feet and standing in front of her mother she seemed to be almost at breaking point. Her voice was getting louder and Sarah was frightened.

'I know the reason I was adopted,' Mary bellowed.

Her face was boiling and her hands were shaking. Emily and Robert were shocked.

'It was nothing to do with money. It was nothing to do with you playing the caring parent either,' she shouted.

Sarah was speechless. Her mouth open and her eyes wide with fear. Emily and Robert were bewildered wondering what other terrible secret their mother had kept from them.

'I was born out of rape!' she suddenly said as loud as her voice would allow her.

Her sadistic smile chilled Emily and Robert's blood.

Emily screamed!

Robert got to his feet in an instant and tried to pull Mary towards the front door, but she resisted.

Sarah sobbed. She had believed she would take her secret to the grave.

'Stop snivelling, woman. Tell your precious children the truth. Tell them our dad was a rapist.'

Sarah was horror-struck. She did not speak.

'You never warmed to Jimmy, did you? That's why he did it and why he went with Maggie.'

Robert let Mary go and she grinned, while looking at the shock on her siblings' faces.

'How did you find out?' Sarah asked.

'How do you think? Maggie's the only person around here who cares about me.'

Sarah thought, 'Jimmy must have told her,' and buried herself in a cushion on the couch. Mary was relentless in her search for answers and pulled it away from under her head.

'Are Robert and Emily also the children of rape, or am I the lucky one?'

'You'd never understand, Mary. It was different with your brother and sister. They were born out of love.'

Mary was enraged further.

'I still don't understand why you didn't keep me,' she said.

'I knew your face would always remind me what your dad did to me.'

Guilt filled Sarah's, solemn face.

All three siblings were now in tears, but Mary's emotion was deeper.

'It's all been about you, Mum. If you weren't such a cold fish all the family would've been together and Dad would still be alive. I'm going to Maggie's.'

Mary left the Grange, leaving Sarah feeling helpless and unworthy. Outside the forceful wind was getting stronger with every gust. Most people living close to the sea had boarded up their properties and placed sandbags outside their front doors.

Teaming cold rain stung Mary's face and when she arrived at Maggie's cottage her shoes were caked with mud. She was drenched from head to foot.

'I didn't think I'd see you this evening, in this foul weather,' said Maggie.

'I wanted to get out of the house. There was a heated row and I told Emily and Robert I was born out of rape. They were mortified and my mother at last admitted why she didn't keep me. I hate her.'

There was a large open fire in the lounge. Mary took off her wet clothes and sat in Maggie's old dressing gown while they were dried. Maggie was drinking red wine, too much red wine and was not thinking straight. Looking at Mary, many years her junior, she thought she was beautiful.

'She'll never be part of the Jackson family now; she's mine, all mine,' thought Maggie.

As Mary continued to criticise her family, the force of the rain on the windows was immense and the cottage creaks were more profound. She hated the scary sounds and it was difficult for them to hear one another.

'I've been thinking a lot about your family. We both hate them,' said Maggie.

'My mum wishes I hadn't been born.'

'Sarah never wanted me here either,' Maggie replied, slurring her words.

'I detest them all!' said Mary.

'We need each other, I think we have since the day you arrived.'

Maggie was sitting close to her by the fire. There was mischievous intent in her voice, as she made eye contact with Mary and put an arm around her shoulder. She was becoming a little affectionate.

'I don't understand, Maggie, what are you trying to say?'

'What if they weren't here? Imagine if we ran the Grange together, without them sticking their noses in.'

'Do you mean buy them out, Maggie? I don't have enough money and I don't think you have either.'

As they sat together talking, another sudden gust of wind with more strength battered the cottage. The whistling noise was unnerving, like the sound of water rushing into a drain. It only lasted a few seconds, but they held on to one another tightly, waiting for it to pass.

'Blimey, that was frightening!' said Mary.

'It often blows like that.'

'That's the worst I've ever known it to be.'

Maggie lied; it unnerved her too. This storm was different, with the wind swirling around the cottage so violently it threatened to lift it off the ground.

Maggie had wanted this conversation with Mary for some time and tried to stay calm. Then there was a flash of lightning followed almost immediately by a thunderclap. It shook the cottage and the ground around it.

She pulled Mary closer.

'There's more than one way to get your family out of the Grange. There's been, let's say, a few unfortunate incidents around here.'

As Mary considered what was said, the tips of Maggie's fingers were caressing her back and then she stroked her arm.

'We're so close now, we could live together in the Grange.'

Moving her hand up to Mary's face and then moving her fingers down to her neck, Mary was almost frozen. Maggie, now heavily intoxicated, lent forward to kiss Mary and their lips touched. They were joined for a second, but then Mary pushed her away.

'No, I don't want this! Is it what you've been planning Maggie?'

'Planning what?'

'Perhaps my family's right. Maybe you are a scheming bitch! Yes, you only want the Grange, don't you? You don't want me.'

'I want what's best for both of us,' said Maggie.

'No! I think you'd do whatever it takes to get back into the Grange. It's not your home now and never will be again.'

Maggie's gentle approach hardened and she got to her feet. Pacing around the room, she entwined her fingers and cracked her knuckles. She said to herself, 'Ever since Mary arrived I've been kind to her. I thought we were friends, but she's been using me, like Jimmy did.'

Maggie's drinking loosened her tongue.

'You're like all the rest, but the Grange needs me, it's always needed me. Eddie thought he was the boss, but I organised everything. He was a lazy bastard and turned people against me.'

Maggie laughed loudly while she continued to walk menacingly around the room berating Mary's grandfather.

'The silly man took me pheasant shooting. As if I'd want to go after a lot of silly birds. It was easy, there was no one

322

about early in the morning. He showed me how to use his shotgun and then it went off with a bang.'

'Bang!!!' Maggie shouted out.

Mary screamed.

'Everyone thought it was an accident, but I thought it was a shame the gun didn't have two barrels.'

'You killed him! You killed my grandfather!'

Mary was horrified.

'Shut up, you stupid girl, it was his fault. He was standing in the way, but he asked for it.'

Another violent gust of wind blew against the cottage. They were becoming more frequent and even stronger in strength. The creaks were more acute and lasted longer. Cups rattled on hooks in the kitchen cupboards and ornaments fell off shelves. There was a sudden crash, as a roof slate tile hit the ground.

Mary screamed again.

'You did kill him, you killed my granddad!'

'I told you, he neglected me. Did you expect me to sit at home night after night while he was out gallivanting and do nothing about it?'

Mary was sobbing with grief.

'Stop your wailing, girl, he had it coming like your father did.'

'Please, no!'

Mary got more agitated by the second. She was fidgeting and biting her lip.

'He deceived me and I was treated like a piece of meat.'

'You took him away from my mum.'

'If you believe that, you'll believe anything! I gave him everything Sarah wouldn't, but he betrayed me. I chased him into the Windmill and we had a terrible row. He was standing over the edge of the mill shaft on the top floor and I was in such a rage. You can understand that can't you?'

'Oh no! Please, Maggie.'

Mary pleaded with her to stop.

'I remember raising my hand. He tried to prevent me from hitting him and I pushed him back. It was all over so quickly.'

'You killed him too! You killed both my granddad and my father!' Mary shouted.

There were tears streaming down her face.

'Jimmy deserved it, he was a lying toad. It doesn't matter whether I did or not.'

Maggie laughed again, reliving Jimmy's death in her mind, thinking about his body crushed to pieces.

The house shook from side to side as the wind circled and attacked the building from all directions.

Mary was shocked by the revelations and her face was red with rage.

'You're a murderer!' she cried out.

'Who's going to believe you, Mary? Your mother wishes you'd never been born and your brother and sister hate you, along with half of the village.'

'You're right, nobody will, I'll have to take matters into my own hands.'

'What do you mean?'

Mary was intent on getting revenge. Her eyes, now piercing like lasers, scared Maggie.

'If you can get away with what you've done, I'm sure no one will question a little accident down here. You'd hardly be missed and I can't imagine there'd be much of an enquiry.'

Very rarely was Maggie brought to tears, but Mary was terrifying her. There was an eerie silence between them as the noise of the storm intensified still further outside. They heard a rumbling sound in the distance, but Mary was laughing and Maggie, sensing she was in critical danger, tried to placate her.

'Come on, Mary, we're friends now; you can have everything you want with me helping you.'

Mary was not listening. She picked up a porcelain dog and threw it. It smashed against a wall beside Maggie's head.

'It's too late now, you're a scheming murdering bitch!'

Mary locked the front door. The key grated as it was turned in its socket.

'What are you doing?' asked Maggie as Mary took a poker from the fireplace.

It was covered in coal dust and she pushed the end into the flames. After a few seconds, she tightly clasped the object by its handle and walked towards Maggie who was cowering against a wall.

Maggie screamed. She was petrified.

'What are you going to do?' she said seeing the poker glowing with heat.

'You've been using me to get at my family ever since I arrived. You never wanted me in the Grange, did you? You wanted it all for yourself.'

She played with Maggie, by prodding the metal rod towards her stomach, burning a hole in her blouse.

Maggie winced and gasped.

Mary raised the poker as if to strike her head and then laughed out loud, watching Maggie squirm as she lay on the floor with her arms covering her face.

Mary stepped back and threw the poker back into the fireplace.

'You didn't think I was going to leave any evidence, did you?'

There was hatred in her eyes. Mary's large frame dwarfed Maggie's. Taking hold of her arm, she wrenched her up. Maggie was shaking as she was dragged towards the kitchen and screamed even more.

'Mary, please don't do this, I'm your friend not your enemy!'

'Shut up, no one can hear you; it's just me and you in this wretched cottage.'

Maggie resisted by pulling with all the strength in her body. She grabbed a table leg, the back of a chair and finally a door handle. Mary was too strong and, in desperation, Maggie bit her arm. Mary slapped her face and hit her so hard her cheek bled instantly.

'You bite me once more, bitch, and I'll gouge your eyes out!'

From the kitchen, a door led to the garden and the sea. Maggie was still struggling in Mary's clutches and was unable to break free.

'People fall off cliffs, don't they? Only the other day a woman walking with her husband fell down by the coast near Overstrand. I wonder if she jumped or if she slipped. Then again, maybe she was pushed. No one will ever know. All it would've taken is a little nudge.'

Mary was smiling at Maggie with intent, as if it was the final scene in a movie.

'This isn't right. I'll help you get everything you want!' Maggie pleaded relentlessly.

'Oh, I will, I definitely will, but you won't be here to see it.'

Mary pinned her against the wall and opened the outside door. She was about to pull Maggie out of the cottage when there was another violent gust of wind. It was followed by a crumbling sound leading to half of the kitchen falling down the cliff as the ground underneath gave way.

Maggie screamed again, but Mary was undeterred.

'You can make all the noise you like, for what good it'll do.'

Now with the cottage open to the elements, the full thrust of the wind battered them and with the intensity of the rain, they were soaked to the skin.

The earth moved again and more of the foundations gave way. Mary lost her balance on the unstable ground, causing her to release her grip on Maggie. She was falling, but Maggie managed to grab some metal railings that were still secure.

Mary was slipping away.

'Help me!' she screamed and instantaneously, Maggie reached out and clasped her hand. She did not know why she did it, but it was Mary's turn to plead for her life.

'It seems my fortunes have changed,' said Maggie.

She enjoyed seeing the terror in Mary's eyes. She was screaming as she tried to get a foot hold on the edge of the cliff, but it was too wet and she was only in slippers.

Maggie laughed, watching her panic on the end of her arm.

'You didn't think I was really going to go through with it, did you? I wanted to teach you a lesson that's all.'

'Oh, I think you did, Mary. You said accidents happen and now all I have to do is open my hand.'

Maggie's nerves disappeared and her confidence returned. She tormented Mary by releasing her grip slightly, causing a slight movement through her fingers. Maggie's arm was hurting more every second, as the weight of Mary's body was pulling it down.

Mary pleaded for mercy, but Maggie continued to taunt her and laughed out loud.

'My hand is getting very tired. I'm not sure I can hold you much longer.'

'Pull me up, please pull me up!' pleaded Mary.

Maggie laughed again.

'Have you been in the sea lately? It's quite refreshing on a warm summer's day. I'm not sure what it's like in the evening though.'

It was high tide now and water was thrashing about on the rocks below. The cliffs were increasingly unstable, and Maggie was concerned there might be a further landslip any moment.

'Please help me!' begged Mary.

Maggie's eyes opened wide. She looked at Mary for the last time and grinned as she slowly loosened her grip.

'No!' shouted Mary, as her body slid away down the cliff. Her screams and shrieks of pain got less and less as she hit the jagged rocks on the way down.

Maggie made her way back through the remains of the kitchen. She was feeling pleased with herself, but to her horror the front of the house had disappeared. She did not know it had collapsed, as the sound was masked by the storm and waves.

There was a gaping hole between her and safety. It was too far for her to jump and she was frantic as the wind blew hard again. It rushed through the damaged property like a fast express train. This was followed by a cracking sound, and more of the cottage collapsed into the encroaching sea. Maggie knew she was in a perilous position.

Back at the Grange, Sarah watched the storm from a bedroom window, but she did not know the cliff edge had collapsed. It was only when angry black clouds parted for a few seconds that there was enough moonlight for her to see the tragedy unfolding.

'Oh my God! Robert, Emily, come here! The cottage is falling into the sea. Mary's down there we must do something.'

'Why? She hates us, they both do,' said Emily.

'She's my daughter.'

Sarah let out a heart wrenching scream as more of the cottage disappeared.

Robert rushed down the stairs and Sarah watched from the landing as he raced towards the cottage. She was terrified, thinking she may not see Robert again.

Maggie was now standing perfectly still against a brick wall, for fear of causing another landslip, and was petrified. Then in the distance, Robert came towards her. Maggie waved her arms and called out to him. He was almost pushed to the ground by the force of the wind knocking him sideways. The rain was relentless turning small puddles into large ponds.

'Robert, Robert, please help me!' she pleaded.

'Where's Mary?'

'She fell into the sea, I think she's dead.'

The rain was lashing down like a monsoon and the ground was likely to move further at any time. Maggie watched Robert search for anything that would help her escape.

'Please hurry!' Maggie called out.

She was screaming as the wind continued to rip through the remains as more of the property collapsed. There was now only one wall standing.

'I've found an old scaffold board, but it's slippery with mud I'm not sure I can lift it.'

'Please, Robert, you have to I'm so scared.'

'Got it, I'm coming Maggie!' he called out.

She saw him carrying it across the sodden ground. He stood it up on its end and dropped it over the gap. It covered the hole with less than two feet to spare on each side. The board was narrow, uneven and sagged in the middle. The prospect of walking over it would have been daunting for anyone.

Sarah and Emily arrived.

'Where's Mary?' asked Sarah.

'I'm sorry,' said Robert, 'she's gone.'

Sarah collapsed on the ground.

'You've killed her, haven't you?' said Emily.

'The ground gave way underneath. I tried to save her,' Maggie replied.

Emily was incensed and tried to remove the board, but Robert pushed her away.

'We have to save her,' said Sarah. She was shaking from head to toe.

'Why? We know what she's capable of!' said Emily.

She tried to pull Robert away, but Sarah grabbed hold of her arms.

'Come on, Maggie, do it now!' said Robert.

'I can't!'

'You might as well die where you are!' shouted Emily.

Maggie's eyes looked down into the chasm. Every muscle in her body tightened.

'You have to; you'll be going down anyway if you don't risk it. It's only a few feet, I'll hold my end of the board as firm as I can.'

Robert tried to reassure her, as Emily tried to wrestle free from her mother. She wanted to push the board away.

'Come on, Maggie!' said Sarah.

Maggie was panicking as lightning lit up the sky again. The following thunderclap was the loudest she had ever heard. It stirred her and she put one foot on the board. It wobbled and sprung as she ventured further across and it began to sink into the mud behind her. Maggie screeched and froze like a statue before sliding backwards.

'Robert, Robert, I'm going to fall, please help me!' she shouted out.

Desperately she held out her hand, but the gap was too wide. The Jackson family watched as she slipped and lost her balance.

'It didn't have to be like this, we weren't your enemy!' Sarah shouted out.

Maggie plunged headlong into a deep, dark, seemingly bottomless hole and her frantic haunting screams did not save her. She disappeared into the abyss and her voice was silenced.

'It's all over, she must be dead,' said Robert.

'That bitch will never hurt this family again,' said Emily. 'I'm glad she's gone.'

On their way back to the Grange, the storm showed no signs of relenting. Rain pounding a metal roofed shed sounded like gunfire. The wind, gusting indiscriminately, whipped up debris from the ground and small bushes were blown out of their roots.

With the moon hidden again, Sarah and her remaining children trod carefully, as their path home was a stream of rushing water. Sarah cried all the way and when they stepped inside The Grange, she hugged Emily and Robert as if she would never let them go.

Robert was quiet, reliving every moment down by the cottage. Emily was sobbing and shivering in her mother's arms. Sarah's life had been shattered so many times, but she was a survivor and her children needed her. She picked herself up and once more embraced the country life she dreamed about, when living in the East End of London.

ACKNOWLEDGEMENTS.

The Salvation Army. Mother's homes and adoption in the 1940's

F Upson. Funeral Directors. Burials during the Second World War.

Hannah Galley. Horse eventing.

Elly Chambers. Great Bircham Windmill.

Norfolk and Norwich Millennium Library.